By Mario Vargas Llosa

The Cubs and Other Stories
The Time of the Hero
The Green House
Captain Pantoja and the Special Service
Conversation in The Cathedral
Aunt Julia and the Scriptwriter
The War of the End of the World
The Real Life of Alejandro Mayta
The Perpetual Orgy
Who Killed Palomino Molero?
The Storyteller
In Praise of the Stepmother
A Fish in the Water
Death in the Andes

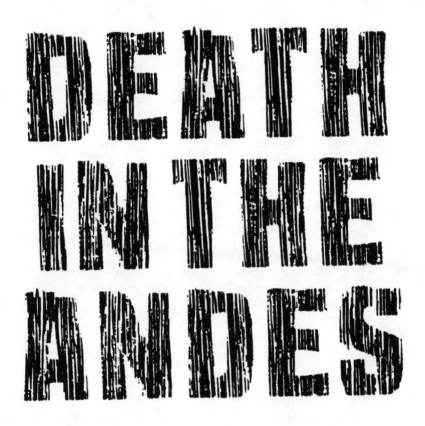

DEATH IN THE ANDES

Mario Vargas Llosa

TRANSLATED BY EDITH GROSSMAN

Farrar, Straus and Giroux

NEW YORK

Library of Congress Cataloging-in-Publication Data
Vargas Llosa, Mario.
[Lituma en los Andes. English]
Death in the Andes / Mario Vargas Llosa ; translated by Edith
Grossman.—1st ed.
p. cm.
I. Grossman, Edith. II. Title.
PQ8498.32.A65L5813 1996   863—dc20   95-40883   CIP

FOR BEATRIZ DE MOURA

a dear friend and an exemplary editor

Cain's City built with Human Blood,

not Blood of Bulls and Goats.

—WILLIAM BLAKE, *The Ghost of Abel*

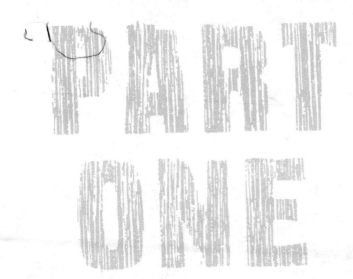

PART ONE

I / WHEN HE SAW the Indian woman appear at the door of the shack, Lituma guessed what she was going to say. And she did say it, but she was mumbling in Quechua while the saliva gathered at the corners of her toothless mouth.

"What's she saying, Tomasito?"

"I couldn't catch it, Corporal."

The Civil Guard addressed her in Quechua, indicating with gestures that she should speak more slowly. The woman repeated the indistinguishable sounds that affected Lituma like savage music. He suddenly felt very uneasy.

"What's she saying?"

"It seems her husband disappeared," murmured his adjutant. "Four days ago."

"That means we've lost three," Lituma stammered, feeling the perspiration break out on his face. "Son of a bitch."

"So what should we do, Corporal?"

"Take her statement." A shudder ran up and down Lituma's spine. "Have her tell you what she knows."

"But what's going on?" exclaimed the Civil Guard. "First the mute, then the albino, now one of the highway foremen. It can't be, Corporal."

Maybe not, but it was happening, and now for the third time. Lituma pictured the blank faces and icy narrow eyes that the people in Naccos—laborers at the camp and comuneros, the Indians from the traditional community—would all turn toward him when he asked if they knew the whereabouts of this woman's husband, and he felt the same discouragement and helplessness he had experienced earlier when he tried to question them about the other men who were missing: heads shaking no, monosyllables, evasive glances, frowns, pursed lips, a presentiment of menace. It would be no different this time.

Tomás had begun to question the woman, writing her answers in a little notebook, using a blunt pencil that he moistened from time to time with his tongue. "The terrorists, the damn terrucos, aren't too far away," thought Lituma. "Any night now they'll be all over us." The disappearance of the albino had also been reported by a woman: they never did find out if she was his mother or his wife. The man had gone out to work, or was on his way home from work, and never reached his destination. Pedrito had gone down to the village to buy the two Civil Guards a bottle of beer, and he never came back. No one had seen them, no one had noticed any fear, apprehension, sickness in them before they vanished. Had the hills just swallowed them up? After three weeks, Corporal Lituma and Civil Guard Tomás Carreño were as much in the dark as on the first day. And now it had happened a third time. Son of a bitch. Lituma wiped his hands on his trousers.

It had begun to rain. The huge drops rattled the tin roof with a loud, unrhythmic noise. It was not yet three in the afternoon, but the storm had blackened the sky, and it seemed as dark as night. In the distance, thunder rolled through the mountains with an intermittent rumbling that rose from the bowels of the earth where the serruchos, these damn mountain people, thought that bulls, serpents, condors, and spirits lived. Do the Indians really believe all that? Sure they do, Corporal, they even pray to them and leave offerings. Haven't you seen the little plates of food by the caves and gullies in the Cordillera? When they told him these things at Dionisio's cantina, or during a soccer game, Lituma never knew if they were serious or making fun of him, a man from the coast. From time to time, through a crack in one of the walls of the shack, a yellowish viper bit at the clouds. Did the mountain people really believe that lightning was the lizard of the sky? The curtains of rain had erased the barracks, the cement mixers, the steamrollers, the jeeps, the huts of the comuneros among the eucalyptus trees on the hill facing the post. "As if they had all disappeared," he thought. There were some two hundred laborers, from Ayacucho and Apurímac, and especially from Huancayo and Concepción in Junín, and Pampas in Huancavelica. Nobody from the coast, as far as he knew. Not even his adjutant was a coastal man. But though he was a native of Sicuani and spoke Quechua, Tomás seemed more like a mestizo. He had brought Pedro Tinoco with him when he came to Naccos. The little mute had been the first to disappear.

Carreño was a man without guile, though somewhat given to melancholy. At night he would confide in Lituma, and he knew how to open himself to friendship. The corporal told him soon after he arrived: "You're the kind of man who should have been born on the coast. Even in Piura, Tomasito." "I know that's a real compliment coming from you, Corporal." Without his company, life in this wilderness would have been grim. Lituma sighed. What was he doing in the middle of the barrens with sullen, suspicious serruchos who killed each other over politics and, as if that weren't enough, went missing too? Why wasn't he back home? He imagined himself at the Río Bar, surrounded by beers and the Invincibles, his lifelong buddies, on a hot Piuran night filled with stars, waltzes, and the smell of goats and carob trees. A wave of sadness made his teeth ache.

"I'm finished, Corporal," said the guard. "The lady really doesn't know too much. And she's scared to death. Can't you tell?"

"Say we'll do everything we can to find her husband."

Lituma attempted a smile and gestured to the Indian that she could go. She continued looking at him, impassive. Tiny and age-less, with bones as fragile as a bird's, she was almost invisible under all her skirts and the shabby, drooping hat. But there was something unbreakable in her face and narrow, wrinkled eyes.

"It seems she was expecting something to happen to her hus-band, Corporal. 'It had to happen, it was bound to happen,' she says. But of course she never heard of terrucos or the Sendero militia."

With not even a nod of goodbye, the woman turned and went out to face the downpour. In a few moments her figure dissolved into the lead-colored rain as she walked back to camp. For a long while the two men said nothing.

Finally, the voice of the adjutant rang in Lituma's ears as if he were offering condolences: "I'll tell you something. You and I won't get out of here alive. They have us surrounded, what's the point of kidding ourselves?"

Lituma shrugged. Usually he was the one who felt demoral-ized, and Carreño had to cheer him up. Today they had changed places.

"Don't brood about it, Tomasito. Otherwise, when they do come, we'll be in such bad shape we won't even be able to defend ourselves."

The wind rattled the sheets of tin on the roof, and little gushes of rain spattered the interior of the cabin. Surrounded by a pro-tective stockade of sacks filled with stones and dirt, their quarters consisted of a single room divided by a wooden screen. On one side was the Civil Guard post, with a board across two saw-horses—the desk—and a trunk where the official record book and service reports and documents were kept. On the other side, next to each other for lack of space, stood two cots. The guards used kerosene lamps and had a battery-operated radio that could pick up Radio Nacional and Radio Junín if there were no atmospheric disturbances. The corporal and his adjutant spent entire afternoons and evenings glued to the set, trying to hear the news from Lima or Huancayo. There were lamb and sheep skins on the packed-dirt floor, and straw mats, a camp stove with a Primus burner, pots, some crockery, their suitcases, and a dilapidated wardrobe—the armory—where they stored rifles, boxes of ammunition, and a submachine gun. They always carried their revolvers and kept them under their pillows at night. Sitting beneath a faded image of the Sacred Heart—an Inca Cola advertisement—they listened to the rain for several minutes.

"I don't think they killed those men, Tomasito," Lituma said at last. "They probably took them away to the militia. The three of them may even have been terrucos. Does Sendero ever disappear people? They just kill them and leave their leaflets behind to let everybody know who did it."

"Pedrito Tinoco a terrorist? No, Corporal, I guarantee he wasn't," said Tomás. "And that means Sendero is right outside the door. The terrucos won't sign us up in their militia. They'll chop us into hamburger. Sometimes I think the only reason you and I were sent here was to be killed."

"That's enough brooding." Lituma stood up. "Fix us some coffee for this shit weather. Then we'll worry about the latest one. What was his name again?"

"Demetrio Chanca, Corporal. Foreman of a blasting crew."

"Don't they say things come in threes? With this one we'll probably solve the mystery of what happened to the other two."

The guard went to take down tin cups from their hooks and light the Primus.

"When Lieutenant Pancorvo told me back in Andahuaylas that they were sending me to this hole, I thought, 'Great, in Naccos the terrucos will finish you off, Carreñito, and the sooner the better,' " Tomás said softly. "I was tired of living. At least that's what I thought, Corporal. But seeing how scared I am now, I guess I don't want to die after all."

"Only a damn fool wants to die before his time," asserted Lituma. "There are some fantastic things in this life, though you won't find any around here. Did you really want to die? Can I ask why, when you're so young?"

"What else could it be?" The guard laughed as he placed the coffeepot over the blue-red flame of the Primus.

The boy was thin and bony but very strong, with alert, deep-set eyes, sallow skin, and jutting white teeth—on sleepless nights Lituma could see them gleaming in the dark.

The corporal ventured a guess, licking his lips. "Some sweet little dame must have broken your heart."

"Who else would break your heart?" Tomasito was visibly moved. "And besides, you can feel proud: she was Piuran too."

"A hometown girl," Lituma approved, smiling. "How about that."

.

The altitude did not agree with *la petite* Michèle—she had complained of a pressure in her temples like the one she got at those horror movies he loved, and of a vague, general malaise—but, even so, she was stirred by the rugged, desolate landscape. Albert, on the other hand, felt marvelously well. As if he had spent his entire life at an altitude of three or four thousand meters, among sharp peaks stained with snow, and occasional flocks of llamas crossing the narrow road. The old bus rattled so much it sometimes seemed about to break apart as it faced the potholes, ruts, and rocks that constantly challenged its ruined body. The young French couple were the only foreigners, but they did not seem to attract the attention of their traveling companions, who did not even look around when they heard them speaking a foreign language. The other passengers wore shawls, ponchos, and an occasional Andean cap with earflaps as protection against the approaching night, and carried bundles, packages, tin suitcases. One woman even had cackling hens with her. But nothing—not the uncomfortable seat or the jolting or the crowding—bothered Albert and *la petite* Michèle.

"*Ça va mieux?*" he asked.

"*Oui, un peu mieux.*"

And a moment later *la petite* Michèle said aloud what Albert had also been thinking: he had been right at the Pensión El Milagro in Lima, when they argued over whether to travel by bus or plane to Cuzco. On the advice of the man at the embassy, she had wanted to fly, but he insisted so much on the overland route that *la petite* Michèle finally gave in. She did not regret it. On the contrary. It would have been a shame to miss this.

"Of course it would," Albert exclaimed, pointing through the cracked pane of the small window. "Isn't it fabulous?"

The sun was going down, and a sumptuous peacock's tail opened along the horizon. An expanse of dark green flatland on their left, with no trees, no houses, no people or animals, was brightened by watery flashes, as if there might be streams or lagoons among the clumps of yellow straw. On the right, however, there rose a craggy, perpendicular terrain of towering rocks, chasms, and gorges.

"Tibet must be like this," murmured *la petite* Michèle.

"I assure you this is more interesting than Tibet," replied Albert. "I told you so: *Le Pérou, ça vaut le Pérou!*"

It was already dark in front of the old bus, and the temperature began to drop. A few stars were shining in the deep blue sky.

"Brrr . . ." *La petite* Michèle shivered. "Now I understand why they all wear so many clothes. The weather changes so much in the Andes. In the morning the heat is suffocating, and at night it's like ice."

"This trip will be the most important thing that ever happens to us, you'll see," said Albert.

Someone had turned on a radio, and after a series of metallic sputterings there was a burst of sad, monotonous music.

Albert identified the instruments. "Charangos and quenas. In Cuzco we'll buy a quena. And we'll learn to dance the huayno."

"We'll put on a costume party at school," fantasized *la petite* Michèle. "*La nuit péruvienne! Le tout Cognac* will come."

"If you want to sleep a little, you can lean on me," Albert suggested.

"I've never seen you so happy." She smiled at him.

"I've dreamed about this for two years," he agreed. "Saving my money, reading about the Incas, about Peru. Imagining all this."

"And you haven't been disappointed." His companion laughed. "Well, neither have I. I'm grateful to you for urging me to come. I think the Coramine Glucose is working. The altitude isn't bothering me as much, and it's easier to breathe."

A moment later, Albert heard her yawn. He put his arm around her shoulders and leaned her head against him. In a little while, in spite of the jolting and bouncing of the bus, *la petite* Michèle was asleep. He knew he would not close his eyes. He was too full of excitement, too eager to retain everything in his memory and recall it later, to write it down in the journal he had scrawled in each night since boarding the train in the Cognac station, and then, later still, to talk about it in detail, with only an occasional exaggeration, to his *copains*. He would show slides to his students with the projector he would borrow from Michèle's father. *Le Pérou!* There it was: immense, mysterious, gray-green, poverty-stricken, wealthy, ancient, hermetic. Peru was this lunar landscape and the impassive, copper-colored faces of the women and men who surrounded them. Impenetrable, really. Very different from the faces they had seen in Lima, the whites, blacks, mestizos with whom they had managed, however badly, to communicate. But something impassable separated him from the serranos, the mountain people. He had made several attempts, in his poor Spanish, to engage his neighbors in conversation, with absolutely no success. "It isn't race that separates us, it's an entire culture," *la petite* Michèle reminded him. These were the real descendants of the Incas, not the people in Lima; their ancestors had carried the gigantic stones up to the aeries of Machu Picchu, the sanctuary-fortress he and his friend would explore in three days' time.

Night had fallen, and in spite of his desire to stay awake, he felt himself succumbing to a sweet lightheadedness. "If I fall asleep, I'll get a crick in my neck," he thought. They were in the third seat on the right, and as he sank into sleep, Albert heard the driver begin to whistle. Then it seemed as if he were swimming in cold water. Shooting stars fell in the immensity of the altiplano. He felt happy, although he regretted that, like a hairy mole on a pretty face, the spectacle was marred by the ache in his neck, his extreme discomfort at not being able to rest his head on something soft. Suddenly, someone shook him roughly.

"Are we in Andahuaylas already?" he asked in a daze.

"I don't know what's going on," *la petite* Michèle whispered in his ear.

He rubbed his eyes and there were cylinders of light moving inside and outside the bus. He heard muffled voices, whispers, a shout that sounded like an insult, and he sensed confused movement everywhere. It was the dead of night, and a myriad of stars twinkled through the broken windowpane.

"I'll ask the driver what's happening."

La petite Michèle did not let him stand up.

"Who are they?" he heard her say. "I thought they were soldiers, but no, look, people are crying."

Faces appeared fleetingly, then disappeared in the movement of the lanterns. There seemed to be a lot of them. They surrounded the bus and now, awake at last, his eyes growing accustomed to the darkness, Albert saw that several had their faces covered with knitted balaclavas that revealed no more than their eyes. And that glinting had to be weapons, what else could it be?

"The man at the embassy was right," murmured the girl, trembling from head to foot. "We should have taken the plane, I don't know why I listened to you. You can guess who they are, can't you?"

Someone opened the bus door and a blast of cold air ruffled their hair. Two faceless silhouettes came in, and for a few seconds Albert was blinded by their lanterns. They gave an order he did not understand. They repeated it, more emphatically.

"Don't be afraid," he whispered into *la petite* Michèle's ear. "It doesn't have anything to do with us, we're tourists."

All the passengers had stood up and, hands on their heads, were beginning to climb out of the bus.

"Nothing will happen," Albert repeated. "We're foreigners, I'll explain it to them. Come on, let's get out."

They climbed down, lost in the press of passengers, and when they were outside, the icy wind cut their faces. They remained in the crowd, very close together, their arms entwined. They heard a few words, some whispers, and Albert could not make out what they were saying. But they were speaking Spanish, not Quechua.

"*Señor, por favor?*" He pronounced the words syllable by syllable, speaking to the man wrapped in a poncho who stood next to him, and a thundering voice immediately roared: "Quiet!" Better not open his mouth. The time would come for him to explain who they were and why they were here. *La petite* Michèle clutched at his arm with both hands, and Albert could feel her nails through his heavy jacket. Someone's teeth were chattering: were they his?

Those who had stopped the bus barely spoke among themselves. They had surrounded the passengers, and there were a good number of them: twenty, thirty, maybe more. What did they want? In the shifting light of the lanterns, Albert and *la petite* Michèle could see women among their assailants. Some in balaclavas, others with their faces bare, some armed with guns, others carrying sticks and machetes. All of them young.

The darkness was shattered by another order that Albert did not understand either. Their traveling companions began to search their pockets and wallets and hand over identification papers. Albert and his friend took their passports from the packs they wore around their waists. *La petite* Michèle was trembling more and more violently, but to avoid provoking them he did not dare to comfort her, to reassure her that as soon as these people opened their passports and saw that they were French tourists, the danger would be over. Perhaps they would take their dollars. They weren't carrying much cash, fortunately. The traveler's checks were hidden in Albert's false waistband and with a little luck might not even be found.

Three of them began to walk among the lines of passengers, collecting documents. When they came to him, Albert handed the two passports to the female silhouette with a rifle over her shoulder, and said haltingly: "French tourists. We no speak Spanish, señorita."

"Quiet!" she yelled as she snatched the passports out of his hand. It was the voice of a young girl, sharp with fury. "Shut up!"

Albert thought how calm and clean everything was up there, in that deep sky studded with stars, and how different it was from the menacing tension down here. His fear had evaporated. When all this was a memory, when he had told it dozens of times to his *copains* at the bistro and to his students at school in Cognac, he would ask *la petite* Michèle: "Was I right or not to choose the bus instead of the plane? We would have missed the best experience of our trip."

They were guarded by half a dozen men with submachine guns, who constantly shone the lanterns into their eyes. The others had moved a few meters away and seemed to be conferring about something. Albert assumed they were examining the documents, subjecting them to careful scrutiny. Did they know how to read? When they saw that they were foreigners, French tourists without much money who carried knapsacks and traveled by bus, they would apologize. The cold went right through him. He embraced *la petite* Michèle and thought: "The man at the embassy was right. We should have taken the plane. When we can talk again, I'll ask you to forgive me."

The minutes turned into hours. Several times he was sure he would faint with cold and fatigue. When the passengers began to sit on the ground, he and *la petite* Michèle imitated them, huddling very close. They were silent, pressing against each other, warming each other. After a long while their captors came back and, one by one, pulling them to their feet, peering into their faces, bringing their lanterns up to their eyes, shoving them, they returned the passengers to the bus. Dawn was breaking. A bluish band appeared over the rugged outline of the mountains. *La petite* Michèle was so still she seemed asleep. But her eyes were very wide. With an effort Albert got to his feet, hearing his bones creak, and he had to help *la petite* Michèle stand by supporting both her arms. He felt exhausted, he had muscle cramps, his head was heavy, and it occurred

to him that she must be suffering again from the altitude sickness
that had bothered her so much when they began the ascent into
the Cordillera. Apparently, the nightmare was ending. The passengers had lined up single file and were climbing into the bus.
When it was their turn, two boys in balaclavas at the door of the
vehicle put rifles to their chests and, without saying a word, indicated that they should move to one side.

"Why?" asked Albert. "We are French tourists."

One of them approached in a menacing way, put his face up
to his, and bellowed: "Quiet! Shhh!"

"No speak Spanish!" screamed *la petite* Michèle. "Tourist!
Tourist!"

They were surrounded, their arms were pinned down, and
they were pushed away from the other passengers. And before they
really understood what was happening, the motor of the bus began
to gurgle and vibrate, its hulk to tremble, and they saw it drive
away, rattling along that road lost in the Andean plateau.

"What have we done?" Michèle said in French. "What are they
going to do to us?"

"They'll demand a ransom from the embassy," he stammered.

"They haven't kept him here for any ransom." *La petite* Michèle
no longer seemed afraid: now she appeared angry and rebellious.

The other traveler who had been detained with them was short
and plump. Albert recognized his hat and tiny mustache. He had
been sitting in the first row, smoking endlessly and leaning forward
from time to time to speak to the driver. He gestured and pleaded,
shaking his head, moving his hands. They had encircled the man.
They had forgotten about him and *la petite* Michèle.

"Do you see those stones?" she moaned. "Do you see, do you
see?"

Daylight advanced rapidly across the plateau, and their bodies,
their shapes, stood out clearly. They were young, they were ad-

olescents, they were poor, and some of them were children. In addition to rifles, revolvers, machetes, and sticks, many of them held large stones in their hands. The little man in the hat fell to his knees and swore on a cross that he formed with two fingers, raising his face to the sky. Until the circle closed in on him, blocking him from view. They heard him scream, beg. Shoving each other, urging each other, imitating each other, the stones and hands rose and fell, rose and fell.

"We are French," said *la petite* Michèle.

"Do not do that, señor," shouted Albert. "We are French tourists, señor."

True, they were almost children. But their faces were hardened and burned by the cold, like those roughened feet in the rubber-tire sandals that some of them wore, like those stones in the chapped hands that began to strike them.

"Shoot us," shouted Albert in French, blind, his arms around *la petite* Michèle, his body between her and those ferocious arms. "We're young too, señor. Señor!"

•

"When I heard him start in to hit her, and she began whimpering, I got gooseflesh," said the guard. "Like the last time, I thought, just like in Pucallpa. Just your luck, you poor bastard."

Lituma could tell that reliving the scene agitated Tomás and made him angry. Had Carreño forgotten he was here, listening to him?

"The first time my godfather sent me to be Hog's bodyguard, I felt really proud," the boy explained, trying to calm down. "Just think: I'd be close to a big boss, I'd travel with him to the jungle. But it was a tough night for me in Pucallpa. And it would be the same damn thing now in Tingo María."

"You had no idea that the world is a dirty place," said Lituma. "Where have you been all your life, Tomasito?"

"I knew all about the world, but I didn't like that sadistic shit. I didn't, damn it. I didn't understand it. It made me mad, even scared. How could a man act worse than an animal? That was when I knew why they called him Hog."

There was a sharp whistling sound, and the woman cried out. Over and over again, he hit her. Lituma closed his eyes and pictured her. Plump, full of curves, round breasts. The boss had her on her knees, stark naked, and the strap left purple streaks on her back.

"I don't know which one made me sicker, him or her. The things those women do for money, I thought."

"Well, you were there for money too, weren't you? Guarding Hog while he got off beating up the hooker."

"Don't call her that, Corporal," Tomás protested. "Not even if she was one."

"It's just a word, Tomasito," Lituma said in apology.

The boy spat furiously at the night insects. It was late, and hot, and the trees murmured all around him. There was no moon, and the oily lights of Tingo María could barely be seen between the woods and the hills. The house was on the outskirts of the city, about a hundred meters from the highway to Aguatía and Pucallpa, and sounds and voices could be heard clearly through its thin walls. There was another sharp crack, and the woman cried out again.

"No more, Daddy," her muffled voice pleaded. "Don't hit me anymore."

It seemed to Carreño that the man was laughing, the same lecherous snigger he had heard the last time, in Pucallpa.

"A boss's laugh, the laugh of the man in charge who can do whatever he wants, the guy who'll fuck anything that moves and has plenty of soles and plenty of dollars," he explained, with an old rancor, to the corporal.

Lituma imagined the sadist's slanted little eyes: bulging inside their pouches of fat, burning with lust each time the woman moaned. He didn't find things like that exciting, but apparently some men did. Of course, he wasn't as shocked by them as his adjutant was. What could you do? This fucking life was a bitch. Weren't the terrucos killing people left and right and saying it was for the revolution? They got a kick out of blood, too.

"Finish it, Hog, you motherfucker, I thought," Tomás continued. "Get off, get done, go to sleep. But he went on and on."

"That's enough now, Daddy. No more," the woman pleaded from time to time.

The boy was perspiring and had trouble breathing. A truck roared down the highway, and for a moment its yellowish lights illuminated the dead leaves and tree trunks, the stones and mud in the ditch at the side of the road. When it was dark again, the little glowing lights returned. Tomás had never seen fireflies before, and he thought of them as tiny flying lanterns. If only Fats Iscariote were with him. Talking and joking, listening to him describe the great meals he had eaten, passing the time, he wouldn't hear what he was hearing, wouldn't imagine what he was imagining.

"And now I'm going to ram this tool all the way up to your eyeballs," the man purred, insane with joy. "And make you scream like your mother did when she gave birth to you."

Lituma thought he could hear Hog's slow little snicker, the laugh of a man on whom life has smiled, a man who always gets what he wants. He could imagine him with no problem, but not her; she was a shape without a face, a silhouette that never quite solidified.

"If Iscariote had been with me, talking to me, I would have forgotten about what was going on in the house," said Tomás. "But

Fats was watching the road, and I knew that nothing would make him leave his post, that he'd be there all night dreaming about food."

The woman cried out again, and this time she did not stop weeping. Could those muffled sounds be kicks?

"For the love of God," she begged.

"And then I realized I was holding the revolver in my hand," said the boy, lowering his voice as if someone might hear him. "I had taken it out of the holster and was playing with it, fiddling with the trigger, spinning the barrel. Without even knowing it, Corporal, I swear."

Lituma turned on his side to look at him. In the cot next to his, Tomasito's barely visible profile was softened by the faint light of the stars and moon shining through the window.

"What were you going to do, you poor bastard?"

He had climbed the wooden steps on tiptoe and very quietly pushed at the front door until he felt resistance from the bar. It was as if his hands and feet were no longer controlled by his head. "No more, Daddy," the woman begged monotonously. Blows fell from time to time, and now the boy could hear Hog's heavy breathing. There was no bolt on the door. He just leaned against it and it began to give way: the creaking was lost in the sound of blows and pleading. When it opened wide with a sharp cracking sound, the wailing and beating stopped and somebody cursed. In the semi-darkness Tomás saw the naked man turn around, swearing. A small lantern hung from a nail in the wall, making crazed shadows. The man was enveloped in mosquito netting, pawing at it, trying to get free, and Tomás looked into the woman's frightened eyes.

"Don't hit her anymore, señor," he implored. "I won't permit it."

"You said a dumb thing like that to him?" Lituma mocked. "And to top it off, you called him señor?"

"I don't think he heard me," said the boy. "Maybe nothing came out of my mouth, maybe I was talking to myself."

The man found what he was looking for, and in a half-sitting position, still wrapped in mosquito netting and held back by the woman, he took aim, growling curses as if to encourage himself. It seemed to Tomás that shots were fired before he squeezed the trigger, but no, it was his gun that fired first. He heard the man howl at the same time that he saw him fall backward, dropping the pistol, cringing. The boy took two steps toward the bed. Half of Hog's body had slipped off the far side. His legs were still crossed on top of the sheet. He wasn't moving. He wasn't the one who was screaming, it was the woman.

"Don't kill me! Don't kill me!" she shrieked in terror, covering her face, twisting around, shielding her body with her arms and legs.

"What are you saying, Tomasito?" Lituma was stunned. "Do you mean you shot him?"

"Shut up!" the boy commanded. Now he could breathe. The tumult in his chest had quieted. The man's legs slid to the floor, dragging down part of the mosquito netting. He heard him groan very quietly.

"You mean you killed him?" Lituma insisted. He leaned on one elbow, still trying to see his adjutant's face in the darkness.

"But aren't you one of the bodyguards?" The woman stared at him, blinking, uncomprehending. Now there was utter confusion in her eyes as well as animal fear. "Why'd you do it?"

She was trying to cover herself, crouching over, raising a blood-stained blanket. She showed it to him, accusing him.

"I couldn't take it anymore," Tomasito said. "I couldn't stand him hitting you and enjoying it like that. He almost killed you."

"I'll be damned," Lituma exclaimed, bursting into laughter.

"What? What did you say?" The woman was recovering from

the shock, and her voice was firmer. Tomás saw her scramble off the bed, saw her stumble, saw her silhouette redden for a moment as she passed beneath the light, saw her, in control of herself now and full of energy, begin to pull on clothes she picked up from the floor, talking all the while: "That's why you shot him? Because he was hitting me? Since when is that any of your business? Just tell me that. Who do you think you are? Who asked you to take care of me? Just tell me that."

Before he could answer, Tomás heard Iscariote running and calling in a bewildered voice: "Carreño? Carreñito?" The stairs shook as he pounded up them, and the door opened wide. There he was, shaped like a barrel, filling up the doorway. He looked at him, looked at the woman, at the rumpled bed, at the blanket, at the fallen mosquito netting. He was holding a revolver in his hand, shifting heavily from one foot to the other.

"I don't know," murmured the boy, struggling against the mineral substance his tongue had become. The partially obscured body was moving on the wooden floor. But not groaning anymore.

"You whore, what's going on?" Fats Iscariote was panting, his eyes bulging like a grasshopper's. "What happened, Carreñito?"

The woman had finished dressing and was slipping on her shoes, moving first one leg, then the other. As if it were a dream, Tomás recognized the flowered white dress she had worn that afternoon when he saw her get off the Lima plane in the Tingo María airport, where he and Iscariote had gone to meet her and take her back to Hog.

"Ask him what happened." Her eyes flashed and she moved her hand, pointing at the man on the floor, at him, at the man again.

"She was so angry I thought she was going to come at me and scratch my eyes out," said the boy. His voice had sweetened.

"You killed the boss, Carreño?" The fat man was dumbfounded. "You killed him?"

"Yes, yes," screamed the woman, beside herself. "And now what's going to happen to us?"

"Damn," Fats Iscariote said over and over again, like a robot. He didn't stop blinking.

"I don't think he's dead," stammered the boy. "I saw him move."

"But why, Carreñito?" The fat man leaned over to look at the body. He straightened up immediately and stepped back in dismay. "What did he do to you? Why?"

"He was hitting her. He was going to kill her. Just for fun. I got mad, Fats, I really lost it. I couldn't take all that shit."

Iscariote's moon face turned toward him, and he scrutinized him, craning his neck as if he wanted to smell him too, even lick him. He opened his mouth but said nothing. He looked at the woman, he looked at Tomás, and sweated and panted.

"And that's why you killed him?" he finally said, shaking his curly head back and forth as mindlessly as one of the giant heads at Carnival.

"That's why! That's why!" the woman cried hysterically. "And now what's going to happen to us, damn it!"

"You killed him for having a little fun with his whore?" Fats Iscariote's eyes shifted back and forth in their sockets as if they were made of quicksilver. "Do you have any idea what you've done, you poor bastard?"

"I don't know what came over me. Don't worry, it's not your fault. I'll explain it to my godfather, Fats."

"Stupid fucking amateur." Iscariote held his head. "You moron. What the hell do you think men do with whores, you prick?"

"The police will come, there'll be an investigation," said the woman. "I didn't have anything to do with it. I've got to get out of here."

"But she couldn't move," the boy recalled, his honeyed voice becoming even sweeter, and Lituma thought: "You mean you'd already fallen for her, Tomasito." "She took a few steps toward the door but stopped and came back, as if she didn't know what to do. Poor thing, she was scared to death."

The boy felt Iscariote's hand on his arm. He was looking at him regretfully, compassionately, not angry anymore. He spoke with great resolve:

"You better disappear, and don't show your face at your god-father's, compadre. He'll shoot you full of holes, who knows what he'll do. Go on, make yourself scarce, and let's hope they don't find you. I always knew this wasn't the job for you. Didn't I tell you that the first time we met?"

"A real friend," the boy explained to Lituma. "What I did could've gotten him in hot water, too. And still he helped me get away. A huge fat man, a face as round as a cheese, a belly like a tire. I wonder what's happened to him?"

He held out a plump, friendly hand. Tomás clasped it firmly. Thanks, Fats. The woman, down on one knee, was searching through the clothes of the man who lay motionless on the floor.

"You're not telling me everything, Tomasito," Lituma interrupted.

"I don't have a cent, I don't know where to go," the boy heard the woman saying to Iscariote as he went out into the warm breeze that made the shrubs and tree branches creak. "I don't have a cent. I don't know what to do. I'm not stealing."

He broke into a run, heading for the highway, but slowed to a walk after a few meters. Where would he go? He was still holding the revolver. He put it back in the holster, which was attached to his belt and concealed by his shirt. There were no cars in sight, and the lights of Tingo María seemed very far away.

"Believe it or not, Corporal, I felt calm, relieved," said the boy. "Like when you wake up and realize the nightmare was only a nightmare."

"But why are you keeping the best part to yourself, Tomasito?" Lituma laughed again.

Along with the sounds of the insects and the woods, the boy heard the woman's hurried steps trying to catch up with him. He felt her beside him.

"But I'm not hiding anything, Corporal. That's the whole truth. That's exactly how it happened."

"He didn't let me take a cent," she complained. "That fat shit. I wasn't stealing, just borrowing enough to get to Lima. I don't have a cent. I don't know what I'm going to do."

"I don't know what I'm going to do either," said Tomás.

They stumbled on the winding little path covered with dead leaves, slipped in the ruts made by the rain, felt the brush of leaves and spiderwebs on their faces and arms.

"Who told you to butt in?" The woman immediately lowered her voice, as if regretting her remark. But a moment later she went on berating him, although in a more restrained way. "Who made you my bodyguard, who asked you to protect me? Did I? You fucked up and you fucked me up too, and I didn't even do anything."

"From what you're telling me, you were already hot for her that night," Lituma declared. "You didn't pull out your revolver and shoot him because the stuff he was doing made you sick. Admit that you were jealous. You didn't tell me the most important part, Tomasito."

2 / "ALL THOSE DEATHS just slide right off the mountain people," Lituma thought. The night before, in Dionisio's cantina, he had heard the news of the attack on the Andahuaylas bus,
and not one of the laborers who were eating and drinking there had
a single thing to say. "I'll never figure out what the fuck's going on
here," he thought. Those three missing men hadn't run away from
their families, and they hadn't stolen any machinery from camp.
They had gone to join the terruco militia. Or the terrucos had
murdered them and buried the bodies in some hollow in the hills.
But if the Senderistas were already here and had accomplices among
the laborers, why hadn't they attacked the post yet? Why hadn't
they put him and Tomasito on trial? Maybe they were just sadists
who wanted to break their nerve before they blew them to bits
with dynamite. They wouldn't even have time to pull their revolvers
from under their pillows, let alone get the rifles out of the wardrobe.
They would sneak up and surround the shack while they slept the
nightmare-ridden sleep they had every night, or while Tomás was
recalling his love affair and using Lituma's shoulder to cry on. A
deafening noise, the flash of powder, night turned into day: they'd
blow off their hands and legs and heads all at the same time. Drawn

and quartered like Tupac Amarú, compadre. It could happen any time, maybe tonight. And in Dionisio and the witch's cantina, the serruchos would put on the same innocent faces they put on last night when they heard about the Andahuaylas bus.

He sighed and loosened his kepi. This was the time of day when the mute used to wash their clothes, there, a few meters away, just like the Indian women: beating each article against a rock and wringing it out carefully in the washtub. He worked very conscientiously, soaping shirts and underwear over and over again. Then he would spread the clothes on the rocks with the same meticulous diligence he brought to everything, his body and soul concentrated on the task. When his eyes happened to meet the corporal's, he would stand erect, rigid and alert, waiting for orders. And he bowed all day long. What could the terrucos have done with that poor innocent?

The corporal had just spent two hours making the same obligatory rounds—engineer, foremen, paymasters, crew bosses, co-workers on the shift—that he had made following the other disappearances. With the same result. Nobody knew much about Demetrio Chanca's life, of course. And even less about his current whereabouts, of course. Now his wife had disappeared, too. Just like the woman who came to report the disappearance of the albino Casimiro Huarcaya. Nobody knew where they had gone, or when or why they had left Naccos.

"Don't you think these disappearances are strange?"

"Yes, very strange."

"It makes you think, doesn't it?"

"Yes, it makes you think."

"Maybe it was the spirits who took them away?"

"Of course not, Corporal, who could believe anything like that?"

"And why would the two women disappear, too?"

"Who knows?"

Were they making fun of him? Sometimes he thought that behind those blank faces, those monosyllables spoken reluctantly, as if they were doing him a favor, those opaque, suspicious, narrow eyes, the serruchos were laughing at him for being a coastal man lost up here in the barrens, for the discomfort the altitude still produced in him, for his inability to solve these cases. Or were they dying of fear? A panicked, raw fear of the terrucos. That might be the explanation. Considering everything that was happening every day, all around them, how was it possible he had never heard a single remark about Sendero Luminoso? As if it did not exist, as if there were no bombings, no killings. "What people," he thought. He hadn't been able to make a single friend among the laborers even though he had spent so many months with them, even though he had already moved the post twice to follow the camp. None of that mattered. They treated him as if he came from Mars. In the distance he saw Tomás walking toward him. He had been making inquiries among the campesinos from the Indian community, and the work crew that was opening a tunnel a kilometer from Naccos on the way to Huancayo.

"So?" he asked, certain he would see him run his finger along his throat.

"I found out something," said the guard, sitting down beside him on one of the rocks that dotted the hillside. They were on a headland, halfway between the post and the camp that sprawled along the gorge where the new highway would be located if it was ever completed. They said that Naccos had once been a bustling mining town. Now it would not even exist except for the highway construction. The midday air was warm, and a blinding sun shone in a sky filled with fat, cottony clouds. "That foreman had a fight with the witch a few nights ago."

The witch was Señora Adriana, Dionisio's wife. Fortyish, fiftyish, ageless, she spent her nights in the cantina, helping her husband serve a steady flow of drinks, and if the stories about her were true, she came from the vicinity of Parcasbamba on the other side of the Mantaro River, a region that was half sierra and half jungle. During the day she cooked for some of the laborers, and at night she told their fortunes, reading cards or astrological charts or their palms, or tossing coca leaves into the air and interpreting the shapes they made when they fell. She had large, prominent, burning eyes, and her ample hips swayed as she walked. Apparently she had once been a formidable woman, and there was endless speculation about her past. They said she had been the wife of a big-nosed miner and even had killed a vampire, what the serranos called a pishtaco. Lituma suspected that in addition to being a cook and a fortune-teller, she was something else at night as well.

"Don't tell me the witch turned out to be a terruca, Tomasito."

"Demetrio Chanca had her throw the coca leaves for him. I guess he didn't like what she saw, because he wouldn't pay her. They got into a shouting match. Doña Adriana was really mad and tried to scratch him. An eyewitness told me about it."

"And to get back at the cheapskate, the witch waved her magic wand and made him disappear." Lituma sighed. "Have you questioned her?"

"I made an appointment with her up here, Corporal."

Lituma didn't think he knew who Demetrio Chanca was. He did have some vague knowledge of the albino because the face in the photograph left with them by the woman who made the complaint reminded him of someone he had once exchanged a few words with at Dionisio's. But the first one, Pedrito Tinoco, had lived in the shack with them, and the corporal couldn't get him out of his mind. Carreño had found him begging in the barrens, and brought him to work at the post for meals and tips. He had turned out to be very useful. He had helped them reinforce the roof beam, secure the corrugated sheets, nail up the partition that had collapsed, and erect the barricade of sacks as protection in the event of attack. Until one fine day they sent him down for beer and he disappeared without a trace. "That's how this fucking thing began," Lituma thought. How was it going to end?

"Here comes Doña Adriana," his adjutant informed him.

At a distance her figure was partially dissolved by the white light. The sun, reverberating on the tin roofs below, made the camp look like a string of ponds, a broken mirror. Yes, it was the witch. She was panting slightly by the time she reached them, and responded to their greetings with an indifferent nod, not moving her lips. Her big maternal bosom rose and fell rhythmically, and her large eyes observed the corporal and the guard without blinking. There was no trace of uneasiness in that stare, whose intensity was troubling. For some reason she and her drunken husband always made Lituma uncomfortable.

"Thank you for coming, señora," he said. "As you probably know, there's been a series of disappearances here in Naccos. Three men missing. That's a lot, don't you think?"

She did not answer. Thickset, calm, swimming inside a darned sweater and a wide green skirt fastened by a large buckle, she seemed very sure of herself, or of her powers. Standing solidly in the man's shoes she wore, she waited, her expression unchanging. Could she have been the great beauty they said? Difficult to imagine when you saw this awful-looking hag.

"We asked you to come so you could tell us about the fight you had the other night with Demetrio Chanca. The foreman who's also disappeared."

The woman nodded. She had a round, sour face and a mouth like a scar. Her features were Indian but she had white skin and very light eyes, like the Arabic women Lituma had once seen in the interior of Ayacucho, galloping like the wind on the backs of small, shaggy horses. Did she really whore at night?

"I didn't have any fight with him," she said categorically.

"There are witnesses, señora," the guard Carreño interrupted. "You tried to scratch him, don't deny it."

"I tried to take off his hat so I could get what he owed me," she corrected him impassively. "He made me work for nothing, and I don't let anybody get away with that."

She had a slow, guttural voice, as if gravel rose from the depths of her body to her tongue when she spoke. Back home in the north, in Piura and Talara, Lituma had never believed in witches or magic, but here in the sierra he was not so sure. Why did this woman make him feel apprehensive? What filthy stuff did she and Dionisio do in the cantina with the drunken laborers late at night, when Lituma and his adjutant were in their beds? "Maybe he didn't like what you read in the coca leaves," said Tomás.

"In his hand," the woman corrected him. "I'm also a palm reader and an astrologer. Except that these Indians don't trust the cards, or the stars, or even their own hands. Just coca." She swallowed and added: "And the leaves don't always speak plain."

The sun was shining directly into her eyes but she did not blink; her eyes were hallucinatory, they overflowed their sockets, and Lituma imagined they could even speak. If she really did what he and Tomás suspected she did at night, the men who mounted her would have to face those eyes in the dark. He couldn't have done it.

"And what did you see in his hand, señora?"

"The things that have happened to him," she answered with great naturalness.

"Did you read in his palm that he was going to disappear?"

Lituma examined her in small stages. On his right, Carreño was craning his neck.

The woman nodded, imperturbable. "The walk up here made me a little tired," she murmured. "I'm going to sit down."

"Tell us what you told Demetrio Chanca," Lituma insisted.

Señora Adriana snorted. She had sat down on a rock and was fanning herself with the large straw hat she had just taken off. There was no trace of gray in her straight hair, which was pulled back and fastened at the back of her neck with the kind of colored ribbon the Indians fastened to the ears of their llamas.

"I told him what I saw. That he would be sacrificed to appease the evil spirits that cause so much harm in this region. And that he had been chosen because he was impure."

"Can you tell me why he was impure, Doña Adriana?"

"Because he changed his name," the woman explained. "Changing the name they give you at birth is an act of cowardice."

"I'm not surprised Demetrio Chanca didn't want to pay you." Tomasito smiled.

"Who was going to sacrifice him?" asked Lituma.

The woman made a gesture that could have indicated either weariness or contempt. She fanned herself slowly, snorting.

"You want me to say 'the terrucos, the Senderistas,' don't you?" She snorted again and changed her tone. "This was out of their hands."

"Do you expect me to be satisfied with an explanation like that?"

"You ask and I answer," said the woman calmly. "That's what I saw in his hand. And it came true. He disappeared, didn't he? Well, they sacrificed him."

"She must be crazy," Lituma thought. Señora Adriana was snorting like a bellows. With a plump hand she raised the hem of her skirt to her face and blew her nose, revealing thick, pale calves. She blew again with a good deal of noise. In spite of his apprehension, the corporal chuckled: what a way to get rid of snot.

"Were Pedrito Tinoco and the albino Huarcaya sacrificed to the devil, too?"

"I didn't read the cards for them, or see their hands, or cast their charts. Can I go now?"

"Just a minute." Lituma stopped her.

He took off his kepi and wiped the sweat from his forehead. The round, brilliant sun was in the middle of the sky. This was a northern kind of heat. But in four or five hours the temperature would begin to drop, and by ten o'clock the cold would make your bones creak. Nobody could make sense out of a climate as incomprehensible as the serruchos. He thought again about Pedrito Tinoco. When he had finished washing and rinsing the clothes, he would sit on a rock, not moving, staring into emptiness. He would remain that way, immobile and absorbed, thinking about God knows what, until the clothes were dry. Then he would fold them carefully and bring them to the corporal, bowing. Son of a bitch. Down in the camp, where the tin roofs gleamed and sparkled, the laborers moved about. Like ants. The ones who weren't blasting the tunnel or shoveling dirt were on their break now, eating their cold lunches.

"I'm trying to do my job, Doña Adriana," he said suddenly, surprised at the tone of confidentiality. "Three men have disappeared. Their relatives came to file a report. The terrorists may have killed them. Or forced them into their militia. Or taken them hostage. We have to find out what happened. That's why we're in Naccos. That's why this Civil Guard post is here. What else do you think it's for?"

Tomás had picked up some pebbles from the ground and was

aiming them at the sacks of their fortification. When he hit the target, there was a tiny clanking noise.

"Are you accusing me of something? Is it my fault there are terrorists in the Andes?"

"You're one of the last people who saw Demetrio Chanca. You had an argument with him. What's this about him changing his name? Just give us a clue. Is that too much to ask?"

The woman snorted again with a stony sound. "I told you what I know. But you don't believe anything you hear, you think it's all fairy tales." She looked directly into Lituma's face, and he felt her eyes accusing him. "Do you believe anything I told you?"

"I'm trying to, señora. Some people believe in the supernatural and some people don't. That doesn't matter now. I only want to find out what happened to the three men. Is Sendero Luminoso in Naccos? It's better if I know. What happened to those three could happen to anybody. Even you and your husband, Doña Adriana. Haven't you heard that the terrucos punish corruption? That they whip parasites? Imagine what they'd do to you and Dionisio, who get people drunk for a living. We're here to protect you, too."

Señora Adriana gave a mocking little smile. "If they want to kill us, nobody can stop them." Her voice was quiet. "The same is true, of course, if they want to execute the two of you. You know I'm right, Corporal. As far as that goes, we're exactly the same: it's a miracle we're all still alive."

Tomasito's hand was raised to aim another pebble, but he did not throw it. He lowered his arm and turned toward the woman. "We prepared a nice welcome for them, señora. We'll blow up half the hill. Before a single one of them can set foot in the post, there'll be Senderista fireworks exploding over Naccos." He winked at Lituma and continued speaking to Doña Adriana. "The corporal isn't talking to you the way he talks to a suspect. More like a friend. And you should show the same confidence in him."

The woman snorted and fanned herself again before she nodded. Raising her hand slowly, she pointed at the succession of snow-capped ridges, peaked or rounded, lead-colored or green, massive and solitary, under the blue dome of the sky.

"All these hills are full of enemies," she said softly. "They live inside. Day and night they weave their evil schemes. They do endless harm. That's why there are so many accidents. Cave-ins in the mines. Trucks that lose their brakes or drive off the road on curves. Boxes of dynamite that explode and blow off legs and heads."

She spoke without raising her voice, in a mechanical way, like the litanies in processions or the weeping of professional mourners at wakes.

"If every bad thing is the work of the devil, then there are no accidents in the world," Lituma remarked ironically. "Was it Satan who stoned those two French kids to death on the road to Andahuaylas, señora? Those enemies are devils, aren't they?"

"They send down huaycos, too," she concluded, pointing at the mountains.

Huaycos! Lituma had heard about them. None had happened here, fortunately. He tried to imagine the avalanches of snow, rock, and mud that came down from the top of the Cordillera like a whirlwind of death, flattening everything, feeding on the hillsides they dislodged, filling up with boulders, burying fields, animals, villages, houses, families. Huaycos were schemes of the devil?

Señora Adriana pointed again at the ridges. "Who else could loosen all that rock? Who else could send the huayco to exactly the place where it can do the most harm?"

She fell silent and snorted again. She spoke with so much conviction that Lituma was shaken for a few moments.

"And the men who are missing, señora?" he insisted.

One of Tomás's pebbles hit the mark with a metallic sound that echoed down the mountain. Lituma saw him lean forward to pick up another handful of ammunition.

"There's not a lot you can do against them," Doña Adriana continued. "But you can do something. Soothe them, distract them. Not with those offerings the Indians put by crevices and gorges. Those little piles of stones, those flowers and animals, they don't do any good. Neither does the chicha they pour for them. In the Indian community here they sometimes kill a sheep, a vicuña. All foolishness. Maybe it's all right in normal times, but not nowadays. Human beings are what they like."

It seemed to Lituma that his adjutant was holding back laughter, but he had no desire to laugh at what the witch was saying. Hearing talk like this, even if it was the bullshit of a charlatan or the ravings of a crazy woman, made him jumpy.

"And in Demetrio Chanca's hand you read . . . ?"

"I told him just for fun." She shrugged. "What's written is what happens, no matter what you do."

What would they say at headquarters in Huancayo if he wired this report on the camp radio: "Sacrificed in manner as yet undetermined to placate evil spirits of Andes, stop. Written in lines of hand, witness claims, stop. Case closed, stop. Respectfully, Post Commander, stop. Corporal Lituma, stop."

"I talk and you laugh," the woman said in a quiet, sarcastic voice.

"I'm laughing at what my superiors in Huancayo would say if I sent them the explanation you've given me," said the corporal. "Thanks, anyway."

"Can I go now?"

Lituma nodded. Doña Adriana struggled to her feet and without saying goodbye began moving down the slope toward camp.

From the rear, wearing her shapeless shoes, swaying her broad hips and making her green skirt flutter, her big straw hat bobbing up and down, she looked like a scarecrow. Was she also a devil?

"Have you ever seen a huayco, Tomasito?"

"No, Corporal, and I wouldn't want to. But when I was a kid, outside Sicuani I saw where one had come down a few days earlier and cut a huge furrow. You could see it plain as day, it came right down the length of the mountain like a toboggan. It flattened houses, trees, people of course. It brought down huge boulders. The dust made everything white for days."

"Do you believe Doña Adriana is an accomplice of the terrucos? That she's handing us a load of shit about the devils inside the hills?"

"I can believe anything, Corporal. Life has made me the most believing man in the world."

·

From the time he was a boy, they had called Pedrito Tinoco half-wit, moron, dummy, simpleton, and since his mouth always hung open, they called him flycatcher, too. The names did not make him angry, because he never got angry at anything or anyone. And the people of Abancay never got angry with him, either; sooner or later everybody was won over by his peaceful smile, his obliging nature, his simplicity. They said he wasn't from Abancay, that his mother brought him there a few days after he was born, and stopped in the city only long enough to wrap her unwanted child in a little bundle and leave him in the doorway of the Church of Our Lady of the Rosary. Whether rumor or truth, this was all anyone in Abancay ever knew about Pedrito Tinoco. The townspeople remembered that from the time he was a little boy he had slept with the dogs and chickens that belonged to the priest (who, malicious gossips claimed, was also his father) and cleaned the church for him and was his bell ringer and altar boy until the good cleric died. Then Pedrito Tinoco, who by this time was an adolescent, moved to the streets of Abancay, where he was a porter, a bootblack, a sweeper, a helper, and a stand-in for watchmen, mailmen, and garbagemen, a caretaker of stalls at the market, an usher at the movies and at the circuses that came to town for the Patriotic Festival. Curled into a ball, he slept in stables, sacristies, or under the benches on the Plaza de Armas, and he ate thanks to charitable neighbors. He went everywhere barefoot, wore a threadbare poncho and baggy, grease-stained trousers held up by a rope, and never took off the pointed Andean cap from whose earflaps locks of straight hair escaped that had never been touched by scissors or comb.

When Pedrito Tinoco was conscripted, some Abancayans tried to make the soldiers see that it was unjust. How could he do military service when anyone could tell just by looking at him that he was a half-wit who had never even learned to talk, who just smiled with that face of an overgrown baby who has no idea what you're saying, or who he is, or where he is? But the soldiers would not be persuaded and took him away, along with the other young men they had picked up in the city's cantinas, chicha taverns, movies, and stadium. At the barracks they shaved his head, stripped him naked, hosed him down, giving him the first complete bath of his life, and stuffed him into a khaki uniform and a pair of boots he never got used to—during the three weeks he spent there his companions saw him walking as if he were crippled or paralyzed. At the beginning of his fourth week as a recruit, he ran away.

He wandered the inhospitable hill country around Apurímac and Lucanas, in Ayacucho, avoiding roads and villages, eating grass, searching at night for vizcacha caves, where he took shelter against the whirling gusts of glacial wind. By the time the shepherds found him, he had grown so thin he was nothing but skin, bone, and two eyes maddened by hunger and fear. A few handfuls of stewed corn, a mouthful of dried meat, a swallow of chicha revived him. The shepherds took him back to Auquipata, an old Indian community of highlands, herds, and poor, small plots of ground where a few blighted potatoes and some rachitic ulluco plants barely survived.

Pedrito grew accustomed to Auquipata, and the comuneros allowed him to stay. There too, as in the city, his obliging nature and frugal life won people over. His silence, his eternal smile, his constant willingness to do whatever he was asked, his air of already being in the world of spirits, gave him the aura of a holy man. The comuneros treated him with both respect and distance, for they were aware that no matter how much he shared in their work and fiestas, he was not one of them.

Some time later—Pedrito could not have said how long, for in his life time did not flow as it did in the lives of other people—there was an invasion of outsiders. They came and left and returned, and a meeting was held, which lasted many hours, to discuss their proposals. In Pedrito's uncertain memory, the newcomers were dressed as others had been dressed, back there, before. The varayoks, the elders, explained that the vicuña reserve which the government wanted to create would not violate the community's titled lands but would actually help Auquipata because the comuneros could sell their products to the tourists who would come to see the vicuñas.

A family was hired to tend the flocks when the vicuñas began to be transported to an altiplano half-hidden in the mountains between the Tambo Quemado and San Juan Rivers, a day's travel from the community's center. It had ichu grass, ponds, little streams, caves in the hills, and the vicuñas soon became attached to the place. Trucks brought them from distant regions in the Cordillera to the spot where the road forked toward San Juan,

Lucanas, and Puquio, and from there they were taken up to the altiplano by Auquipatan shepherds. Pedrito Tinoco went to live with them. He helped them build a shelter and plant a potato field and construct a pen for guinea pigs. They had been told that the authorities would periodically bring provisions and furniture for their shack, and pay them a salary. And, in fact, from time to time some official would show up in a red van, ask questions, and give them money or food. Then they stopped coming. And so much time went by without anyone visiting the reserve that one day the caretakers tied their belongings into bundles and returned to Auquipata. Pedrito Tinoco stayed with the vicuñas.

He had established a more intimate relationship with these delicate creatures than he ever had with anyone of his own species. With a dazed, almost mystical attention, he spent the days observing them, learning their habits, their movements, their games, their manias, doubling over with laughter when he saw them chase each other, bite each other, frolic with each other in the dried grass, growing sad when one of them lost its footing on a precipice and broke its legs, or a female bled to death during a difficult birth. Like the Abancayans and the Auquipata comuneros, the vicuñas adopted him, too. They viewed him as a kindly, familiar figure. They let him approach without starting away, and sometimes the more affectionate ones would stretch out their necks, asking him with their intelligent eyes to pull their ears, scratch their backs and bellies, or rub their noses, which was the thing they liked best. Even the males in mating season, when they turned surly and would not permit anyone near their band of four or five concubines, allowed Pedrito to play with the females, though they did keep their great eyes on him, ready to intervene in case of danger.

Once some outsiders came to the reserve. They were from far away, they did not speak Quechua or Spanish but made sounds that were as strange to Pedrito Tinoco as their boots, scarves, helmets, and hats. They took photographs and went on long hikes, studying the vicuñas. But despite Pedrito's best efforts, the animals would not allow them to approach. He put the strangers up in his shelter and waited on them. When they left, they gave him some canned food and a little money.

These visits were the only anomalies in Pedrito Tinoco's life, composed of daily routines that followed natural rhythms and events: rains and hailstorms in the afternoon and at night, the harsh sun in the morning. He set traps for vizcachas, but for the most part he ate potatoes from his small field, and occasionally killed and cooked a guinea pig. And he salted and sun-dried strips of meat from the vicuñas that died. Occasionally he went down to a fair in the valleys to trade potatoes and ullucos for salt and a little sack of coca. Once some shepherds from the community came up to the reserve. They stayed in Pedrito Tinoco's shelter and gave him the news from Auquipata. He listened very attentively, trying to remember the things and people they were talking about. The place they came from was a blurred dream. The shepherds stirred forgotten depths in his memory, fleeting images, traces of another world, of a person he no longer was. And he could not understand what they meant by the turmoil, the curse that had fallen on the land, the people being killed.

The night before that dawn, there was a hailstorm. These storms always took a few young vicuñas. Huddled under his poncho in the shelter while rain splashed through the cracks in the roof, he had spent almost the entire night thinking about the ones that would freeze to death or be charred by lightning. He fell asleep when the storm began to ease. He woke to the sound of voices. He stood up, went out, and there they were: about twenty of them, more people than Pedrito had ever seen on the reserve. Men, women, young people, children. His mind associated them with the noisy barracks, because these people also carried rifles, submachine guns, knives. But they were not dressed like soldiers. They had made a fire and were cooking food. He welcomed them, smiling with his witless face, bowing, lowering his head as a sign of respect.

They spoke to him first in Quechua and then in Spanish.

"You shouldn't bend down like that. You shouldn't be servile. Don't bow as if we were señores. We're all equals. We're the same as you."

He was a young man with hard eyes and the expression of someone who has suffered a great deal and who hates a great deal. How could that be, when he was almost a boy? Had Pedrito Tinoco said something or done something to offend him? To make up for his mistake, he ran to his shelter and brought back a little sack of dried potatoes and some strips of dried meat. He handed them the food and bowed.

"Don't you know how to talk?" a girl asked in Quechua.

"He must have forgotten how," said one of the men, looking him up and down. "Nobody ever comes up to these isolated places. Do you at least understand what we're saying to you?"

He made an effort not to miss a word and, above all, to guess how he could serve them. They asked him about the vicuñas. How many there were, how far the reserve extended in this direction, and that, and that, where they watered, where they slept. With many gestures, repeating each word two, three, ten times, they told him to be their guide and help them round up the animals. By jumping and imitating the movements of the vicuñas when it rains, Pedrito explained that they were in the caves. They had spent the night there, huddled together, on top of each other, warming each other, trembling when the thunder rolled and the lightning flashed. He knew, he had spent many hours there lying with them, holding them, feeling their fear, shivering like them with cold and repeating in his throat the sounds they made when they talked to one another.

"Up in those hills"—one of them understood at last. "That must be where they sleep."

"Take us there," ordered the young man with the hard eyes. "Come with us, mute, and add your grain of sand."

He was at the head of the group and led them through the countryside. It had stopped raining. The sky was clean and blue, and the sun gilded the surrounding mountains. From the straw and the muddied earth covered with puddles, a sharp odor rose through the damp air and made Pedrito happy. He dilated his nostrils and breathed in the scent of water, earth, and roots, which seemed to make amends to the world after a storm, to soothe all those who had feared, in the violent downpours and claps of thunder, that their lives would end in cataclysm. The walk took a long time because the ground was slippery and their feet sank in the mud up to their ankles. They had to take off their shoes, their sneakers, their Indian sandals. Had he seen any soldiers, any police?

"He doesn't understand," they said. "He's a half-wit."

"He understands but he can't speak," they said. "So much solitude, living with vicuñas. He's like a wild man."

"That must be it," they said.

When they reached the edge of the hills, Pedrito Tinoco pointed, jumped, gestured, made faces, indicating that if they did not want to frighten them they had to stay very quiet in the bushes. Not talking, not moving. They had sharp ears, good eyes, and were suspicious and fearful and started trembling as soon as they smelled strangers.

"We should wait here and be quiet," said the boy with hard eyes. "Spread out, and no noise."

Pedrito Tinoco saw them stop, open out like a fan, and, keeping a good distance from each other, crouch behind the plumes of ichu grass.

He waited for them to get settled, to hide, to stop making

noise. He tiptoed toward the caves. In a little while he could see the gleam of their eyes. The ones who stayed in the entrances, keeping watch, observed him as he approached. They considered him, their ears rigid, twitching their cold noses to confirm the familiar scent, a scent that carried no threat to males or females, adults or calves. Taking great pains to keep his movements cautious and calm so as not to arouse that chronic skittishness of theirs, Pedrito Tinoco began to cluck his tongue, vibrating it very softly against his palate, imitating them, talking to them in the one language he had learned to speak. He reassured them, announced his presence, called to them. Then he saw a grayish blur streak between his legs: a vizcacha. He was carrying his slingshot and could have hit it but didn't to avoid startling the vicuñas. He felt the weight of the strangers' eyes on his back.

They began to come out. Not one by one but in families, as they always did. The male and his four or five females tending to him, and the mother with her recent calf weaving between her legs. They sniffed the water in the air, examined the disturbed earth and flattened straw, smelled the plants that the sun was beginning to dry and that they would eat now. They moved their heads to the right and the left, up and down, their ears erect, their bodies vibrating with the distrust that was the dominant trait in their nature. Pedro Tinoco watched them pass by, brush against him, stretch and shake when he tugged at the warm cave of their ears or buried his fingers in their wool to pinch them.

When the shooting began, he thought it was thunder, another storm approaching. But he saw the sheer terror in the eyes of the creatures closest to him, and he saw how they went mad, stampeding, running into each other, falling, getting in each other's way, blinded and stupefied by panic, unable to decide whether they should flee to open country or return to the caves, and he saw the first ones whimper and fall, bleeding, their haunches opened, their bones splintered, their muzzles eyes ears torn apart by bullets. Some fell and stood up and fell again, and others were petrified, their necks craning as if they were trying to rise up and escape through the air. Some of the females bent down to lick their dying calves. He, too, was paralyzed, looking around, trying to understand, tilting his head from one side to the other, his eyes staring, his mouth hanging open, his ears tortured by the shooting and the whimpering that was worse than when the females gave birth.

"Be sure not to hit him!" the boy-man bellowed from time to time. "Careful, careful!"

They not only shot them, but some ran to cut off the ones that attempted to escape, surrounding them, cornering them, finishing them off with rifle butts and knives. At last Pedro Tinoco reacted. He began to jump, to roar with his chest and stomach, to wave his arms like propellers. He advanced, retreated, put himself between their weapons and the vicuñas, pleading with his hands and his shouts and the shock in his eyes. They did not appear to see him. They went on shooting and chasing the ones that had managed to get away and were running through the straw toward the ravine. When he reached the boy-man, he knelt and tried to kiss his hand, but the boy-man shoved him away in a rage.

"Don't do that," he berated him. "Stop it, get out of the way."

"It's orders from the high command," said another, who was not angry. "This is war. You can't understand, mute, you have no idea."

"Cry for your brothers and sisters, cry for those who suffer," advised a girl, consoling him. "For those who've been murdered and tortured, for the ones who've gone to prison, the martyrs, the ones who sacrificed themselves."

He went from one to the other, trying to kiss their hands, pleading with them, going down on his knees. Some moved him away gently, others with repugnance.

"Have a little pride, have some dignity," they said. "Think about yourself instead of the vicuñas."

They were shooting them, chasing them, killing off the wounded and dying. It seemed to Pedro Tinoco that night would never come. One of them blew up two calves lying quiet next to their mother, sent them flying with a stick of dynamite. The air was filled with the smell of gunpowder. Pedro Tinoco no longer had the strength to cry. He sprawled on the ground, his mouth open, looking at one, looking at another, trying to understand. After a while, the boy with the cruel expression came over to him.

"We don't like doing this," he said, modulating his voice and putting a hand on the mute's shoulder. "It's orders from the high command. This reserve belongs to the enemy. Ours and yours. A reserve devised by imperialists. In their world strategy, this is the role they've assigned us: Peruvians raise vicuñas. So their scientists can study them, so their tourists can take pictures of them. As far as they're concerned, you're worth less than these animals."

"You should leave this place, little father," one of the girls said in Quechua, embracing him. "Police will come, soldiers will come. They'll kick you and cut off your manhood before they put a bullet in your head. Go away, far away."

"Maybe then you'll understand what you don't understand now," the boy-man explained again as he smoked a cigarette, looking at the dead vicuñas. "This is war, nobody can say it's not their business. It's everybody's business, even mutes and deaf people and half-wits. A war to put an end to señores. So nobody has to kneel or kiss anybody's hands or feet."

They stayed there for the rest of the afternoon and the entire night. Pedrito Tinoco saw them cook a meal, post sentries on the slopes that faced the road. And he heard them sleep, wrapped in their ponchos and shawls, leaning against each other in the caves on the hillside, like the vicuñas. The next morning, when they left, telling him again that he should leave if he didn't want the soldiers to kill him, he was still in the same spot, mouth hanging open, body wet with dew, unable to understand this new, immeasurable mystery, surrounded by dead vicuñas on which birds of prey and carrion eaters were feasting.

•

"How old are you?" the woman suddenly asked him.

"I wonder about that, too," exclaimed Lituma. "You never told me. How old are you, Tomasito?"

Carreño, who had begun to doze, was wide awake now. The truck was not jolting them quite as much, but the motor kept roaring as if it would explode on the next uphill curve. They were ascending into the Cordillera, with stands of tall vegetation to the right and on the left the almost bare rock of slopes, with the Huallaga River thundering at their base. They were sitting in the back of an ancient truck that had no canvas to protect them if it rained, surrounded by sacks and crates of mangoes, lucumas, cherimozas, maracuyas, which were draped in sheets of plastic. But in the two or three hours it had taken to drive away from the jungle and climb into the Andes on the way to Huánuco, the storm had not broken. The night turned colder with the altitude. The sky teemed with stars.

"Oh God, before they come and kill us, let me fuck a woman just one more time," Lituma pleaded. "Son of a bitch, since I came to Naccos I've been living like a eunuch. And your stories about the Piuran get me hot, Tomasito."

"Still wet behind the ears, I'll bet," she added after a pause, as if talking to herself. "So even if you carry a gun and go around with gangsters, you don't know anything at all, Carreño. That's your name, isn't it? The fat man called you Carreñito."

"The women I knew were scared babies, but she had so much nerve," the adjutant said excitedly. "Even after what happened in

Tingo María, she had her self-control back in no time. Faster than I did, I can tell you. She was the one who talked the truck driver into taking us to Huánuco, and for half of what he had asked. Just argued with him like his equal."

"I'm sorry to change the subject, but I have a feeling they'll attack tonight, Tomasito," said Lituma. "Like I could see them climbing down the hill right now. Do you hear something outside? Should we get up and have a look?"

"I'm twenty-three," he said. "I know everything I need to know."

"But you don't know that men sometimes need to play games to get their kicks," she replied, somewhat defiantly. "Do you want me to tell you something that'll turn your stomach, Carreñito?"

"Don't worry, Corporal. I have good ears, and I swear nobody's on the hill."

The boy and the woman sat side by side among sacks of fruit. The aroma of the mangoes grew more intense as the night deepened. The motor's spasmodic roar had drowned out the hum of the insects, the rustling of the leaves, the singing of the river.

"The truck jolted so much it threw us against each other," the adjutant recalled. "Every time I felt her body, I trembled."

"So nowadays they call it trembling?" Lituma joked. "It used to be known as getting horny. You're right, there's nothing out there, it's just my nerves. You know, I was getting a hard-on listening to you, and that sound put it right back to sleep."

"He wasn't even really hitting me," the woman murmured, and Carreño gave a start. He thought she was smiling, because he could see the gleam of her teeth. "He cursed, and I begged and cried, and you thought he was beating me. Didn't you know it was just to get excited, to get him excited? You're such a baby, Carreñito."

"Shut up or I'll throw you off the truck," he interrupted, filled with indignation.

"You should've said, 'Shut up or I'll kick your ass,' 'Shut up or I'll beat you to a pulp,' " said Lituma. "That would've been pretty funny, Tomasito."

"That's what she said, Corporal. And we both burst out laughing. And then neither of us could stop. We'd get serious for a minute and then begin laughing again."

"Yes, it would've been funny if I hit you," the boy acknowledged. "And I admit, I want to sometimes when you start putting me down for trying to help you. Let me tell you something. I don't know what's going to happen to me now."

"And what about me?" she replied. "At least you pulled that dumb trick because you wanted to, but you got me into this mess and didn't even ask my opinion. They're going to look for us, maybe they'll kill us. And nobody's going to believe what really happened. They'll say that you work for the police and I was your accomplice."

"Didn't she know you were in the Civil Guard?" Lituma asked in surprise.

"And I don't even know your name," the boy recalled.

There was a sudden silence, as if the motor had been turned off, but it immediately began to roar and boil again. Tomás thought those little lights up there were an airplane.

"Mercedes."

"Is that your real name?"

"I only have one," she said angrily. "And in case you were wondering, I'm not a whore. I was his girlfriend. He took me out of a show I was working in."

"At the Vacilón, a club in downtown Lima," the guard explained. "She wasn't the only one. Hog had a string of girlfriends. Iscariote introduced him to five at least."

"What a life." Lituma sighed. "Five at the same time! A change of woman every day, every night, like underwear or shirts. And here we are, Tomasito, starving to death."

"My back was aching," his adjutant went on, absorbed in his memories. "There was no way to persuade the driver to let us ride in the cab. He was afraid we'd attack him. We were covered with bruises. And I was eaten up by doubts when I thought about what Mercedes had said. Could it be true, was all her crying just an act to get him excited? What do you think, Corporal?"

"I don't know what to say, Tomasito. It probably was an act. He pretended to beat her, she pretended to cry, then he got hot and got off. I've heard about guys like that."

"What a pig, a real pig," his adjutant growled. "He deserved to die, damn it."

"And in spite of everything you fell in love with Mercedes. Love's really complicated, Tomasito."

"Don't I know it," murmured the guard. "If it wasn't for love I wouldn't be in the damn barrens waiting for some motherfucking fanatics to decide to come and kill us."

"Did you hear something? I'm going to have a look around, just in case." Lituma listened intently. He stood, holding his revolver, and went to the door of the shack. He peered in all directions and came back to his cot, laughing. "No, it's not them. I thought I saw the mute taking a shit in the moonlight."

What would happen to him now? Better not think about it. Just get to Lima and then he'd see. Could he face his godfather after this? It would be a bitter pill to swallow. He had always behaved like a gentleman and this is how you repay him. That's called being a real asshole, Carreño. Yes, but he didn't care. He felt better now, bouncing around with each jolt of the truck and touching her sometimes; much better than back in Tingo María, shaking, sweating, choking, leaning against the walls of that house, listening to his filthy shit. All those moans, pleas, blows, threats, just an act, just a lie? False. Or, unexpectedly, true.

"I didn't regret a thing, Corporal, and that's the truth," Tomás declared. "Whatever happened to me would happen. Because I was already crazy about her, just like you guessed."

The motion and the sweet aroma of the mangoes made them both drowsy. Mercedes tried to rest her head against a sack, but the bouncing of the truck made that impossible. Carreño heard her grumble, saw her bury her face in her hands as she shifted again and again in an effort to find a comfortable position.

"Let's make a deal," he heard her say at last, trying to be casual. "You lean on my shoulder for a while, and then I'll lean on you. If we don't get some sleep, we'll be dead on our feet by the time we get to Huánuco."

"Well now, things are getting interesting," remarked Lituma. "Tell me once and for all about the first time you fucked her, Tomasito."

"Right then and there I stretched out my arm and made a little place for her," Tomás said joyfully. "I felt her body coming close to mine, I felt her head resting on my shoulder."

"And, of course, you got a hard-on," said Lituma.

The boy didn't take the hint this time, either.

"I put my arm around her, I rested my hand on her," he explained. "Mercedes was sweating. So was I. Her hair brushed my face, tickled my nose. I felt the curve of her hip right next to mine. When she spoke, her lips touched my chest, and I could feel her warm breath right through my shirt."

"Son of a bitch, the one who's getting a hard-on here is me," said Lituma. "So what do I do now, Tomasito? Jerk off?"

"Go out and take a leak, Corporal. The cold will make it go down."

"Are you religious? A good Catholic? Can't you accept that a man and a woman do certain things? Was it sin or something that made you kill him, Carreñito?"

"I felt happy having her so close," his adjutant admitted. "I kept my mouth closed tight, stayed very still, listened to the truck struggling up the Cordillera, and that's how I could stand how much I wanted to kiss her."

"Don't get angry because I asked," Mercedes insisted. "It's just that I'm trying to understand why you killed him, and nothing comes to me."

"Go to sleep and don't think about it," the boy said. "Like me. I don't remember anymore. I've forgotten about Hog and Tingo María. And don't bring religion into it."

It was the dead of night over the great peaks of the Andes, which seemed to grow higher with each curve in the road. But down in the jungle they were leaving behind, day was breaking in a thin bluish-white streak along the horizon.

"Did you hear that? Did you?" Lituma sat up abruptly in his cot. "Grab your revolver, Tomasito. I'll swear those are footsteps coming up the hill."

3 / "MAYBE THEY GOT RID of Casimiro Huarcaya because they thought he was a pishtaco," said Dionisio the cantinero. "He spread the rumor himself. I don't know how many times I heard him bellow like a wild boar, right there where you're standing: 'I'm a pishtaco and so what? One of these days I'll slice up your fat and suck out your blood. All of you.' Maybe he was a little high, but everybody knows drunks tell the truth. The whole cantina heard him. By the way, are there any pishtacos in Piura, Corporal, sir?"

Lituma raised the glass of anisette that the cantinero had just poured, said "Cheers" to his adjutant, and drank it in one swallow. The sweet-tasting warmth went down to his belly and raised his spirits, which had been dragging on the ground all day.

"Personally, I've never heard of pishtacos in Piura. Now, spirit-chasers are a different story. I knew one in Catacaos. He would go to houses where there were souls in torment and talk to them and get them to leave. Of course, a spirit-chaser isn't much compared to a pishtaco."

The cantina was in the very center of the camp, surrounded by the barracks where the laborers slept. It had a low ceiling, benches and crates that served as chairs and tables, a dirt floor, and pictures of naked women tacked to the plank walls. The place was always crowded at night, but it was still early—the sun had just set—and in addition to Lituma and Tomás there were only four other men, all wrapped in scarves, and two wearing hard hats; they were sitting at a table and drinking beer. The corporal and the guard each carried his second glass of anisette to the adjoining table.

"I can see that what I said about the pishtaco hasn't convinced you." Dionisio laughed.

He was a fat, flabby man with a sooty face that looked as if it had been streaked with coal, and greasy, kinky hair. He was stuffed like a sausage into a blue sweater that he never took off, and his eyes were always bloodshot and burning, for he drank along with his customers. Though he never became completely drunk. At least Lituma had never seen him in the state of total intoxication that so many laborers reached on Saturday nights. He usually played Radio Junín at top volume, but tonight he hadn't turned on the radio yet.

"Do you believe in pishtacos?" Lituma asked the men at the next table. Four faces, half hidden by shawls, turned toward him. They all seemed made from the same mold—skin burned by hot sun and cutting cold, evasive, inexpressive eyes, noses and lips livid with harsh weather, unruly hair—and it was difficult for him to tell them apart.

"Who knows?" one of them answered at last. "Maybe."

"I do," one of the men in a hard hat said after a moment. "They must exist if so many people talk about them."

Lituma narrowed his eyes. He could see him. A stranger. Half gringo. At first glance you didn't know what he was because he looked just like everybody else in this world. He lived in caves and committed his crimes at night. Lurking along the roads, behind boulders, hiding among haystacks or under bridges, waiting for solitary travelers. He would approach with cunning, pretending to be a friend. His powder made from the bones of the dead was all ready, and at the first careless moment he threw it in his victims' faces. Then he could suck out their fat. Afterward he let them go, emptied, nothing but skin and bone, doomed to waste away in a few hours or days. These were the benign ones. They needed human fat to make church bells sing more sweetly and tractors run more smoothly, and now, lately, to give to the government to help pay off the foreign debt. The evil ones were worse. They not only slit their victims' throats but butchered them like cattle, or sheep, or hogs, and ate them. Bled them drop by drop and got drunk on the blood. Son of a bitch, the serruchos believed this stuff. Did that witch Doña Adriana really kill a pishtaco?

"Casimiro Huarcaya was an albino," murmured the laborer who had spoken first. "What Dionisio said might be true. Maybe they took him for a pishtaco and knocked him off before he could cut out their fat."

His companions celebrated his remarks with whispers and giggles. Lituma felt his pulse quicken. Huarcaya had broken rocks and shoveled dirt and sweated alongside these men on the unfinished highway; now he was either dead or kidnapped. And these fuckers allowed themselves the luxury of making jokes.

"You don't give a shit about any of this," he said accusingly. "What happened to the albino could happen to you. And suppose the terrucos attack Naccos tonight and start their people's trials the way they did in Andamarca? How'd you like to be stoned to death for being traitors or faggots? How'd you like to be whipped for being drunkards?"

"Well, I'm not a drunkard, or a traitor, or a faggot, so I wouldn't like it at all," said the man who had spoken earlier.

His companions congratulated him with titters and nudges.

"What happened in Andamarca is a sad business." One of the

men who had not said anything yet spoke seriously. "But at least they were all Peruvians. I think what happened in Andahuaylas is worse. Those French kids, you know, what can you say? Why mix them up in our troubles? Not even foreigners are safe."

"I believed in pishtacos when I was a kid," Carreño interrupted, speaking to the corporal. "My grandmother used to scare me with stories about them when I made her mad. I grew up suspicious of every stranger who came through Sicuani."

"And do you think the pishtacos dried and sliced up the mute, and Casimiro Huarcaya, and the foreman?"

The guard drank from the glass of anisette.

"Like I told you before, Corporal, the way things are going, I'm ready to believe anything that comes along. As a matter of fact, I'd rather deal with pishtacos than terrucos."

"You're right to believe," the corporal agreed. "If you want to understand what goes on around here, you're better off believing in devils."

Those French kids in Andahuaylas, for example. They took them off the bus and beat their faces to a pulp, according to Radio Junín. What was the point of being so brutal? Why not just shoot them and be done with it?

"We've gotten used to cruelty," said Tomasito, and Lituma noticed that his adjutant looked pale. The anisette had made his eyes shine and weakened his voice. "I'm speaking for myself now, and I mean every word. Did you ever hear of Lieutenant Pancorvo?"

"Can't say I have."

"I was in his squad when the terrucos slaughtered the vicuñas in Pampa Galeras. We caught one, and he wouldn't open his mouth. 'You can quit acting so innocent and looking at me like you don't understand,' the lieutenant told him. 'I'm warning you: if I start the treatment, you'll sing like a canary.' And we gave him the treatment."

"What was the treatment?" Lituma asked.

"We burned him with matches and lighters," Carreño explained. "Starting with his feet and then the rest of him, little by little. No lie, with matches and lighters. It was very slow. His flesh started to cook, he smelled like roast pork. I was pretty green in those days, Corporal. It made me sick to my stomach and I almost passed out."

"Imagine what the terrucos will do to you and me if they take us alive," said Lituma. "And you gave him the treatment, too? After something like that, how could you hand me a song and dance about Hog smacking that girl around in Tingo María?"

"That wasn't the worst of it." Tomasito was deathly pale now, and stumbling even more over his words. "It turned out he wasn't even a terruco. He was retarded and didn't talk because he couldn't. He didn't know how. Somebody from Abancay recognized him. 'Listen, Lieutenant, he's a half-wit from my town, how can Pedrito Tinoco talk if he's never made a sound in his life?' "

"Pedrito Tinoco? You mean our Pedrito Tinoco? The little mute?" The corporal drank from a fresh glass of anisette. "Are you kidding me, Tomasito? Son of a bitch, son of a bitch."

"He was the caretaker on the reserve." Tomás nodded and took a drink, too; he held the glass in shaking hands. "We fixed him up the best we could. The squad took up a collection for him. We all felt bad, even Lieutenant Pancorvo, and me more than all of them put together. That's why I brought him here. Didn't you ever see the scars on his feet, his ankles? That's when I lost my cherry, Corporal. After that, nothing could scare me or make me feel bad. I became hard like everybody else. I didn't tell you before because I was ashamed. And without the anisette I wouldn't have told you tonight, either."

To keep from thinking about the mute, Lituma tried to imagine the faces of the three missing men smashed to a bloody pulp, the eyes bursting out of their sockets, the bones pulverized, like those French kids, or burned over a slow fire, like Pedrito Tinoco. Son of a bitch, he couldn't think about anything else.

"Let's get out of here." He swallowed the rest of the anisette and stood up. "Before it turns any colder."

As they were leaving, Dionisio blew them a kiss. The cantinero was circulating among the tables, which were crowded with laborers now, clowning the way he did every night: doing dance steps, filling his patrons' glasses himself with pisco or beer, encouraging them to dance with each other since there were no women. His unashamed camping always irritated Lituma, and when the cantinero went into action, the corporal left. They said good night to Doña Adriana, who was tending bar. She responded with an exaggerated, somewhat sarcastic bow. She had just tuned in Radio Junín, and Lituma recognized the bolero "Moonbeam." He had once seen a movie by that name, and Ninón Sevilla, a blonde with long legs, had danced in it. Outside, the generator that provided light for the barracks had just been turned on. A few silhouettes in hard hats or ponchos moved around the area and responded with a grunt or a nod when the police officers greeted them. Lituma and Carreño covered their mouths and noses with scarves, and set their kepis firmly on their heads so they would not blow off. The wind whistled with a melancholy sound that rebounded off the hills, and they hunched over as they walked and kept their heads down.

Suddenly, Lituma came to an abrupt stop. "Son of a bitch! It makes me sick to my stomach," he exclaimed indignantly.

"What does, Corporal?"

"All of you torturing the poor mute there in Pampa Galeras." He raised his voice, trying to see his adjutant's face in the lantern light. "Doesn't something that barbaric give you a guilty conscience?"

"It did at first, I felt awful," Carreño said softly, his head down. "Why do you think I brought him to Naccos? Up here I was making amends. What happened to him wasn't my fault, was it? And we treated him fine here, we gave him food and a roof over his head, didn't we, Corporal? Maybe he's forgiven me. Maybe he knows that if he'd stayed up there in the barrens, they would've killed him by now."

"To tell the truth, I'd rather hear about your adventures with Mercedes, Tomasito. The story of what happened to the mute makes me feel like shit."

"I wish I could forget it too, I swear."

"The things I've found out in Naccos," Lituma grumbled. "Being a Civil Guard in Piura and Talara was a piece of cake. The sierra is hell, Tomasito. And no wonder, it has so many serruchos."

"Why do you hate mountain people so much, if you don't mind my asking?"

They had begun to climb the slope to the commissary, and since they had to bend over to walk, they took the rifles from their shoulders and carried them in their hands. As they moved away from the camp, they were plunged further into darkness.

"Well, you're a serrucho and I don't hate you. I like you a lot."

"Thanks for the compliment." The guard laughed. And a moment later: "You shouldn't think that people in camp are unfriendly because you're from the coast. It's because you're a cop. They're cold to me, too, and I'm from Cuzco. They don't like anybody in uniform. They're scared that if they get close to us the terrucos will put them on trial for being informers."

"To tell the truth, you have to be pretty dumb to join the Civil Guard," Lituma commented. "The pay is lousy, nobody can stand you, and you're the first one they blow up with dynamite."

"Well, a few take advantage of the uniform, and that gives all of us a bad name."

"In Naccos you can't even take advantage of the uniform," Lituma complained. "Damn. Poor Pedrito Tinoco. The week he disappeared, we hadn't given him his tip yet."

He stopped to take out a cigarette. He offered one to his adjutant. They had to make a shelter with their bodies and their kepis to light the cigarettes because the gusting wind blew out the matches. The wind was everywhere, howling like a pack of hungry wolves. The guards resumed their deliberate pace, testing the slippery rocks with the toe of their boots before putting down their weight.

"After you and I leave, I'm sure all kinds of faggot shit goes on in the cantina," said Lituma. "What do you think?"

"It makes me so sick I don't even like to go there," the adjutant replied. "But you'd die of loneliness if you never left the post, never went out for a drink. Sure, disgusting stuff goes on. Dionisio makes them all drunk and then he gives it to them up the ass. You want to know something, Corporal? I don't feel sorry when Sendero executes a faggot."

"The funny thing is, I feel a little sorry for all these serruchos, Tomasito. Even though they're so hard to get along with. They have a sad life, don't you think? They work like mules and hardly make enough to live on. So let them enjoy themselves a little, if they have the chance, before the terrucos cut off their balls or some Lieutenant Pancorvo shows up and gives them the treatment."

"And isn't our life just as sad, Corporal? But we don't get drunk like animals or let that pervert put his hands all over us."

"Wait a few months and then who knows, Tomasito."

The afternoon rainstorm had left the ground covered with puddles. They made slow progress, and were silent for a long while.

"You'll probably tell me to mind my own business, Tomasito," Lituma said suddenly. "But since I like you, and the anisette has loosened my tongue, I'll say it anyway. I heard you crying last night."

He noticed that the rhythm of the boy's walking changed, as if he had stumbled. They were lighting their way with lanterns.

"Men cry too, when they have to," Lituma went on. "So don't be ashamed. Tears don't mean a man's a faggot."

They continued climbing the hill, but the young guard did not say a word. The corporal made an occasional comment.

"Sometimes, when I think to myself: 'Lituma, you'll never get out of Naccos alive,' I start to feel desperate. And then I want to cry, too. So don't be ashamed. I didn't say it to make you feel bad, but because it's not the first time. I heard you the other night as well, even though you were crying into the mattress. I don't like to see you suffering like that. Is it because you don't want to die in this godforsaken place? If that's the reason, I understand. But maybe it's not good for you to think about Mercedes so much. You tell me about her, you confide in me, but then you fall apart. Maybe you shouldn't talk about her anymore, Tomasito, maybe you should just forget about her."

"No, it's a relief to tell you about Mercedes." His adjutant spoke at last in a muffled voice. "So, I cry in my sleep? Well, I guess I'm not so hard after all."

"Let's put out the lanterns," Lituma whispered. "I've always thought that if they were going to ambush us, it would happen on this curve."

•

They entered Andamarca along the two roads leading into the settlement—the ones that come up from the Negromayo River, cross the Pumarangra, and skirt Chipao—and along a third, a trail worn by people from the rival community of Cabana, which climbs the gorge of the Stream That Sings (its name in the archaic Quechua spoken in the area). They came at first light, before the campesinos had left to tend to their fields, or the shepherds to pasture their flocks, or the itinerant peddlers to continue on to Puquio or San Juan de Lucanas in the south, or to Huancasancos and Querobamba. They had walked all night or slept just outside town, waiting for a little light before they invaded the village. They did not want anyone on the list to get away under cover of darkness.

But one did, one of those they most wanted to put on trial: the lieutenant governor of Andamarca. And in such an absurd way that afterward people found it hard to believe. Because of a severe attack of diarrhea, Don Medardo Llantac spent the whole night scurrying out of the only bedroom in the house on the extension of Jorge Chávez Boulevard where he lived with his wife, mother, and six of his children, and squatting down by the outside wall of the building, which was next to the cemetery. He was there, straining, emptying his gut in a pestilential stream and cursing his stomach, when he heard them. They kicked the door open and shouted his name. He knew who they were and what they wanted. He had been waiting for them ever since the provincial subprefect practically forced him to become lieutenant governor of Andamarca. Without bothering to pull up his trousers, Don Medardo threw himself to the ground, crawled like a worm to the cemetery, and slithered into a grave that had been dug the night before, pushing away the slab that served as a tombstone and then pulling it back into place. He spent the morning and afternoon huddling on the ice-cold remains of his cousin, Don Florisel Aucatoma, not seeing anything but hearing a good deal of what happened in that village where he was, in theory, the highest-ranking political official.

The members of the militia were familiar with the town, or had been well informed by their accomplices among the residents.

They posted guards at all points of egress while synchronized columns walked along the five parallel streets of shacks and cottages spread in rectangular blocks around the church and town square. They wore sneakers or Indian sandals, a few were barefoot, and their steps could not be heard on the Andamarca streets: they were all either dirt or asphalt except for the main thoroughfare, Lima Avenue, which was paved with rough cobblestones. In groups of three or four they went directly to where those on the list were sleeping and pulled them from their beds. They captured the mayor, the justice of the peace, the postmaster, the owners of the three stores and their wives, two men who had been discharged from the army, the pharmacist and moneylender Don Sebastián Yupanqui, and two technicians sent by the Agrarian Bank to instruct the campesinos in the use of irrigation and fertilizers. They shoved and kicked them onto the square in front of the church, where the rest of the militia had assembled the village.

By then day had broken and, except for three or four who still wore balaclavas, their faces were uncovered. Older boys and men predominated in their ranks, but there were also women and children, some of whom could not have been older than twelve. Those who did not carry machine guns, rifles, or revolvers had old shotguns, clubs, machetes, knives, slingshots, and sticks of dynamite on bandoliers, like miners. They also carried red flags with the hammer and sickle, which they raised over the bell tower of the church, on the flagpole of the town hall, and at the top of a pisonay tree with red flowers that overlooked the village. While the trials were being held—they did this in an orderly way, as if they had done it before—some of them painted the walls of Andamarca with slogans: Long live the armed struggle, the people's war, the Marxist–Leninist guiding principles of President Gonzalo, Death to imperialism, revisionism, the traitors and informers of the genocidal, anti-worker regime.

Before they began, they sang hymns to the proletarian revolution, in Spanish and Quechua, proclaiming that the people were
breaking their chains. Since the Andamarcans did not know the
words, they mingled with them, making them repeat the verses
and whistling the melodies for them.

Then the trials began. In addition to those on the list, others,
accused of stealing, abusing the weak and the poor, committing
adultery, and engaging in the vices of individualism, had to face
the tribunal composed of the entire village.

They took turns speaking, in Spanish and in Quechua. The
revolution had a million eyes, a million ears. No one could hide
from the people and escape punishment. This scum, these dogs,
had tried and now here they were, on their knees, begging for
mercy from those they had stabbed in the back. These hyenas
served the puppet government that murdered campesinos, shot
workers, sold the country to imperialism and revisionism, and la-
bored day and night to make the rich richer and the poor poorer.
Hadn't this excrement gone to Puquio to beg the authorities there
to send the Civil Guard, supposedly to protect Andamarca? Hadn't
they incited their neighbors to betray the Revolution's sympathizers
to the military patrols?

They took turns and patiently explained the crimes, real and
inferred, that these servants of a government drenched in blood,
these accomplices of repression and torture, had committed against
each and every one of them, and their children and their children's
children. They instructed them, they encouraged them to take part,
to speak without fear of reprisal, for the armed power of the people
protected them.

Little by little, breaking out of their timidity and confusion,
spurred on by their own fear, by the atmosphere of exaltation, and
by darker motivations—old quarrels, buried resentments, silent
envy, family hatreds—the townspeople began to speak. It was true,

Don Sebastián was mean to anyone who couldn't pay for medicine in cold hard cash. If you didn't pay that same day, he kept your security no matter how you begged and pleaded. Once, for example . . . By midday, many Andamarcans had found the courage to walk to the middle of the square and present their complaints and re-criminations and point the finger at bad neighbors, bad friends, bad kin. They grew impassioned as they made their statements; their voices trembled when they recalled the sons and daughters they had lost, the animals killed by drought and disease, and how every day brought fewer buyers, more hunger, more sickness, more children in the cemetery.

They were all condemned by a forest of hands. Many relatives of the accused did not raise their hands when it was time to vote, but they were frightened by the fermenting anger and hostility and did not dare to speak out in their defense.

The sentence was carried out by forcing them to kneel and rest their heads on the low wall around the well. They were held down while a line of neighbors filed past, smashing them with stones taken from the construction site next to the village hall. The militia did not take part in the executions. No gun fired. No knife stabbed. No machete hacked. Only hands, stones, and sticks were used, for were the weapons of the people to be wasted on rats and scorpions? By taking action, by participating, by carrying out the people's justice, the Andamarcans would become conscious of their own power. This was a destiny they could not avoid. They were no longer victims, they were beginning to be liberators.

Then came the trial of bad citizens, bad husbands, bad wives, social parasites, degenerates, whores, faggots, the shame of An-damarca, putrefying garbage that the feudal capitalist regime, sup-ported by North American imperialism and Soviet revisionism, encouraged in order to still the combative spirit of the masses. This, too, would change. The purifying wildfire of the Revolution would burn away egotistical bourgeois individualism, and the collectivist spirit and class solidarity would flourish.

The townspeople seemed to listen more than they really listened, to understand more than they really understood. But after the events of the morning they were agitated enough, confused and bewildered enough, to take part with no hesitation in this second ritual, which they would remember, and their children and grandchildren would remember, as the stormiest in the history of Andamarca.

Señora Domitila Chontaza, encouraged by the exhortations of the succession of armed women and men who took turns speaking, was the first to point an accusing finger. Every time her husband took a drink he kicked her across the floor and called her "devil's shit." Her husband, a hunchback with hair like a porcupine's, swore it wasn't true. Then he contradicted himself and whined that when he drank, an evil spirit took possession of his body, the anger came, and he had to get rid of it by beating her. The forty strokes left his curved back bloody and swollen. Fear more than physical pain was behind his vows that he would never taste another drop of alcohol, his abject "Thank you, thank you very much" to each of the neighbors who beat him with whips made of leather or animal gut. His wife dragged him away to put poultices on his wounds.

Some twenty men and women were tried, sentenced, whipped or fined, obliged to return their ill-gotten gains, to indemnify those whom they had overworked or deceived with false promises. How many accusations were true, and how many were inventions dictated by envy and rancor, the result of an excitation in which they all felt compelled to take part by revealing the cruelties and injustices they had suffered? Not even they could have answered the question when, some time in the middle of the afternoon, they put Don Crisóstomo on trial. He had been the bell ringer back in the days when the tower of the Andamarca church had a bell and the church had a priest, and he was accused by a woman who had caught him just outside the village pulling down a boy's trousers. Others confirmed the charge. It was true, he couldn't keep his hands to himself, he was always touching the boys and trying to get them inside his house. One man, his voice breaking with emotion, confessed in an electric silence that when he was a boy Don Crisóstomo had used him the way you use women. He had never had the courage to speak before because he was ashamed. Others, who were right here, could tell stories like his. The bell ringer was sentenced to a beating with sticks and stones, and his corpse joined the bodies of those who had been on the list.

It was growing dark when the trials ended. Don Medardo Llantac took advantage of that moment to move away the slab covering the grave of his cousin Florisel, crawl out of the cemetery, and run through the countryside like a soul pursued by the devil, heading for Puquio. He reached the provincial capital a day and a half later in a state of exhaustion, his eyes still full of horror, and reported what had happened in Andamarca.

Fatigued, confused, not looking into one another's faces, the Andamarcans felt the way they did after the fiesta for their patron saint, after three days and nights of drinking all they could drink, and eating, dancing, stamping their heels, fighting, praying, not sleeping—it was a struggle to accept the idea that the great dazzling explosion of unreality was over, that they had to go back to their daily routines. But now they felt even greater dislocation and deeper malaise as they faced the unburied corpses swarming with flies and beginning to rot under their very noses, the bruised backs of those whom they had whipped. They all suspected that Andamarca would never be the same.

The tireless members of the militia continued to take turns speaking. Now it was time to organize. There could be no victory for the people without the iron-willed, enduring participation of the masses. Andamarca would be a support base, one more link in the chain that already ran the length of the Cordillera of the Andes and was sending out branches to the coast and the jungle. Support bases were the rear guard for the vanguard. Important, useful, indispensable, they existed, as their name indicated, to support the fighters: to feed them, heal them, hide them, dress them, arm them, to give them information about the enemy and provide replacements for those who made the ultimate sacrifice. Everyone had a job to perform, a grain of sand to contribute. They should subdivide by neighborhoods, multiply by streets, blocks, families, add new eyes and ears, legs, arms, and brains to the million already at the disposal of the Party.

Night had fallen when the neighbors elected five men and four women to be in charge of organization. To advise the residents and act as liaison to the high command, Comrade Teresa and Comrade Juan would remain in Andamarca. They should assimilate them, behave as if they had been born here and had buried their dead here.

Then they cooked a meal and ate and went to various houses and slept alongside the Andamarcans, many of whom, bewildered, disbelieving, uncertain, frightened at what they had done, seen, and heard, did not close their eyes that night.

They assembled them again at dawn. From among the younger ones they chose some boys and girls for the militia. They sang their hymns, shouted their victory cries, waved their red flags. Then they broke into the units they had been in when they entered the village, and the neighbors saw them separate and move away, some crossing the Negromayo River and others heading toward Chipao and Pumarangra, disappearing among the terraces of green fields beneath the lead-colored ocher of the mountains.

The patrol of National and Civil Guards reached Andamarca forty-eight hours after the Senderistas left. They were under the command of a young, muscular second lieutenant from the coast who had a crew cut and wore dark glasses; his men addressed him only by his nickname, Trigger. With them came the lieutenant governor, Don Medardo Llantac, who had put on years and taken off kilos.

The corpses were still in the square, unburied. The Andamarcans lit a bonfire to keep away the vultures, but despite the flames, dozens of turkey buzzards mounted guard around the bodies, and there were more flies than in the butcher shop on the days they slaughtered a cow. When Don Medardo and the second lieutenant asked why they had not buried the dead, they did not know what to say. No one had dared to take the initiative, not even the victims' relatives, for they were paralyzed by a superstitious terror of bringing down the militia again or unleashing another catastrophe if they touched the bodies, even to bury them—these neighbors whose heads, faces, and bones they had just crushed as if they were mortal enemies.

Since there was no justice of the peace—he was one of those who had been executed—the second lieutenant had Don Medardo Llantac himself record what had happened, and ordered several residents to sign the document as witnesses. Then they carried the dead to the cemetery, dug graves, and buried them. Only then did their relatives react with normal grief and anger. The widows, children, brothers, sisters, nieces, nephews, and stepchildren wept, embraced, cursed, and raised their fists to heaven, asking for revenge.

After the square was disinfected with buckets of creosote, the second lieutenant began to demand explanations. Not in public, but behind closed doors in the community hall, calling for the families one by one. He had posted sentries on the roads out of town and given strict orders that no one was to leave without his permission. (But Comrade Juan and Comrade Teresa escaped as soon as they caught sight of the patrol approaching along the Puquio road.)

The relatives went in and came out after fifteen minutes, after half an hour, hanging their heads and crying, confused and uncomfortable, as if they had said more or less than they should have, and regretted it.

In the village the atmosphere was gloomy, the silence grim. The townspeople insisted on concealing their fear and uncertainty behind angry faces and a refusal to speak, but they were betrayed by their sleepwalker's gait as they paced the straight little streets of Andamarca far into the night. Many women spent the day praying and reciting litanies in the dilapidated church on the square whose roof had caved in during the last earthquake.

The second lieutenant questioned people all day and half the night without a break, not even for lunch—he had a bowl of soup with dried beef brought in, and he ate as he carried out his investigations—and one of the few things the residents knew in the course of that extraordinary second day was that a frenetic Don Medardo Llantac remained at the officer's side, giving him information about those who came in to make statements, meddling in the interrogations, demanding names and precise details.

That night, Andamarca's false civility shattered. Arguments, disputes, accusations, insults, and threats erupted in the houses, on the corners, in the streets, all around the square, where everyone congregated to spy on those leaving the community hall. Fistfights broke out and there were shoving and scratching matches. The National Guard and Civil Guard did not intervene, either because they had been instructed not to or because they had received no orders and did not know how to respond to the unbridled hostility of a free-for-all. They watched with contempt or indifference and did not lift a finger to separate the Andamarcans as they called one another murderers, accomplices, terrorists, slanderers, traitors, cowards, and then raised their hands against their neighbors.

Those who were questioned had to tell everything—doing their best to lessen their own responsibility by exaggerating the responsibility of others—and the second lieutenant was able to reconstruct in broad strokes what had occurred at the trials, because on the following day the five men and four women named as leaders of the support base were locked up in the town hall.

At midmorning the second lieutenant assembled the Andamarcans in the village square—turkey buzzards still prowled the corner where the executions had taken place—and spoke to them. They did not all understand the officer's rapid coastal Spanish with its dropped consonants, but even those who missed a good part of his speech understood that he was berating them. For collaborating with the terrorists, for taking part in this parody of justice, for carrying out a grotesque, criminal massacre.

"All of Andamarca should be tried and punished," he repeated several times. Then, with patience, though not showing any signs of understanding, he listened to the residents who had the courage to formulate obscure excuses: it wasn't true, no one had done anything, it had all been the work of the terrucos. They had threatened them, señor. They had forced them, they had put machine guns and pistols to their heads and said they would slaughter the children like pigs if they didn't pick up the stones. They contradicted and interrupted each other, disagreed with each other, and eventually accused and insulted each other. The second lieutenant watched them with a pitying look.

The patrol remained in Andamarca all day. That afternoon and evening the National Guard and Civil Guard carried out searches and confiscated jewelry, ornaments, any objects that seemed valuable, and the bags and packets of money they found hidden under mattresses and in the false bottoms of trunks and wardrobes. But none of the neighbors denounced the looting to the second lieutenant.

The next morning, when the patrol was preparing to leave, taking the prisoners with them, Don Medardo Llantac and the officer argued in front of the residents. The lieutenant governor wanted a few men from the patrol to remain in town. But the second lieutenant had been ordered to bring the entire patrol back to the provincial capital. The villagers had to organize their own defense and set up squads to protect the streets.

"And what will we do for weapons?" Medardo Llantac shouted. "We'll have sticks and they'll have rifles. Is that how you expect us to fight them?"

The second lieutenant replied that he would talk to his superiors. He would try to convince them to reopen the Civil Guard post that had been closed for almost a year. Then he left with the prisoners, who were tied together in single file.

After a time, the relatives of the nine who had been arrested went to Puquio, but the authorities could not tell them anything. There was no record of a group of prisoners from Andamarca in any police station or any office of the political-military command. As for the young second lieutenant whose nickname was Trigger, he had probably gone elsewhere, since he was not one of their officers and nobody in Puquio knew him. By then Don Medardo Llantac and his wife had left without telling even his mother or his children where they were going.

•

"I know you're awake and dying to tell me what happened," said Lituma. "Okay, Tomasito, tell me."

The truck drove into Huánuco at dusk, twenty hours after leaving Tingo María. They'd had two flat tires: the road was badly rutted by the rains, and Tomás climbed down to help the driver, a Huancayan who didn't ask indiscreet questions. At a checkpoint on the outskirts of Acomayo, as they hid among sacks and crates of fruit, they heard him say "None" when the Civil Guard asked how many passengers he was carrying. They made two more stops to have breakfast and lunch at shabby little taverns along the highway, and Tomás and Mercedes got down, too, but did not talk with the driver. He dropped them off across from the Central Market.

"I thanked him for not giving us away at the Acomayo checkpoint," said Tomás. "We had told him we were running away from a jealous husband."

"If you're running away from something else too, don't stay around here," the driver advised, instead of saying goodbye. "All the coca from the jungle passes along this highway, and Huánuco is full of stool pigeons on the lookout for dealers."

He waved and drove away. It was dark, but the streetlights had not yet been turned on. Many of the stalls in the market were closed; at the ones that were still open, people were eating by the dim light of candles. The place smelled of oil, frying food, and horse droppings.

"I feel like I have bruises on every bone and muscle," said Mercedes. "I'm stiff and tired. But most of all I'm hungry."

She yawned and rubbed her arms. Her flowered dress was covered with dirt.

"Let's find a place to sleep," said Carreño. "I'm half dead, too."

"Damn, that's pretty cute," whispered Lituma. "To sleep or to do something else, Tomasito?"

They asked the people who were sipping steaming bowls of soup and were given the addresses of a pensión and a small hotel. They had to step carefully, for the ground was covered with sleeping beggars and tramps, and on the dark streets enraged dogs leaped out to bark at them. They decided against the Pensión Lucinda because it was next to a police station. Three blocks farther on, forming the street corner, they found the Hotel Leoncio Prado, a two-story building with adobe walls, a corrugated tin roof, and little false balconies. There was a restaurant with a bar on the ground floor.

"The woman at reception asked me for my voter's identification but didn't ask Mercedes, and she made us pay in advance," said Tomás, lingering over the details. "She didn't seem to care that we weren't carrying suitcases. She had us wait in the hallway while she got the room ready."

"Just one room?" Lituma exulted. "Just one little bed for the two of you?"

"The restaurant was empty," the boy went on, not hearing, drawing out his story. "We ordered sodas and some soup. Mercedes was yawning and kept rubbing her arms."

"Do you know what I'd regret most if the terrucos killed us tonight, Tomasito?" Lituma interrupted. "Having to leave this life without seeing a naked broad again. I've felt like a eunuch ever since I set foot in Naccos. It doesn't seem to bother you much, remembering your Piuran is enough for you, isn't it?"

"All I need now is to get sick," Mercedes complained.

"That was an excuse," Lituma protested. "I hope you didn't believe her."

"It's because the truck was so uncomfortable. You'll feel better after a little soup and a good sleep," the boy assured her.

"I hope so," she replied. And sat with her eyes closed, shivering, until they brought the food.

"And that meant I could look at her all I wanted," said Tomasito.

"So far, I haven't been able to picture her," said Lituma. "I still can't see her. You saying 'She's terrific-looking,' 'She's a knockout' isn't any help. At least give me a few details."

"A round little face, cheeks like two apples, full lips, a nice nose," Tomás recited. "A little nose that quivered when she talked, sniffing like a puppy's. She was so tired she had dark circles under those long eyelashes."

"Damn, you had it worse than a love-sick calf," Lituma said in amazement. "And you still do, Tomasito."

"Even though her hair was messy, even though her makeup had worn off and she was dirty from the trip, she didn't look ugly," the boy insisted. "She was still real pretty, Corporal."

"At least you have memories of Mercedes to comfort you," Lituma complained. "I didn't bring any from Piura. Not a single girl in Piura or Talara misses me, not a single woman in the world for me to miss."

They had the soup in silence, and then they were served breaded steak and rice, which they had not ordered. But they ate it all the same.

"Suddenly her eyes filled with tears, even though she was trying not to cry," said Tomás. "She was trembling, and I knew it was because of what could happen to us. I wanted to comfort her, but I didn't know how. The future looked black to me, too."

"Skip that part and get to the bed," Lituma pleaded.

"Dry your eyes," said Carreño, handing her his handkerchief. "I won't let anything happen to you, I swear it."

Mercedes wiped away the tears and did not speak until they had finished eating. Their room was on the second floor, at the end of the hall, and the beds were separated by a wooden bench that served as a night table. The lightbulb dangled from a cord draped in cobwebs, and it barely lit the faded, uneven walls and the floorboards that creaked under their feet.

"The manager gave us two towels and a piece of soap," Tomasito continued, relishing every detail. "She said that if we wanted to shower we should do it now because there was no water during the day."

She walked out and Mercedes followed, with a towel over her shoulder. She came back a good while later, and the boy, who was lying on the bed as taut as a guitar string, gave a start when he heard her come into the room. She had the towel wrapped around her head like a turban, her dress was unbuttoned, and she was carrying her shoes.

"A great shower," he heard her say. "The cool water revived me."

He picked up the other towel and went to shower, too.

"What an asshole!" Lituma was indignant. "What the hell were you waiting for? Suppose she fell asleep?"

There was no shower head, but the water was strong and cool. Tomás soaped and rubbed his body and felt his weariness lifting. He dried himself, put on his shorts, and wrapped the towel around his waist. The light in the room was turned off. He left his clothes on the bureau, where Mercedes had folded hers, felt his way to the empty bed, and lay down under the spread. His eyes gradually grew accustomed to the dark. Uneasy and overwrought, he strained his ears, trying to hear her. She was breathing slowly, deeply. Was she asleep already? He thought he could smell her body, there, so close to him. Tomás was restless, and took a deep breath. Should he go to see his godfather, should he try to explain? "This is how you repay everything I've done for you, you piece of shit." He would have to leave the country, somehow.

"I thought about everything and nothing, Corporal." His adjutant's voice trembled. "I felt like smoking but didn't get up, so I wouldn't wake her. It was so strange to be lying next to her. So strange to think, 'If I stretch out my hand, I can touch her.' "

"Get on with it," Lituma grumbled. "You have me on pins and needles, Tomasito."

"Did you do it because you liked me?" Mercedes asked suddenly. "When you picked me up at the Tingo María airport, with the fat man? Did you notice me then?"

"I saw you before that," Carreño whispered, feeling as if talking made his mouth hurt. "Last month, when you went to Pucallpa to spend the night with Hog."

"You were his bodyguard in Pucallpa? That's why I thought your face looked familiar when I saw you in Tingo María."

"In fact, she didn't remember that I had picked her up on the first trip, too," said the adjutant. "That I was the one standing guard all night in Pucallpa, in that house between the river and the woods. Listening to him beat her. Listening to her beg."

"If this doesn't end with some fucking, I'm going to beat you," Lituma warned.

"Sure, that's why your face looked familiar, that's it," she went on. "So it wasn't disgust and it wasn't religion that made you go crazy. You'd already noticed me. It was because you liked me. You were jealous. Is that why you shot him, Carreñito?"

"I was blushing so hard my face burned, Corporal. 'If she goes on talking like this, I'll slap her mouth shut,' I thought."

"You fell in love with me," Mercedes declared, half annoyed, half pitying. "Now I get it. When men fall in love, they'll do anything. Women are colder."

"You think you're so much because you've been around, because you're experienced," the boy finally responded. "I don't like it when you treat me like I was still in short pants."

"That's exactly what you are, Carreñito. A kid in short pants." She laughed and then became serious. She continued talking, pronouncing her words carefully. "But if you liked me, if you fell in love with me, why haven't you told me? Now that I'm with you, I mean."

"She was absolutely right," exclaimed Lituma. "Why didn't you do anything? What were you waiting for, Tomasito?"

The sound of frantic barking on the street made her stop talking. They heard "Shut up, you shits" and a stone hitting something. The dogs calmed down. The boy, his entire body covered in perspiration, saw her stand up and walk around the bed. Seconds later, Mercedes's hand was buried in his hair. She began to play with it, very gently.

"What are you saying?" Lituma's voice choked.

"Why didn't you go straight to my bed when you came back from the bathroom, Carreñito? Wasn't that what you wanted?" Mercedes's hand moved down from his hair to his face, stroked his cheeks, and came to rest on his chest. "It's beating so hard! Boom boom boom. You're so strange. Were you embarrassed? Do you have a problem with women?"

"Wh-wh-what?" Lituma repeated, sitting up in the darkness, peering at Tomasito.

"I'd never take advantage of you, I'd never hit you," the boy stammered, seizing Mercedes's hand, kissing it. "Besides . . ."

"You're lying," Lituma repeated, incredulous. "It can't be, it can't be."

"I've never been with a woman," the boy confessed at last. "You can laugh if you want."

Mercedes didn't laugh. Carreño felt her sit up and lift the spread, and he moved over to make a place for her. When he felt her body next to his, he embraced her.

"A virgin at twenty-three?" Lituma said. "My boy, I don't know what you're doing in the Civil Guard."

As he kissed her hair, her neck, her ears, he heard her say very quietly: "I finally think I'm beginning to get it, Carreñito."

4 / WERE THEY MAKING any progress on that highway? Lituma had the impression it was moving backward instead. In the months he had been here, there had been three work stoppages, and in all of them the same process was repeated like a broken record. The project was going to be halted at the end of this week, or this month, the government had already given notice to the construction company, a union meeting was called, and the laborers took over the installations and equipment and demanded guarantees. Nothing happened for a period of time. The engineers left and the camp remained in the hands of the foremen and the paymaster, who socialized with the strikers and shared the communal meal prepared at dusk in the empty field surrounded by barracks. There was no violence, and the corporal and his adjutant never had to intervene. The work stoppages would end mysteriously, without defining the future of the highway. The company, or the ministerial representative sent to mediate the dispute, would agree not to fire anyone and to pay the workers for the days they had been on strike. Work was resumed in slow motion. But Lituma always thought that instead of picking up where they had left off, the laborers retraced their steps. Because of landslides on the hills

where they were blasting, or because flooding after the rains had washed away the track and destroyed the roadbed, or for whatever reason, the corporal had the impression that they were still excavating, dynamiting, steamrolling, and laying down layers of gravel and tar in the same section they had been working on when he first came to Naccos.

He was on a rocky elevation at the foot of a snowfield, a kilometer and a half from the camp, and down below, in the clean dawn air, he could see the tin roofs of the barracks gleaming in the early-morning sun. "Near the mouth of the abandoned mine," the man had told Tomasito. There it was, partially obscured by rotting beams that had once marked the entrance to the shaft but had collapsed, and by rocks and boulders that had rolled down from the peak and now blocked three-quarters of the opening.

What if this meeting was an ambush? A trick to separate him from Carreño? They'd attack them singly, disarm them, torture them first, then kill them. Lituma imagined his corpse riddled with bullets or hacked to pieces by machetes, wearing a sign scrawled in red paint: "This is how the dogs of the bourgeoisie die." He took the Smith & Wesson .38 out of its holster and looked around: rocks, sky, a few very white clouds in the distance. Not even a damn bird in the air.

Last night the man had come up behind Tomasito while he was watching a soccer game between two teams of laborers, and, pretending to comment on the plays, had whispered: "Somebody has information about the guys who disappeared. He'll give it to the corporal personally if there's a reward." Was there one?

"I don't know," Carreño said.

"Smile," said the man. "Look at the ball and point, don't make problems for me."

"Okay," said the guard. "I'll ask the corporal."

"Tomorrow at sunrise, at the abandoned mine. Tell him to go

alone." The man grinned, gesturing and making faces as if he had his eye on every kick. "Smile, point at the ball. Most important, forget all about me."

Carreño had been very excited when he came to give him the news: "Finally we have something to go on, Corporal."

"We'll see, Tomasito. I hope you're right. Do you have any idea who he is?"

"He looked like a laborer. I don't think I've seen him before." The corporal woke while it was still dark, and saw the sun come up on his way to the mine. He had been there a long time. His excitement had faded. If it wasn't a trap, it might be some serrucho motherfucker's idea of a joke at the expense of a man in uniform. To have him up here like a damn fool, holding his revolver and waiting for a ghost.

He heard a "Good morning" behind him.

He whirled around, the Smith & Wesson cocked, and saw Dionisio.

"Easy, easy." The cantinero smiled and made reassuring gestures with his hands. "Put down that revolver, Corporal, sir, be careful it doesn't go off."

He was short and stocky, and the neck of his habitual blue sweater was pulled up to his chin. That fat, sooty face, those greenish teeth, that shock of gray hair, those narrow eyes burning with drunken fever, those hands like shovels: Lituma found it all unsettling. What was he doing here?

"It's not a good idea to sneak up on me like that," he grumbled. "You could've been shot."

"We're all on edge, what with everything that's going on," the cantinero murmured. He had a honeyed, servile way of talking, but this was belied by glazed eyes that were self-confident, even contemptuous. "Especially you cops. And with good reason, of course."

Dionisio had always awakened an insurmountable distrust in Lituma, now more than ever. But he concealed it, walked over to the cantinero, and shook his hand.

"I'm waiting for somebody," he said. "You'll have to leave."

"You're waiting for me," replied Dionisio, amused. "And here I am because I came."

"You're not the one who talked to Tomasito yesterday."

"Forget about him, and forget my name and my face," the cantinero said as he squatted on his heels. "You'd better sit, they can see us from down there. This is confidential."

Lituma sat next to him, on a flat rock. "So, you have information for me about the missing men?"

"I'm risking my neck to have this meeting, Corporal, sir," Dionisio said in a hushed voice.

"We all risk our necks, every day," Lituma replied. A shadow appeared high above them. It soared without moving its wings, suspended in midair, moved by some gentle, invisible current; at that height, it could only be a condor. "Even the poor animals. Did you hear about that family in Huancapi? They even executed the dogs."

"Last night there was a guy in the cantina who'd been there when the terrucos came." Something in Dionisio's tone sounded satisfied, even euphoric, to Lituma. "They held their people's trial, like they always do. The lucky ones were whipped, the rest had their heads bashed in."

"All we need now is for them to suck people's blood and eat them raw."

"It'll come to that," the cantinero declared, and Lituma saw that his eyes blazed with uneasiness. "A bird of evil omen," he thought.

"Well, to get back to our problem here," he said. "If you know what the hell is going on and can tell me about it, I'd be grateful.

Death in the Andes

These disappearances. They're driving me crazy. You can see I'm being frank with you. Was it Sendero? Did Sendero kill them? Or take them away? And don't tell me how it was pishtacos or the spirits of the mountains, like Doña Adriana did, okay?"

The cantinero began to scratch at the ground with the twig he had been chewing a moment before, and did not look at him. Lituma had always seen him wearing that greasy blue sweater. And he had been struck by the gray streak in his hair. The mountain people almost never had gray hair. Even the really old ones, the tiny wizened Indians who looked like children or dwarfs, kept their black hair. They didn't go bald or turn gray. Probably because of the climate. Or all the coca they chewed.

"Nobody works for nothing," the cantinero whispered. "The information I have would destroy Naccos. A lot of heads would roll. I'm risking my neck if I tell you. Have you thought about some kind of compensation? You know what I'm saying."

Lituma searched his pockets for cigarettes. He offered one to Dionisio and lit it for him.

"I won't play games with you," he admitted dryly. "If you're expecting money, I don't have a cent. Anybody can see how my adjutant and I live. Worse than the laborers, not to mention the foremen. And worse than you. I'd have to consult headquarters in Huancayo. They'll take their time answering, if they even bother to answer. I'd have to send the message over the company radio, and the operator, which means all of Naccos, would find out. In the end, this is what they'll tell me: 'This guy who's asking for a reward, cut off one of his balls and make him talk. If he doesn't talk, cut off the other one. And if he still doesn't talk, shove a bayonet up his ass.' "

Dionisio burst into laughter, twisting his flabby body and clapping his hands. Lituma laughed too, reluctantly. The winged shadow descended, swooped in a majestic curve over their heads,

---

and began to fly away with a certain disdain. Yes, it was a condor. He knew that in some villages in Junín, at the fiesta for their patron saint, they would capture them alive and tie them to bulls so the birds could peck at the animals while the serruchos fought them. That must be something to see.

"You're a decent Civil Guard," Dionisio asserted. "Everybody in camp says so. You never abuse your authority. There aren't too many like you. Take it from somebody who knows the sierra like the palm of his hand. I've traveled every inch of it."

"You mean the laborers think I'm okay? How would it be if they didn't?" Lituma said mockingly. "So far, I haven't made a single friend in camp."

"The proof is that you and your adjutant are still alive," Dionisio declared as casually as if he were saying that water is liquid or that it's dark at night. He paused, scratched the ground again with his twig, and added: "But those three, Pedrito, Demetrio, Casimiro, nobody had a good opinion of them. Did you know that Demetrio Chanca wasn't his real name?"

"Then what was it?"

"Medardo Llantac."

They fell silent, and as they smoked, Lituma felt the skin crawl all over his body. Dionisio knew everything. Now he'd learn the truth, too. What had they done to them? It was bound to be something awful. And who did it? And why? The day advanced quickly, and a pleasant warmth replaced the coolness of dawn. The color of the hills seemed to intensify, and sunlight and snow made some of the peaks glisten. Down in the camp, in the translucent air, Lituma could see tiny figures moving about.

"I'd like to know what happened," he said softly. "I'd be grateful if you could tell me. Everything, every single thing. It keeps me awake at night. Why did Demetrio Chanca stop calling himself Medardo Llantac?"

"He changed his name because he was running from the ter-rucos. And maybe from the cops. He came to Naccos because he didn't think anybody would find him here. The laborers say he was a hard foreman to work for."

"Then they're the ones who killed him, why beat around the bush? Because all three are dead, aren't they? Did the terrucos kill them? Are there a lot of Senderistas in camp?"

The cantinero's head was lowered, and he kept scratching at the ground with his twig. Lituma could see the white streak running through dark, unkempt hair. He remembered the boozy celebration of the Patriotic Festival in the crowded cantina. Dionisio, drunk as a lord, his eyes malevolent, was urging the men to dance together: the same story every night. He went from group to group, hopping, dancing, drinking from all the glasses and bottles, pouring shots of pisco, sometimes imitating a bear. Suddenly he had lowered his trousers. Lituma could hear Doña Adriana's laughter again, and the guffaws of the laborers, could see the cantinero's fat, sweaty buttocks. He felt the same disgust he had experienced that night. What sickening things happened later, after he and Tomasito had gone? The white-streaked head nodded. The twig came up, drew a half circle in the air, and pointed at the entrance to the abandoned mine.

"The three bodies are in that mine shaft?"

Dionisio did not say yes or no. His plump hand returned to its former position, and with a certain impatience, the twig began scratching at the pebbles again.

"I wouldn't advise you to go down there to look for them," he said in a tone that struck Lituma as more insidious than amiable. "It's a miracle those shafts haven't collapsed. They'll cave in at the first false step. Besides, the tunnels are full of gases. Yes, they must still be in there, in that labyrinth, if the muki hasn't eaten them yet. You know who the muki is, don't you? The devil of the mines, he takes revenge for the hills that are misused by human greed. He only kills miners. I'd better not say any more, Corporal, sir. As soon as you know, you're a dead man. You wouldn't last an hour. I was going to tell you for money, even though I knew it meant sending you to be slaughtered. We need money to get away from here. You know that. They're closing in, they could come any time. After you and your adjutant, my wife and I are second on their list. Maybe first. They don't hate just cops. They hate anybody who drinks and fucks, anybody who makes other people drink and fuck. Anybody who has a little fun in spite of hard times. They'll stone us to death, too. We have to get out. But with what? It's lucky you don't have money to buy the secret from me. That saved your life, Corporal, sir!"

Lituma ground out the cigarette with his foot. Maybe the cantinero was right, maybe his ignorance had kept him alive. He tried to picture them hacked to pieces at the bottom of those damp, eternally dark tunnels, in passageways filled with explosive fumes and sulfurous poisons. Maybe Señora Adriana had told the truth. Maybe they were killed for superstitious reasons. Sendero didn't throw people down mine shafts, Sendero left the corpses in plain view so everybody could see. The cantinero knew exactly what had happened. Who could have done something like that? What if he put the Smith & Wesson in Dionisio's mouth and threatened him? "Talk or you'll find yourself at the bottom of a mine shaft, too." That's what Lieutenant Silva in Talara would have done. He gave a brief chuckle.

"Let me in on the joke, Corporal."

"It sets my nerves on edge, that's why I'm laughing," Lituma explained. "Don't forget, I knew one of them very well. Pedrito Tinoco helped us fix up the post, and he lived with us from the time my adjutant brought him to Naccos. He never hurt a soul."

He rose to his feet and took a few steps, breathing deeply.

Again he felt the oppressive, crushing presence of the immense mountains, the deep sky of the sierra. Everything here moved upward. With every cell of his body he longed for the deserts, the endless Piuran flatlands studded with carob trees, flocks of goats, white sand dunes. What are you doing here, Lituma? And again, as he had so often over the past few months, he felt certain he would not leave Naccos alive. He'd end up like the other three at the bottom of a shaft.

"It's a waste of time to try to understand, Corporal, sir," said the cantinero, who was sitting now on the flat stone previously occupied by Lituma. "People are hotheaded on account of what's going on. And when people are like that, anything can happen."

"You're all very gullible, very naïve," replied Lituma. "You believe anything, like stories about pishtacos and mukis. In civilized places, nobody believes things like that anymore."

"You people from the coast are very sophisticated, aren't you," said Dionisio.

"It's too easy to blame the disappearances on Satan, like your wife does."

"Poor Satan." Dionisio laughed. "Adriana is just going along with the crowd. Isn't he always blamed for every bad thing that happens? Why are you so surprised?"

"Come on, you don't think Satan's so bad," Lituma remarked, observing him.

"If it wasn't for him, men wouldn't have learned how to enjoy life." Dionisio challenged him with his sardonic eyes. "Or are you opposed to people boozing, like those fanatics?"

"As far as I'm concerned, everybody can fuck and live it up as much as they want to," Lituma replied. "It's what I'd like to be doing here. But there's nobody to do it with."

"What are you waiting for? Why don't you fuck your adjutant?" Dionisio laughed. "The kid's not bad-looking."

"I don't like that faggot shit," Lituma said angrily.

"It's just a joke, Corporal, sir, don't get mad," said the cantinero, standing up. "Well, since we can't do business, I'll leave you in the dark. I'll say it again, you're better off. And I'm worse off. I know I'm in your hands now. If you decide to tell anybody about this conversation, I'm a dead man."

He said this without a trace of concern, as if he had no doubt the corporal could never betray him.

"I know how to keep my mouth shut," Lituma said. "I'm sorry we couldn't make a deal. But it's not up to me. I may wear a uniform, but I'm a nobody."

"Let me give you some advice," said Dionisio. "Just tie one on and forget about it. People are happy when they don't think. Anything I can do for you, I'm there in the cantina. See you soon, Corporal, sir."

He gestured vaguely with his hand and walked away, not along the path that led down to the camp, but circling around the mine. Lituma sat down on the rock again and, with perspiring hands, lit his second cigarette of the morning. The cantinero's words whirled inside his head, like those dark birds flying toward the snowfields. No question about it: the terrorists had a lot of allies in camp. That's why Dionisio was frightened and wanted to get away, even if he had to sell out some of his patrons. Did those three refuse to go along with something, or somebody, is that why they ended up at the bottom of the shaft? If the terrucos set fire to the post one night and he and Tomasito were burned to a crisp, headquarters would send condolences to their families and mention them in the order of the day. Some consolation.

He took drag after drag on his cigarette, and his mood changed from anger to demoralized gloom. No, it couldn't have been Sendero. It must have been some stupid serrucho witchcraft. He stood and walked toward the mine entrance partially blocked by stones.

Were they in there? Or was this just a tall tale invented by a drunk who wanted to pick up a few soles any way he could and get out of Naccos? He and Tomasito would have to go down and see what they could find.

He tossed the cigarette away and started the climb down. Carreño must be fixing breakfast by now. Tomasito had his mystery, too. Suddenly starting to cry at night. Was it just on account of the Piuran? Pretty funny, come to think of it. The world falling apart, executions, disappearances, devils, mukis, pishtacos, and Civil Guard Tomás Carreño cried because some broad left him. Well, she was his first lay, the one who took his cherry, the only girl that green kid ever fucked.

·

Early that morning, as she did whenever she was leaving on a trip, Señora d'Harcourt woke while it was still dark, just seconds before the alarm went off. And with the same tingle of excitement she always felt each time she traveled to the countryside, either for work or for pleasure (they were indistinguishable as far as she was concerned), even though she had been doing it for nearly thirty years now. She dressed quickly, tiptoed out of the room so as not to wake her husband, and went down to the kitchen to make coffee. She had left her packed bag by the front door the night before. As she was rinsing her cup, Marcelo appeared in the kitchen doorway, wearing his bathrobe and yawning, his feet bare, his hair tousled.

"No matter how hard I try, I always seem to make noise," she apologized. "Or does my unconscious mind betray me? Perhaps I really want to wake you."

"I'll give you anything if you don't go to Huancavelica." He yawned again. "Shall we negotiate? I have my checkbook right here."

"The moon and stars, just for openers." She laughed, handing him a cup of coffee. "Don't be silly, Marcelo. I'm safer up there than you are, going to the office. Statistically speaking, the streets of Lima are more dangerous than the Andes."

"I've never believed in statistics." Yawning and stretching, he watched her, observing the orderliness with which she arranged cups, saucers, and spoons in the cupboard. "These trips of yours are going to give me an ulcer, Hortensia. If they don't give me a heart attack first."

"I'll bring you some nice fresh cheese from the sierra." She brushed a lock of hair off his forehead. "Go back to bed and dream about me. Nothing will happen, don't be silly."

Just then they heard the jeep from the Ministry pull up outside, and Señora d'Harcourt hurried to leave. She kissed her husband, reassuring him that there was nothing to worry about, and reminding him to send the envelope with the photographs from the Yanaga–Chemillén National Park to the Smithsonian. Marcelo accompanied her to the door, and when he said goodbye, he told Cañas, the engineer, what he always told him: "Bring her back safe and sound, Señor Cañas."

The streets of Lima were deserted and wet. In a few minutes the jeep reached the central highway, where traffic was still fairly light.

"Does your wife get as nervous as my husband does when you travel, Señor Cañas?" asked Señora d'Harcourt. In the milky glow of dawn, they were leaving the lights of the city behind them.

"A little," the engineer said, nodding. "But Mirta's not very good at geography, and she has no idea that we're going into the lion's den."

"The lion's den?" said the driver, and the jeep bucked. "You should have told me before, Señor Cañas, and I wouldn't have come. I'm not going to risk my neck for the miserable salary they pay me."

"Pay us." Cañas laughed.

"Pay the two of you," declared Señora d'Harcourt. "I don't earn a red cent. I do all this for the sake of art."

"You know you love it, señora. You'd pay them to do the work."

"Well, yes, that's true," she admitted. "It fills my life. It must be that plants and animals have never deceived me, but people sometimes do. And you love it, too, Señor Cañas. You wouldn't stay at the Ministry if it weren't for something more significant than your salary."

"You're to blame, señora. I've told you before: I read your articles in *El Comercio*. You whetted my appetite and made me want to travel through Peru and see the wonderful things you described. It's your fault I studied agronomy and ended up in the Forestry Agency. Doesn't your conscience bother you?"

"Thirty years of preaching and at last I have a disciple." Señora d'Harcourt clapped her hands. "Now I can die happy."

"You have a good many," Cañas declared with conviction. "You've made us see what a privileged land we live in. And how badly we treat it. I don't think any Peruvian knows this country as well as you."

"If we're paying compliments, it's my turn now," said Señora d'Harcourt. "My life has changed since you came to the Ministry. Finally, someone who understands the environment and fights the bureaucrats. It's not just words, Señor Cañas. Thanks to you, I don't feel like an orphan anymore."

When they reached Matucana, the sun was beginning to break through between the hills. It was a dry, cold morning, and for the rest of the trip, as they crossed the frozen peaks of La Oroya and the temperate Jauja Valley, the engineer and Señora d'Harcourt were planning how to obtain new backers for the reforestation project in the Huancavelica sierra, which had been sponsored by the FAO and Holland: they were going now to inspect the early results. It was a victory they had celebrated together a few months earlier at a Chinese restaurant in San Isidro. Close to four years of meetings, memos, conferences, articles, letters, negotiations, recommendations. And finally success. The project was under way. Instead of being limited to herding and subsistence farming, indigenous communities would begin to raise trees. In a few years, if they could keep their funding, leafy queñua forests would once again give shade to those caves filled with magical inscriptions, drawings, messages from remote ancestors, and as soon as there was peace again, archaeologists from all over the world could come to decipher them. It was essential for more countries and foundations to give money. They needed teachers to show the campesinos how to use animal dung instead of wood for cooking and heating; there had to be an experimental station and at least ten more nurseries. In short . . . Señora d'Harcourt was a practical woman, but she sometimes let herself be carried away by her imagination, restructuring reality to match her desires even though she knew reality all too well, for she had spent half her life doing battle with it.

They reached Huancayo in the early afternoon and stopped to have a quick lunch and allow the driver to fill the jeep's tank and check the motor and tires. They went into a restaurant on a corner of the square.

"I almost convinced the Spanish ambassador to come along," Señora d'Harcourt told the engineer. "He couldn't because he had to meet with some kind of delegation from Madrid. He promised me he'd come the next time. And make inquiries to see if the Spanish government will help us. It seems ecology is becoming fashionable there, too."

"I'd like to visit Spain," said Cañas. "My maternal grandfather came from Galicia. I must still have relatives over there."

They could barely talk during the second part of the trip

because of the violent jarring and bouncing on the ruined highway. The ruts and fallen rock between Acostambo and Izcuchaca were so severe that they almost turned back; they clutched at their seats and at the roof, but with each pothole they crashed into each other and were almost thrown from the jeep. The driver was enjoying it, shouting "Look out below!" and "Wild bull on the loose!" It was dark by the time they reached Huancavelica. They had put on sweaters, woolen gloves, and scarves to protect themselves from the cold.

The prefect, who had received instructions from Lima, met them at the Hotel de Turistas. He waited while they cleaned up, and invited them to have supper with him there in the hotel. They were joined by the two technicians from the Ministry who would accompany them, and the garrison commander, a short, cordial man who saluted in military fashion and then shook hands.

"It's a great honor to welcome someone so important, señora," he said, removing his cap. "I always read your page in *El Comercio*. And I've read your book on the Huaylas Canyon. What a shame I don't have it with me now so you could sign it."

He told them the patrol was ready; they could start their inspection at seven the next morning.

"A patrol?" Señora d'Harcourt questioned the engineer with her eyes.

"I explained to you that we didn't want an escort," Cañas said to the prefect.

"And I conveyed that information to the commander," the prefect replied with a shrug. "But the crew doesn't give orders, the captain does. This is an emergency zone under military authority."

"I'm very sorry, señora, but I can't allow you people to go up there without protection," the commander informed them. He was a young man, with a carefully trimmed mustache, and he was making an effort to be pleasant. "It's a dangerous area, the subversives call it 'liberated territory.' I can't assume the responsibility. I assure you the patrol will not interfere in any way."

Señora d'Harcourt sighed and exchanged dejected looks with the engineer. She would have to explain it to the commander, as she had explained it to prefects, subprefects, captains, majors, commanders, Civil Guards, National Guards, and ordinary soldiers, ever since violence began to fill these mountains with corpses, fear, and phantoms.

"We're not political and we have nothing to do with politics, Commander. Our concern is nature, the environment, the animals and plants. We don't work for this government; we work for Peru. All of Peru. The military as well as those hotheads. Don't you understand? If they see us surrounded by soldiers, they'll have a false impression of what we are and what we do. I appreciate your good intentions, but I assure you we don't need anyone to take care of us. Our best protection is to go alone and prove we have nothing to hide."

The commander was not convinced. It had been rash enough to travel overland from Huancayo to Huancavelica, where there had been dozens of assaults and ambushes. He apologized for insisting. They might think him impertinent, but it was his obligation, and he wanted no recriminations later.

"We'll sign a paper freeing you of all responsibility," Cañas proposed. "Don't take offense, Commander, but for our work we shouldn't be identified with the military."

The discussion ended only when Señora d'Harcourt declared that if the officer insisted on a patrol, she would cancel the expedition. The commander drew up a document and had the prefect and the two technicians sign it as witnesses.

"You're a hard man," Señora d'Harcourt commented in a conciliatory way when she said good night. "But thank you for your kindness. Let me have your address, and I'll send you a little book of mine on the Colca Valley that's coming out soon. It has some very nice photographs."

Señora d'Harcourt went to Mass the next morning at the Church of Saint Sebastian, where she spent some time looking at its majestic colonial arches and antique retables of sleepy-eyed archangels. They left in two vehicles, she and the engineer in the jeep, the technicians and the prefect in an old black Ford. On the road to the Santa Barbara mines, they encountered a patrol of soldiers who carried their rifles with fixed bayonets and seemed ready to fire. A few kilometers farther on, the road became an indistinct trail, and the jeep reduced its speed so as not to leave the Ford too far behind. For an hour or two they drove up and down hill through semi-desert, passing a succession of barren mountains; on the slopes, in occasional touches of life and color, a few huts came into view, and fields planted in potatoes, barley, beans, oca, and mashua. The Ford was no longer in sight.

"The last time I was here, there weren't so many painted slogans and red flags," Cañas observed. "What the commander said must be true. It seems they control this area."

"I just hope that doesn't interfere with the reforestation project," said Señora d'Harcourt. "That would be too much. Four years to get the project off the ground, and when it finally happens . . ."

"I haven't put in my two cents yet, and that's a fact," the driver interjected. "But if you ask me, I would've felt a lot happier with that escort."

"Then they would have thought we were their enemies," said Señora d'Harcourt. "And we're not, we're not anybody's enemies. We're working for them, too. Don't you understand?"

"I understand, señora," the man grumbled. "I only hope they do. Haven't you seen on TV how brutal they are?"

"I never watch television," replied Señora d'Harcourt. "That must be why I feel so calm."

At dusk they reached the Indian community of Huayllarajcra, where one of the nurseries was in operation. The campesinos came there for the queñua seedlings and planted them around their fields and along the banks of lagoons and streams. The village center—the small church with a tile roof and collapsed tower, the little adobe school, the cobblestoned square—was almost deserted. But the mayor and elders of Huayllarajcra, their staffs of authority in hand, showed them around the nursery, which had been built by communal labor. They seemed enthusiastic about the reforestation program and said that until now all the comuneros had lived in the highlands, isolated from one another, but if the plans to bring them together became a reality, they would have electricity and drinkable water. In the fading light they could still make out the vast expanse around them, with its patchwork of cultivated fields and a terrain that grew stonier as it rose and disappeared into the clouds. The engineer took a deep breath and spread his arms wide.

"I lose all my Lima neuroses in this landscape," he exclaimed, pointing around him in excitement. "Don't you, señora? We should have brought a little bottle of something for the cold."

"Do you know when I saw this for the first time? Twenty-five years ago. On the very spot where you're standing. It's marvelous, isn't it."

Next to the nursery was a shack where meals were served. Cañas and Señora d'Harcourt had stayed there on previous occasions and would do so now. But the family that used to live in the house had been reduced to one old woman, who could not explain where her kinfolk had gone, or why. The place was empty except for a small cot. The woman said nothing and busied herself with tending the fire, stirring the pot, keeping her back to them. The mayor and elders returned to their houses. They were alone in the village center. The two watchmen at the nursery had gone into their hut and barred the door. The little reed corral, where Señora d'Harcourt recalled seeing sheep and chickens, was empty, the stakes pulled out of the ground. A ragged piece of red flannel fluttered on a stick set into the heaps of straw on the roof.

By the time the prefect and the technicians drove into Huay-llarajcra in the Ford, the stars were shining in a deep black sky. The engineer and Señora d'Harcourt were unpacking. They had set up their sleeping bags in a corner and inflated their air pillows, and were heating coffee on a portable Primus stove.

"We thought you had an accident," Cañas greeted them. "I was ready to go out and look for you."

But the prefect was a different person; the helpful, good-natured little man from Huancavelica was beside himself. They had, in fact, had a flat tire, but that wasn't why he was frantic.

"We have to go back immediately," he ordered as he climbed out of the car. "We absolutely cannot spend the night here, absolutely not."

"Have some coffee and a biscuit and enjoy the view," the engineer tried to calm him. "You can't see this anywhere else in the world. Take it easy, friend."

"Don't you know what's going on?" The prefect raised his voice. His chin trembled, and he squeezed his eyes open and shut as if his vision had blurred. "Haven't you seen the slogans painted all along the road? Isn't there a red flag right over our heads? The commander was right. It's sheer recklessness. We can't expose our-selves like this. And you least of all, señora."

"We've come here to do work that has nothing to do with politics," she tried to reassure him. "But if you feel unsafe, you can go back to the city."

"I'm no coward." The prefect's voice changed and he spoke with wounded pride. "But this is foolhardy. We're in danger. None of us can spend the night here. Not me, not the technicians, not the engineer. Listen to me, we've got to leave. We can come back with the patrol. Don't put other people's lives at risk, señora."

Cañas turned toward the two technicians, who were listening in silence.

They were fairly young and wore poor men's clothing. They seemed uncomfortable and exchanged glances, not saying anything.

"Please, don't feel obliged," Señora d'Harcourt intervened. "If you'd rather go back, you can."

"Are you staying, Señor Cañas?" one of them finally asked in a northern accent.

"Absolutely," he said. "We've fought too long to establish this project, to get money from the FAO and the Dutch. I'm not going to retreat just when it's getting under way."

"Then we'll stay, too," said the one who had asked the question. "God's will be done."

"I'm very sorry, but I'm leaving," declared the prefect. "I hold political office. If they come, I'm done for. I'll ask the commander to send the patrol for you."

"Under no circumstances," she replied, offering him her hand. "You can go, but don't do anything else. I'll see you in Huancavelica in a few days. Have a good trip back. And don't worry about us. Somebody up there is taking better care of us than any patrol could."

They unloaded the technicians' blankets and packs and watched the Ford drive away into the darkness.

"It's crazy to travel alone at night along those roads," murmured one of the technicians.

For some time they worked in silence, making preparations to spend the night in the small house. After serving them a very spicy soup with chunks of yuca, the old woman lay down on her cot. They arranged their sleeping bags and blankets side by side, then built a fire and sat next to it, watching the stars twinkle and multiply. They had ham, chicken, and avocado sandwiches, and Señora d'Harcourt passed around pieces of chocolate for dessert. They ate slowly, talking about the next day's itinerary and their families in Lima, and the northern technician, who came from Pacasmayo, spoke of his fiancée in Trujillo: last year she won second prize in the folk-dance competition. Then the conversation centered on how bright, how infinite in number, the stars were when viewed from the Andean peaks.

Señora d'Harcourt abruptly changed the direction of their talk. "I've been traveling in Peru for thirty years, and I never dreamed that things like this could happen one day."

The engineer, the technicians, and the driver were silent, reflecting on her words. Later they went to sleep, fully dressed.

They arrived at dawn, just as the party of travelers was waking up. There were about fifty of them: men, women, many young people, a few children, most of them campesinos but also some urban mestizos, in jackets, ponchos, sneakers, sandals, jeans, and sweaters with crude embroidered figures in the style that decorates pre-Hispanic pottery. On their heads they wore mountain caps with earflaps, berets, hats, and some hid their faces with balaclavas. They were poorly armed: only three or four carried Kalashnikovs; the others had shotguns, revolvers, hunting carbines, or simple machetes and sticks. The old cook had disappeared.

"You don't need to point those guns at us," said Señora d'Harcourt, stepping forward. "We're not armed, and we won't try to run away. Can I speak to your leader? To explain what we're doing here?"

No one answered her. No order was given, but they all seemed well trained, for in twos or threes they separated from the larger group and surrounded each of the five, searched them carefully, and took everything they had in their pockets. They tied their hands behind their backs with lengths of rope or animal gut.

"We're not your enemies, we're not political, we don't work for the government, we work for all Peruvians," said Señora d'Harcourt, extending her hands to make her captors' work easier. "Our job is to defend the environment, our natural resources. To keep nature from being destroyed, so that in the future all the children of the sierra will have food and work."

"Señora d'Harcourt has written many books about our plants, our animals," explained the engineer. "She's an idealist. Like you. She wants a better life for the campesinos. Thanks to her, this region will be covered with trees. That's a wonderful thing for the comuneros, for Huancavelica. For you and your children. It's good for all of us, regardless of politics."

They allowed them to speak without interruption, but they did not pay the slightest attention to what they said. They had mobilized, placing sentries at various positions that allowed them to keep an eye on the road leading into the village and the trail that climbed along the snowfields. It was a cold, dry morning, with a clear sky and a cutting wind. The high walls of the hillsides seemed renewed.

"Our struggle is like yours," said Señora d'Harcourt, her voice calm, her expression revealing no sign of alarm. "Don't treat us like enemies; we're not your enemies."

"Could we talk to your leader," Engineer Cañas asked from time to time, "or with any person in charge? Let me speak to him."

After some time had passed, a group of them entered the shack, and those who remained outside sent the members of the traveling party in, one by one. The questions were asked in loud voices. Those outside could follow portions of the dialogue. These were slow, repetitive interrogations: personal information mixed with political considerations and occasional queries regarding other people and foreign affairs. The first one questioned was the driver, followed by the technicians, and then the engineer. It was growing dark by the time he came out. Señora d'Harcourt realized with some surprise that she had been standing for ten hours with nothing to eat or drink. But she did not feel hunger, or thirst, or fatigue. She thought about her husband, grieving more for him than for herself. She watched Cañas walk out. His expression had changed, as if he had lost the certainty that had animated him during the day, when he had tried to speak to them.

"They hear, but they don't listen, and they don't want to understand what you say to them," she heard him murmur as he walked past her. "They're from another planet."

When she entered the shack they had her sit on the ground, in the same position the three men and one woman had assumed. Señora d'Harcourt addressed the one who wore a leather jacket and a scarf around his neck, a young man with a full beard and cold, gray, penetrating eyes. She told him about her life in some detail, from her birth almost sixty years ago in that remote Baltic country she did not remember and whose language she did not speak, to her nomadic childhood in Europe and America, moving from school to school, language to language, country to country. Until, not yet twenty and recently married to a young diplomat, she came to Peru. She told him about her love at first sight for the Peruvians, and, above all, about her awe and wonder at the deserts, the jungles, the mountains, the trees, the animals, the snows, in this country that was now her country, too. Not only because her passport said so—she had taken the nationality of Marcelo, her second husband—but because she had earned the right to call herself Peruvian after many years of traveling the length and breadth of this country, studying and fostering its beauty in lectures, articles, and books. She would go on doing this work until the end of her days because it had given meaning to her life. Did they understand that she was not their enemy?

They listened without interrupting, but their faces showed no interest at all in what she said. Only when she stopped speaking, after explaining how difficult it had been for her and that generous, self-sacrificing young man, the engineer Cañas, to begin the reforestation program in Huancavelica, did they begin to ask her questions. Without enmity or antipathy, with dry, mechanical phrases in neutral, routinized voices, as if, thought Señora d'Harcourt, all the questions were a useless formality because they already knew the answers. They asked how long she had been an informer for the police, the army, the Intelligence Agency; they asked about her trips, her inspection tours. She gave them all the details. The Military Institute of Geography had asked her to serve as a consultant to the Permanent Commission that was redrawing and improving the atlas, and this had been her only connection to the Armed Forces except for an occasional lecture at the Military Academy, the Naval Academy, or the Center for Advanced Military Studies. They wanted to know about her contacts with foreign governments, the ones she worked for, the ones that sent her instructions. She explained that it wasn't a question of governments but of scientific institutions, the Smithsonian in Washington, the Museum of Man in Paris, the British Museum in London, and a few foundations or ecological centers, from which she occasionally obtained funds for small projects ("It was never very much"). But while she talked, corrected, specified, and although her responses stressed the fact that none of her contacts was political, that all these connections and relationships were scientific, purely scientific, the expressions and glances of her interrogators filled her with the overwhelming certainty of an insuperable incomprehension, a lack of communication more profound than if she had been speaking Chinese and they spoke only Spanish.

Death in the Andes

When it seemed to be over—her mouth was dry and her throat burned—Señora d'Harcourt felt very tired.

"Are you going to kill me?" she asked, hearing her voice break for the first time.

The one in the leather jacket looked into her eyes without blinking.

"This is war, and you are a lackey of our class enemy," he explained, staring at her with blank eyes, delivering his monologue in an expressionless voice. "You don't even realize that you are a tool of imperialism and the bourgeois state. Even worse, you permit yourself the luxury of a clear conscience, seeing yourself as Peru's Good Samaritan. Your case is typical."

"Can you explain that to me?" she said. "In all sincerity, I don't understand. What am I a typical case of?"

"The intellectual who betrays the people," he said with the same serene, icy confidence. "The intellectual who serves bourgeois power and the ruling class. What you do here has nothing to do with the environment. It has to do with your class and with power. You come here with bureaucrats, the newspapers provide publicity, and the government wins a battle. Who said that this was liberated territory? That a part of the New Democracy had been established in this zone? A lie. There's the proof. Look at the photographs. A bourgeois peace reigns in the Andes. You don't know this either, but a new nation is being born here. With a good deal of blood and suffering. We can show no mercy to such powerful enemies."

"May I at least intercede on behalf of Cañas?" Señora d'Harcourt stammered. "He's young, almost the same age as you. I've never known a more idealistic Peruvian, one who works with so much . . ."

"The session is over," said the young man in the jacket as he rose to his feet.

When they walked outside, the sun was setting behind the

hills and the nursery of seedlings was disappearing in a great fire whose flames heated the air and made their cheeks burn. Señora d'Harcourt saw the driver climbing into the jeep. A short while later, he drove off in the direction of Huancavelica.

"At least they let him go," said the engineer, who stood beside her. "I'm glad, he's a decent guy."

"I'm so sorry, Señor Cañas," she murmured. "I feel so guilty about you. I don't know how to beg your . . ."

"Señora, it is a great honor for me," he said in a firm voice. "I mean, being with you at the end. They've taken the two technicians over there, and since they hold a lower rank they'll shoot them in the head. You and I, however, are people of privilege. They just explained it to me. A question of symbols, apparently. You're a believer, aren't you? I'm not, so please pray for me. Can we stand together? I'll bear up better if I can hold your hand. Let's try, all right? Move closer, señora."

.

"And what were you saying in your sleep, Tomasito?" Lituma asked.

When the boy opened his eyes with a start, the sun was shining into the room, which seemed smaller and shabbier than it had the night before. Mercedes, combed and dressed, sat looking at him from a corner of the bed with narrowed, inquisitive eyes. A little mocking smile floated across her face.

"What time is it?" he asked, stretching.

"I've been watching you sleep for hours." Mercedes opened her mouth and laughed.

"Go on, cut it out," said the boy, feeling uncomfortable. "At least today you woke up in a good mood."

"I wasn't just watching you sleep; I was listening, too." "Her teeth were as white as a little mouse's, they gleamed in Mercedes's dark face, Corporal." "You talked and talked. I thought you were just pretending to be asleep. But I came over and you were dead to the world."

"What the hell were you saying, Tomasito?" Lituma insisted.

"You can't imagine the beautiful fuck I was having, Corporal."

"You learned pretty fast, you figured things out pretty quick." Mercedes laughed again, and he, to hide his confusion, pretended to yawn. "You kept saying the pretty things you told me last night."

"Now it was time for flirting," Lituma remarked with amusement.

"Well, when you're asleep you can say anything," Carreño said defensively.

Mercedes became serious and looked straight into his eyes. She put out her hand, burying her fingers in his hair, and Tomás felt her stroking it the way she had the night before.

"Do you really feel those things for me? Those things you said all night and kept saying when you were asleep?"

"She had such an open way of talking about intimate things, you never saw anything like it," Tomás murmured with emotion. "It really shocked me, Corporal."

"You thought it was sweeter than honey, you liar," Lituma corrected him. "My paisana had you wrapped around her little finger."

"Or were you just hot for me, and now that I gave you what you wanted, are you cooling down?" Mercedes added, devouring him with her eyes.

"Talking in broad daylight about the things you whisper into someone's ear in the dark, I don't know, Corporal. I swear, it almost made me angry. But the feeling left as soon as she started to play with my hair."

"I know you don't like me to talk about what happened," said Mercedes, becoming serious again. "But I still don't get it, how you could see me only a couple of times and not even say a word to me and then fall in love like that. Nobody ever said those things to me, hour after hour, even when he was finished. Nobody ever got down on his knees and kissed my feet, like you did."

"You got down on your knees and kissed her feet?" Lituma was astonished. "That's not love, that's worship."

"My face is burning, honey, I don't know what to do with myself," the boy joked.

He looked for the towel that he remembered leaving at the foot of the bed the night before. It was on the floor. He picked it up, wrapped it around his waist, and got out of bed. As he passed Mercedes, he bent down to kiss her.

With his mouth on her hair, he whispered: "What I told you is what I feel. What I feel for you."

"A hard-on is what you felt," Lituma grew animated. "Did you fall into bed again?"

"I just got my period, so don't get all excited," said Mercedes.

"It'll be hard for me to get used to the way you talk," Carreño said, laughing and letting her go. "Do you think I'll ever get used to it, or do I have to change you?"

She patted him on the chest.

"Go on, get dressed, let's get some breakfast. Aren't you hungry after everything you did last night?"

"I once went to bed with a whore who had her period, at the Green House in Piura," Lituma recalled. "She only charged me half. The Invincibles drove me crazy, saying it would give me syphilis."

Carreño was laughing as he left the room. The shower and sink were dry, but there was a washbasin filled with water, and he gave himself a sponge bath. He dressed, and they went down to the restaurant. The tables were crowded now, and a good many faces turned to look at them. It was afternoon, and people were having lunch. They sat at the only free table. The boy who waited on them said it was too late for breakfast. They decided to be on their way. They paid for the night, and the manager told them that the bus and jitney offices were near the Plaza de Armas. Before going there, they stopped at a pharmacy to buy sanitary napkins for Mercedes. And in the market they bought alpaca sweaters for the cold in the Cordillera.

"It was lucky Hog paid me in advance," said Tomás. "Imagine if we didn't have a cent in our pockets."

"Didn't that dealer have a name?" asked Lituma. "Why do you always call him the man, Hog, the boss?"

"Nobody knew his name, Corporal. I don't even think my godfather knew."

They had cheese sandwiches in a small café and went to the offices to make their inquiries. They decided to take a car that was leaving at five and would reach the capital at noon the next day. The guards at the checkpoints along the highway would be less vigilant at night. It was a little after one. They lingered on the Plaza de Armas, where the heat seemed less intense in the shade of the great trees. Carreño had his shoes shined. The vast square swarmed with shoeshine boys, peddlers, street photographers, and tramps who basked in the sun or slept on the benches. There was a heavy traffic of trucks loaded with fruit arriving from the jungle or leaving for the sierra and the coast.

"And now what's going to happen when we get to Lima?" Mercedes asked.

"We'll live together."

"So you decided everything all by yourself."

"Well, if you want, we'll get married."

"That's called moving fast," Lituma interrupted. "Were you really serious about getting married?"

"In church, with a veil and a white dress?" asked Mercedes, intrigued.

"Whatever you want. If you have family in Piura, I'll go there with my mother to ask for your hand. Because I don't have a father. Anything you want, honey."

"Sometimes I envy you." Lituma sighed. "It must be fantastic to fall in love like that."

"Now I know it's true." Mercedes leaned against him, and the boy put his arm around her shoulders. "You really are crazy about me, Carreñito."

"More than you'll ever know," he whispered in her ear. "I'd kill another thousand Hogs if I had to. We'll get out of this, you'll see. Lima's a big place. Once we get there, they'll never catch us. But something else is worrying me. You already know how I feel. But what about you? Are you in love with me, even a little?"

"No, no I'm not," Mercedes answered immediately. "I'm sorry to disappoint you, but I can't say what isn't true."

"And she started in about how she didn't like to lie"—Tomasito grew sad—"and how she wasn't one of those girls who fall in love one two three. We were in the middle of that when all of a sudden, out of the blue, there was Fats Iscariote standing in front of us."

"Have you gone crazy? What are you doing here? You think this is any time to be smooching in public with the girlfriend of the man you just bumped off, you stupid—"

"Calm down, Fats, take it easy," Carreño said.

"He was absolutely right," Lituma acknowledged. "They must've been looking for you in Tingo María, in Lima, everywhere. And you were just living it up."

"We only have one life and we have to live it, Corporal," said Tomás. "And since the night before, I was living it to the hilt with my sweetheart. What did I care about Hog, or if they were after me, or would send me to jail? Nobody could take that happiness away from me."

Iscariote's eyes bulged, and the basket of tamales in his hand shook with his rage. "You can't be this dumb, Carreño."

"You're right, Fats. Don't get so upset. Do you want to know something? I'm really happy to see you. I thought I'd never see you again."

Iscariote wore a tie and jacket, but his shirt was too tight, and he tugged at the collar so much he seemed determined to pull it off. His bloated face gleamed with perspiration, and he needed a shave. He looked around in alarm. The shoeshine boys observed him with curiosity, and a tramp lying on a bench and sucking a lemon stretched out his hand, begging for money. Iscariote dropped to the bench next to Mercedes but stood up immediately, as if he had received an electric shock.

"Everybody's looking at us." He pointed at the Hotel de Turistas. "We're better off inside, room 27. Just go up without asking for me. I stepped out for a minute to buy tamales."

He strode away, not looking back. They waited a few minutes, took a turn around the square, and followed him. In the Hotel de Turistas, a woman mopping the lobby floor showed them where the staircase was. Room 27 was next to the stairs, and Carreño knocked and then pushed the door open.

"He was fat, he ate like a pig, and he was the dealer's bodyguard," Lituma concluded. "That's all you've told me about Iscariote."

"He had some kind of connection to the police," said his adjutant. "My godfather introduced us, and I never knew much about his life. He didn't work full-time for Hog. Just occasional jobs, like me."

"Lock it," the fat man ordered but did not stop chewing. He had taken off his jacket and was sitting on the bed, holding the little basket between his legs and eating tamales with his hands. His handkerchief was tucked like a napkin into his collar. Tomás sat next to him, and Mercedes took the only chair in the room. The leafy tops of the trees on the square, and the old gazebo with its faded balustrade, were visible through the window. Not saying a word, Iscariote offered them the basket; there were two tamales left. They declined.

"They used to taste better than this," said Iscariote, stuffing half a tamale into his mouth. "I'd like to know what you're doing in Huánuco, Carreñito."

"We're leaving this afternoon, Fats." Tomás patted him on the knee. "They may not be very good, but you sure can put them away."

"I get hungry when I'm nervous. My hair stood on end when I saw you in the square. Well, to tell you the truth, everything makes me hungry."

He had finished eating. He stood, went to his jacket, and took out a pack of light-tobacco cigarettes. He lit one.

"I talked on the phone to my contact, the one they call Mameluke," he said, blowing smoke rings. "I filled him in on everything. How the boss had been shot and how you and the dame disappeared. He got an attack of hiccups. What do you think his reaction was? 'So he sold him out to the Colombians. And the whore too, that's for sure.'" The half smile on Iscariote's face abruptly turned into a grimace. "Did the Colombians pay you, Carreñito?"

"He was a little bit like you, Corporal. He couldn't get it through his head that anybody could kill for love."

"Iscariote, Mameluke, Hog." Lituma laughed. "Those names are right out of a movie."

The fat man nodded, his expression wary. Behind a new set of smoke rings, his slanted eyes, half buried in the fat pockets of his cheeks, examined Mercedes from head to foot.

"Were you already fucking her?" he asked, with an admiring whistle.

"A little more respect," Mercedes protested. "Who do you think you are, you elephant . . ."

"She's with me now, so treat her the right way." Carreño took the woman's arm possessively. "Mercedes is my fiancée now, Fats."

"All right, let's not make a big deal out of nothing," Iscariote apologized, looking from one to the other. "I only want to be sure of one thing. Are the Colombians behind this?"

"I didn't have anything to do with it," Mercedes said quickly.

"It was just me, Fats," the boy swore. "I know it's hard for you to believe. But it was just like I told you. A spur-of-the-moment thing."

"At least tell me if she was already your girlfriend," Iscariote insisted. "At least tell me that, Carreñito."

"We never even talked. I only caught a glimpse of her when we picked her up and dropped her off at the airport, in Pucallpa and in Tingo María. That's how it was, Fats, you have to believe me."

Iscariote continued smoking, shaking his large head, overwhelmed by so much stupidity.

"It's so crazy," he murmured, "it must be true. So you killed him because—"

"All right, all right," the boy interrupted, laughing. "Let them think the Colombians paid me, what difference does it make?"

Iscariote flicked the cigarette out the window and watched it zigzag through the air before landing among the pedestrians on the Plaza de Armas.

"Hog wanted them off his back, he was tired of the Colombians taking the lion's share. I heard him say it a lot of times. Somebody

could have tipped them off, and then they had him killed. Doesn't
that make sense?"

"It does," the boy acknowledged. "But it isn't true."

Iscariote scrutinized the crests of the trees on the square. "It
could be true," he said at last with a vague gesture. "Anyway, it's
the truth that does you the most good. Do you understand what
I'm saying, Carreñito?"

"Not a word," said Lituma in surprise. "What was he cooking up?"

"This elephant is one smart cookie," said Mercedes.

"She understood." Iscariote sat down again on the bed next to
Carreño. He put a hand on his shoulder. "Give the corpse to the
Colombians as a gift, Tomasito. Didn't Hog want out? Didn't he
want to set up on his own, do the refining and exporting himself,
write them off? You did them a favor when you got rid of a com-
petitor. They'll have to do something for you, damn it. What are
they drug lords for if they can't take care of you?"

He stood, looked through his jacket, and lit another cigarette.
Tomás and Mercedes started smoking, too. They were silent for a
moment, dragging on their cigarettes and exhaling mouthfuls of
smoke. Outside, the bells in various churches began to ring. Harsh
or high-pitched, with long or brief echoes, the sound filled the
room, and Mercedes crossed herself.

"As soon as you get to Lima, put on your uniform and go see
your godfather," said Iscariote. "Say 'I got rid of him, now
they don't have to worry about him. I did a big favor for the
Colombians, Godfather, and you can present them with the bill.'
The commander knows them. He's in touch with them. He gives
them protection, too. You'll turn a bad thing into something
good, Carreñito. And your godfather will forgive you for what
you did."

"That fat man was pretty sharp," said Lituma admiringly. "Damn, what an imagination."

"Well, I don't know," said the boy. "Maybe you're right. Maybe that's what I should do."

Mercedes looked from one to the other, disconcerted. "What's this about putting on your uniform?" she asked.

"Fats had thought it all out," the boy explained. "He had his plan. Make the Colombians think I killed Hog to get in good with them. Iscariote's dream was to work for the international Mafia and get to New York one day."

"This way, something good will come out of something bad, for you, and even for me," Iscariote said with satisfaction. "Will you go to your godfather and tell him what I said, Carreñito?"

"I promise I'll go, Fats. Let's stay in touch in Lima."

"If you get there," said Iscariote. "That's still up in the air. You won't have me as a guardian angel every time you do some damn stupid thing."

"That fat man is becoming more interesting than you fooling around with the Piuran," Lituma exclaimed. "Tell me more about him."

"A great guy, Corporal. And a great friend, too."

"Until it's time for you to leave, you'd better not go around engaging in indecent behavior on public thoroughfares," Iscariot recommended. "Didn't they teach you that when you put on the uniform?"

"What uniform is he talking about?" Mercedes asked Tomás again in an irritated voice.

Iscariote burst out laughing, then abruptly turned to face her and asked an unexpected question: "How did you do my friend to make him fall for you like this? What's your secret?"

"How, how did she do it?" Lituma cut him off. "Doggie-style?"

But Mercedes ignored him and continued to question the boy. "What's this about a uniform, what does he mean?"

"She's your fiancée and you haven't told her yet that you're in the Civil Guard?" Iscariote asked mockingly. "That's a bad deal you made, comadre. Trading a drug boss for an ordinary cop."

"The son of a bitch was right, Tomasito." Lituma laughed. "Your Piuran made a rotten deal."

5 / "DO YOU MEAN we're under arrest?" asked Señora Adriana.

It was pouring, and her voice could barely be heard in the clatter of heavy raindrops on the tin roof. She was sitting on a sheepskin on the floor, staring at the corporal, who was perched on a corner of the desk. Dionisio stood next to her, his expression remote, as if nothing going on around him was his concern. His eyes were bloodshot and glassier than usual. The guard Carreño stood as well, leaning against the wardrobe-armory.

"You understand, there's nothing else I can do." Lituma nodded as he spoke. He was not happy in these Andean storms, with their thunder and lightning; he had never gotten used to them. It always seemed to him that they would become more and more violent until they exploded in a cataclysm. And he was not happy either about detaining the drunken cantinero and that witch. "It would be better if you helped us out, Doña Adriana."

"And why are we under arrest?" she insisted, showing no sign of emotion. "What have we done?"

"You didn't tell me the truth about Demetrio Chanca, or,

should I say, Medardo Llantac. That was the foreman's name, wasn't it?" Lituma took out the radiogram he had received from Huancayo in reply to his inquiry, and waved it in front of the woman's face. "Why didn't you tell me he was the mayor of Andamarca, the one who escaped the Senderista massacre? You knew why he came here to hide."

"Everybody in Naccos knew," the woman said calmly. "Worse luck for him."

"Why didn't you tell me when I questioned you last time?"

"Because you didn't ask me," she replied just as calmly. "I thought you knew, too."

"No, damn it, I didn't." Lituma raised his voice. "But now that I do, I also know that after your fight with the unlucky bastard it was easy to take your revenge and turn him over to the terrucos."

For a long while Doña Adriana looked at him with pitying irony, her prominent eyes scrutinizing him. Finally she began to laugh.

"I don't have dealings with the Senderistas," she exclaimed sarcastically. "They like us even less than they liked Medardo Llantac. They weren't the ones who killed him."

"Who was it, then?"

"I already told you. Destiny."

Lituma felt like hitting both of them, her and her drunken sot of a husband. No, she wasn't pulling his leg. She might be as crazy as they come, but she knew exactly what had happened; she had to be an accomplice.

"At least you know that three corpses are rotting in a shaft in the abandoned mine, isn't that true? Didn't your husband tell you? He told me. And he could confirm it if he wasn't falling-down drunk."

"I don't recall telling you anything," Dionisio muttered, grimacing and playing the fool. "I guess I was a little high. But now I'm in fine shape, and I don't remember ever talking to you, Corporal, sir."

He laughed, contorting his soft body a little and then becoming distracted again, adopting an impassive attitude, eyeing the objects in the room with interest. Carreño walked to the bench behind the woman and sat down.

"Every finger in Naccos is pointing at the two of you," he declared, but Señora Adriana did not turn to look at him. "They all say you planned what happened to them."

"And just what is it that happened to them?" She guffawed in a badgering way.

"That's what I want you to tell us, Doña Adriana," said Lituma. "Forget about devils, evil spirits, black and white magic, and all those witches' stories you recite for the laborers. Just tell me straight out what happened to those three men. Why is there talk in camp that you and your husband are responsible?"

She laughed again, joylessly and with a touch of contempt. As she sat on the sheepskin, her body distorted by her posture and her bulky clothing, there was something sinister and disturbing about the woman. She did not seem frightened at what could happen to her. Lituma thought that Doña Adriana was so certain of her fate she could even permit herself the luxury of feeling sorry for them when he and Carreño fumbled like blind men. As for the cantinero, he was the most cynical man he had ever seen. Now he claimed not to remember wanting to sell him the secret; he even had the gall to deny their conversation at the abandoned mine, when he let him know unequivocally that the missing men were at the bottom of a shaft. From that time until the radiogram arrived from Huancayo, Lituma and Tomasito had not considered the terrucos responsible for the disappearances. But now they weren't so sure. The terrucos must have been looking for that Andamarcan

mayor with his false name, no question about it. Which means . . .
In any case, as Tomasito said, every finger pointed at these two.
Gradually, by putting some pressure on one laborer, a little more
on another, and connecting what still others had hinted at, they
knew beyond any doubt that the cantinero and his wife were seriously involved, and in any case certainly knew every detail of
what had happened. The rain continued, coming down harder.

"You need somebody to blame for the disappearances," Dionisio exclaimed suddenly, as if coming back to the real world to
confront Lituma. "You're barking up the wrong tree, Corporal, sir.
We have nothing to do with it. Adriana may read people's fates,
but she doesn't decide them."

"What happened is beyond you, beyond us," his wife interrupted. "I already told you. Destiny, that's what it's called. It exists,
even if people wish it didn't. Besides, you know very well that the
camp gossip is garbage."

"It's not garbage," said Carreño, still sitting behind her. "Before she left Naccos, Demetrio's wife, I mean Medardo Llantac's
wife, told us that the last time she saw her husband he said he was
going to have a drink at the cantina."

"Don't all the laborers and foremen come to our place?" Dionisio exclaimed, waking up again. "Where else can they go? Is there
another cantina in Naccos?"

"To tell the truth, we have no concrete accusations against
you," Lituma acknowledged. "That's right. Either because they
only know part of the story, or because they're afraid. But with a
little pressure, they all imply that the two of you had a hand in
the disappearances."

Señora Adriana laughed her bitter, defiant laugh, grimacing
and stretching her mouth wide into the kind of face adults make
to amuse children.

"I don't put ideas into anybody's head," she said quietly. "I take out the ideas they already have inside and make people look at them. But these Indians don't like to see themselves in the mirror."

"I just pour their drinks and help them forget their troubles," Dionisio interrupted again, turning his glazed, unfocused eyes toward Lituma. "What would happen to the laborers if they didn't even have a cantina where they could drown their sorrows?"

There was a distant lightning flash followed by thunder. The four did not speak until the noise stopped and the only sound was the rain. The entire hillside leading down to the camp was a quagmire rutted by streams of water. Through the half-opened door, Lituma saw curtains of rain and a backdrop of dark storm clouds. The camp and the surrounding hills had vanished into a gray blur. And it was only three in the afternoon.

"Is it true what they say about you, Doña Adriana?" Carreño exclaimed suddenly. "That when you were young, you and your first husband, a miner with a nose this big, killed a pishtaco?"

This time the witch turned to look at the guard. They took each other's measure for a long while, in silence, until Tomasito finally blinked and lowered his eyes.

"Give me your hand, boy," Señora Adriana murmured gently.

Lituma saw the guard pull back and begin to smile, but he immediately became serious again. Dionisio watched in amusement, crooning quietly to himself. Doña Adriana waited, her hand extended toward him. Seen from behind, her head looked like a ruffled feather duster. The adjutant's eyes were asking him what he should do. Lituma shrugged. Tomasito allowed the woman to take his right hand between both of hers. The corporal craned his head forward slightly. Doña Adriana blew on the guard's hand and wiped it, and brought it up to her large, bulging eyes: to Lituma they seemed about to pop out of their sockets and roll around the floor of the shack. Tomasito turned pale and looked at her suspiciously, but allowed her to continue. "He ought to tell her to go to hell and put an end to this farce," Lituma thought, not moving. Dionisio was lost again in some dream, and with half-closed eyes hummed one of those tunes that mule drivers sang to while away their boredom on long trips. Finally, the witch released the guard's hand, exhaling as if she had just made a great effort.

"Boy, you have a broken heart," she said softly. "Your face already told me so."

"Every fortune-teller in the world says that," Lituma declared. "Let's get back to serious business, Doña Adriana."

"And your heart is this big," she added, as if she had not heard Lituma, separating her hands and sketching a gigantic heart. "She's a lucky girl to have somebody who loves her so much."

Lituma attempted a laugh.

"She's trying to soften you up, Tomasito, don't let her do it," he said. But the guard did not laugh. Or listen to him. He was very serious, staring at her, fascinated. She took his hand again and blew on it, peering at it with her bulging eyes. The cantinero continued to sing the same song under his breath, swaying and hopping in time to the music, indifferent to everything else.

"It's a love that has brought you misfortune, that makes you suffer," said Doña Adriana. "Your heart bleeds every night. But at least that helps you to go on living."

Lituma did not know what to do. He felt uncomfortable. He did not believe in witches, much less in the wild rumors about Adriana that circulated through the camp and the Indian community of Naccos, like the story that she and her first husband had killed a pishtaco with their bare hands. All the same, he felt disoriented and confused whenever the supernatural was involved. Could you read people's fates in the lines of their hands? In cards or in coca leaves?

"Everything will work out, so don't despair," Señora Adriana concluded, releasing the guard's hand. "I don't know when. You may have to suffer a little while longer. Some hungers are never satisfied, they always demand more and more. But the thing that's making your heart bleed now, that's going to work out fine."

She exhaled a second time, and turned back to Lituma.

"Señora, are you trying to get on our good side so we'll forget about the disappearances?"

The witch gave her little laugh again. "I wouldn't read your future even if you paid me, Corporal."

"And I wouldn't let you. Son of a bitch, what's wrong with him?"

Animated by his own fantasy, singing in a louder voice and keeping his eyes shut tight, Dionisio, in a state of great concentration, had begun to dance in place. When Carreño grasped his arm and shook it, the cantinero stopped moving and opened his eyes, gazing at each of them in astonishment, as if seeing them for the first time.

"Quit acting, you're not that drunk," Lituma chided him. "Let's get back to business. Are you finally going to tell me what happened to those guys? Then I'll let you go."

"My husband and I didn't see a thing," she said, her eyes and voice hardening. "Go shake the truth out of the ones who say we did anything wrong."

"Besides, what's done is done, and there's no way to change it, Corporal, sir," Dionisio intoned. "Just accept it. You can't fight destiny, it's useless, understand, it can't be done." The rain came to an abrupt stop, and immediately the world was filled with bright afternoon sunlight. Lituma could see a rainbow crowning the hills around the camp, hovering over the eucalyptus grove. The ground, covered with puddles and gleaming rivulets, looked like quicksilver. And on the horizon, along the Cordillera where rock and sky met, there was that strange color, somewhere between violet and purple, which he had seen reproduced on so many Indian skirts and shawls and on the woolen bags the campesinos hung from the ears of their llamas; for him it was the color of the Andes, of this mysterious, violent sierra. The witch's words had left Carreño pensive and withdrawn. Of course, Tomasito: she told you what you wanted to hear.

"Where are you going to keep us prisoner?" Señora Adriana cast a scornful glance around the shack. "In here? Are the four of us going to sleep on top of each other?"

"Well, I know this isn't the classy kind of station you're used to," said Lituma, "but you'll have to settle for what we have. It isn't good enough for us, either. Isn't that right, Tomasito?"

"Yes, Corporal," the guard whispered, waking up.

"At least let Dionisio go. Who else will keep an eye on the cantina? They'll steal everything, and that junk pile is all we have."

Lituma examined her again, intrigued. Thick and shapeless, buried inside the rags of a secondhand clothes dealer, with only her flaring hips to remind the world that this was a woman, the witch spoke without a trace of emotion, as if she were complying with a formality, demonstrating that she really did not care what happened to her. Dionisio seemed even more contemptuous of his fate. His eyes were half closed again, he had distanced himself from the world. As if the two of them were above it all. Son of a bitch, they were still acting superior.

"We'll make a deal," Lituma said at last, suddenly overcome by a sense of defeat. "Give me your word you won't leave camp. Not even twenty meters. On that condition, I'll let you live at the cantina while we investigate."

"Where would we go?" Dionisio opened his eyes. "If we could have gone, we'd have left by now. Aren't they out there, hiding in the hills, with their stones all ready? Naccos has turned into a jail, and all of us are prisoners. Don't you know that yet, Corporal, sir?"

The woman struggled to her feet, holding on to her husband. And without saying goodbye to the guards, the two of them left the shack. They moved away, walking carefully, searching out the stones or higher ground where it wasn't so muddy.

"You're pretty happy about what the witch told you, Tomasito."

Lituma offered him a cigarette. They smoked and watched the silhouettes of Dionisio and Adriana on the slope grow smaller and finally disappear.

"Did all that about your broken heart impress you?" Lituma exhaled a mouthful of smoke. "Bah, everybody feels that, some more, some less. Or do you think you're the only man who ever suffered on account of a girl?"

"You said you never went through it, Corporal."

"Maybe not, but I've been head over heels in love," said Lituma, feeling somehow diminished. "It's just that I get over it fast. Almost always with hookers. Once, in Piura, in the Green House I told you about, I was crazy about a little brunette. But to tell you the truth, I never wanted to kill myself over a woman."

They smoked in silence for a time. Down at the foot of the slope, a tiny figure began to climb the path to the post.

"I don't think we'll ever know what happened to those three men, Tomasito. No matter how much everybody in camp hints that Dionisio and Doña Adriana are involved, the truth is I'm not convinced."

"I have a hard time believing it, too, Corporal. But then, why do all the laborers wind up accusing them?"

"Because all the serruchos are superstitious and believe in devils, pishtacos, and mukis," said Lituma. "And since Dionisio and his wife are half witches, they tie them in with the disappearances."

"I didn't believe in any of that until now," the guard attempted to joke. "But after what Doña Adriana read in my hand, I ought to believe. I liked what she said about a big heart."

By this time Lituma could make out the person climbing the hill. He wore a miner's helmet that glinted in what was now a sunlit afternoon with a brilliant, cloudless sky. Who would believe that just a few minutes earlier there had been violent downpours, thunder, heavy black clouds?

"Ah, hell, the witch bought you off," Lituma continued the joke. "Maybe you made those three disappear, Tomasito."

"Who knows, Corporal?"

And they broke into nervous, insincere laughter. In the meantime, as he watched the approach of the man in the helmet, Lituma could not stop thinking about Pedrito Tinoco, the little mute who ran errands for them and cleaned their quarters, who had seen with his own eyes the slaughter of the vicuñas in Pampa Galeras. Ever since Tomasito told him the story, he had Pedrito on his mind almost all the time. Why did he always picture him in that spot between the barricade and those gray rocks, washing clothes? The man in the helmet had a pistol in his belt and carried a club similar to the ones the police used. But he wore civilian clothes: blue jeans and a heavy jacket with a black armband around the right sleeve.

"There's no question that a lot of people around here know exactly what happened even if they won't open their mouths. You and I are the only suckers who don't know what's going on. Don't you feel like an asshole up here in Naccos, Tomasito?"

"What I feel is jumpy as a grasshopper. Sure they all know something, but they lie and try to shift the blame onto the cantinero and his wife. I even think they all got together to make us believe that Dionisio and Doña Adriana planned it. That way they throw us off the track and don't get any of the blame. Shouldn't we just close this case, Corporal?"

"It's not that I care so much about solving it, Tomasito. I mean, as far as the job is concerned. But I'm a person with a lot of curiosity. It's gnawing at me, and I want to know what happened to them. And after what you told me about the mute and Lieutenant Pancorvo, I won't sleep easy until I find out."

"People are really scared, have you noticed? At the cantina, on the job, all the work crews. Even the Indians who haven't left the community yet. There's tension in the atmosphere, like something was about to happen. Maybe it's the rumor that they're stopping work on the highway, that they'll all lose their jobs. And all the killing everywhere. Nobody's nerves can take it. The air's overheated. Don't you feel it?"

Yes, Lituma felt it. The laborers' faces were intent, their eyes darted right and left as if trying to spot an enemy waiting to ambush them, and their talk at the cantina or on the work crews was intermittent and melancholy, and stopped altogether in his presence. Was it the disappearances? Were they frightened because any one of them could be the fourth?

"Good afternoon, Corporal," said the man in the miner's helmet, greeting them with a nod. He was a tall, strong mestizo with a full beard. His heavy-soled miners' boots were muddied up to the ankle, and he kicked them against the side of the doorway, trying to clean them off before entering the shack. "I've come from La Esperanza. To see you, Corporal Lituma."

La Esperanza was a silver mine, about a four-hour trek to the east of Naccos. Lituma had never been there, but he knew that several laborers in camp had miners' licenses issued by the company.

"The terrucos attacked last night and did a lot of damage," he explained, taking off his helmet and shaking his long, greasy hair. His jacket and trousers were soaked. "They killed one of my men and wounded another. I'm chief of security at La Esperanza. They stole explosives, payroll money, and a lot of other things."

"I'm really sorry, but I can't leave," Lituma apologized. "There are only two of us at the post, my adjutant and myself, and we have a serious problem here to take care of. I'd have to ask for instructions from headquarters in Huancayo."

"The engineers already took care of that," the man replied, very respectfully. He took a folded sheet of paper from his pocket and handed it to him. "They talked to your superiors by radio. And Huancayo said you should take charge. La Esperanza is within your jurisdiction."

A disheartened Lituma read and reread the telegram. That's exactly what it said. They had better equipment at the mine than in this filthy camp. And he was stuck here, cut off, blind and deaf to what was happening in the outside world. Because the camp radio worked poorly, or too late, or never. Whose crazy idea was it to establish a Civil Guard post in Naccos instead of at La Esperanza? But if it had been there, he and Tomasito would have been obliged to face the terrucos. So they were close by. The noose was tightening a little more around his neck.

Carreño was preparing coffee on the Primus. The man from the mine, whose name was Francisco López, dropped onto the sheepskin where Doña Adriana had been sitting. The pot started to bubble.

"It's not that you can do anything now," López explained. "They got away, naturally, and took all their loot with them. But a police report has to be filed before the insurance will reimburse the company."

Tomás filled the tin cups with boiling coffee and handed them around.

"If you want, I'll take a run over to La Esperanza, Corporal."

"No, that's okay, I'll go. You take charge of the post. And if I'm late getting back, say an Our Father for me."

"There isn't any danger, Corporal," Francisco López reassured him. "I came in a jeep, but I had to leave it down where the road ends. It's not very far, less than an hour if you drive fast. Only I got caught in the rain. I'll bring you back as soon as you finish the paperwork."

Francisco López had worked in security for three years at La Esperanza. This was the second assault. The first time, six months earlier, there had been no casualties, but the terrorists had taken explosives, clothing, provisions, and all the medical supplies.

"The lucky thing is that the engineers were able to hide," he explained, sipping his coffee. "Along with a friend of theirs, a gringo who's visiting the mine. They climbed into the water tanks. If the terrucos had found them, they'd be six feet under by now. Engineers, administrators, executives: they never get off. And foreigners sure as hell don't."

"Don't forget the police," said Lituma in a hollow voice.

Francisco López made a joke: "I didn't want to be the one to say it. I didn't want to be the one to scare you. They never do anything to the workers, though, unless they think they're scabs."

He spoke with absolute naturalness, as if these things were normal, as if it had always been this way. Son of a bitch, maybe he was right.

"With everything that's going on, they're talking about closing La Esperanza," López added, blowing on his coffee and taking another sip. "The engineers don't want to go there anymore. And paying the revolutionary quota pushes costs up too high."

"If you're paying the quota, why the assault?" asked Lituma.

"That's what we'd like to know," Francisco López said. "It doesn't make sense."

He continued to blow on his coffee and sip from the cup, as if this conversation, too, were the most normal thing in the world.

.

His straw-colored hair and light, limpid eyes had been a nightmare for Casimiro Huarcaya in his childhood. Because in the small Andean village of Yauli where he was born, everyone was dark, and especially because his parents and brothers and sisters all had black hair, dark skin, dark eyes. Where had this albino in the Huarcaya family come from? The jokes at his expense, made by his classmates at the little state school, forced Casimiro into frequent fights, for despite his good nature he would go blind with rage every time they suggested, for the sake of watching him get angry, that his father was not his father but some outsider passing through Yauli, or even the devil himself, because, as everybody in the Andes knows, when the devil comes to work his evil on earth he sometimes takes the shape of a limping gringo stranger.

And the question Casimiro could never get out of his mind was whether his own father, the potter Apolinario Huarcaya, had his suspicions, too, regarding his origins. He was sure he had been the cause of arguments between his parents, and Apolinario, who was kind to his other children, not only gave him the hardest jobs to do but whipped him if he made the slightest mistake.

Yet, in spite of teasing at school and difficult relationships at home, Casimiro matured with no serious complexes. He was strong, clever with his hands, alert, and he loved life. Ever since he was a boy, he had dreamed of growing up fast and leaving Yauli for a big city like Huancayo, Pampas, or Ayacucho, where his blond hair and light eyes would not attract so much attention.

Shortly before his fifteenth birthday, he ran away from his village with an itinerant peddler whom he had helped with loading, unloading, and selling his merchandise at the market whenever he came to Yauli. Don Pericles Chalhuanca had a small truck as old as Methuselah, which had been patched and repatched a thousand times. In it he made the rounds of all the Indian communities and campesino villages in the central part of the Andes, selling city goods—patent medicines, tools, clothing, pots and pans, shoes— and buying cheese, ullucos, beans, fruit, or weavings and pottery, which he then took to the cities. Don Pericles was a skilled mechanic as well as a peddler, and at his side Casimiro memorized the secrets of the truck and learned to repair it whenever it broke down—at least several times a trip—on the terrible sierra roads.

He was completely happy with Don Pericles. The old man dazzled him with tales of his adventurous life as an unrepentant rooster in other men's henhouses—the women he had seduced, made pregnant, and abandoned in countless districts, hamlets, and settlements in the departments of Apurímac, Huancavelica, Ayacucho, Cuzco, and Cerro de Pasco, where, he boasted, "I've sown plenty of bastards, my own flesh and blood." On their travels he pointed out some of them to Casimiro with a sly wink. Many greeted the trader respectfully, kissing his hand and calling him godfather.

But what the boy liked best was their outdoor life, with no schedules or predetermined routes, at the mercy of harsh or kind weather, fairs, fiestas for patron saints, the orders they received, the indispositions of the little truck: these were the factors that decided their daily fate, their itinerary, how many nights they spent in each place. Don Pericles had a permanent home, one without wheels, in the Pampas countryside, which he shared with a married niece and her children. When they were there, Casimiro slept in the house as if he were part of the family. But most of the time he lived in the back of the truck, under the heavy canvas and surrounded by merchandise, where he had built a shelter of cowhides. If it rained, he slept in the cab or underneath the vehicle.

The business was not especially profitable, at least not for

Pericles and Casimiro, because all their earnings were swallowed up by the truck, which always needed replacement parts or new treads for the tires, but it did provide them with a living. In the years he spent with Don Pericles, Casimiro came to know the central region of the Andes like the palm of his hand, all its hamlets, communities, fairs, ravines and valleys, as well as the secrets of the trade: where to buy the best corn and sell needles and thread, where people waited for lamps and percale as if they were manna from heaven, and which ribbons, barrettes, necklaces, and bracelets the girls found irresistibly attractive.

At first Don Pericles treated him like an apprentice, then a son, and finally a partner. As he aged and the boy grew into a man, the burden of work shifted to his shoulders until, after some years, Casimiro did all the driving and decided what they would buy and sell, and Don Pericles became merely the titular head of the partnership.

Luckily, they were in Pampas when the old man suffered the stroke that left him paralyzed and unable to speak, for this meant they could take him to the hospital and save his life. But Don Pericles could not go back on the road, and Casimiro was obliged to travel alone. He did so for some time, in the immortal truck, until one day he had to quit because Don Pericles's niece and her children demanded unheard-of sums of money from him for the right to continue to use the vehicle. And so he returned it to them, and although he visited Don Pericles regularly until the old man died, bringing a little present whenever he happened to be in Pampas, from then on he was lord and master of his own business. The young man was strong and resilient, hardworking and cheerful, and he had friends all over the sierra. He could spend his nights drinking and dancing at the village fiestas, responding with clever jokes to drunken taunts about his yellow hair, and be open for business at the market the next morning before any other merchant.

He had replaced the truck with a thirdhand van that he bought from a Huancayo farmer, to whom he paid monthly installments with strict punctuality.

Once, when he was selling buckles and earrings in a tiny hamlet in Andahuaylas, he caught sight of a girl who seemed to be waiting to talk to him alone. She was young, her hair hung in braids, and she had the haughty, timid face of a small animal. It seemed to him he had seen her before. Then, when he had no more customers, the girl approached Casimiro, who was sitting on the tailgate of the van. "I know," he said, laughing. "You want one of those barrettes and you don't have any money."

She shook her head in confusion. "You made me, you know, pregnant, Papay," she whispered in Quechua, lowering her eyes. "Don't you even remember me?"

Casimiro had a foggy recollection: was this the girl who had climbed into the van at the fiesta for the Archangel Gabriel? He'd had a good deal of chicha to drink that day, and he was not sure if hers was the blurred face in his memory.

"And who says it was me?" he asked angrily. "How many other men did you go with during the fiesta? Do you think I'm that easy to catch? That you can saddle me with a kid who could be anybody's?"

He could not go on shouting at her, because the girl ran off. Casimiro remembered that Don Pericles had advised, in a situation like this, to get behind the wheel and drive away. But a few hours later, when he closed up shop, he began to look for the girl. He felt troubled, and he wanted to make peace with her.

He found her along the road, just outside the settlement, on a path lined with willows and prickly pears, and noisy with the croaking of frogs. She was going back to her village, deeply offended. Huarcaya finally placated her, convinced her to get into the van, and drove her to the outskirts of the community where she lived. He did his best to comfort the girl, gave her some money, and told her to see one of those midwives who also perform abortions. She nodded, tears in her eyes. Her name was Asunta, and when he asked her age she said eighteen, but he thought she was younger.

He passed that way again a month later, asked for the girl, and found her house. She lived with her parents and a swarm of brothers and sisters, who were suspicious and gruff with him. Her father, who owned his own plot of land in the community, had been in charge of the fiesta. He understood Spanish, although he replied to Casimiro's questions in Quechua. Asunta had not found anyone who would give her one of those concoctions, but she told Huarcaya not to worry. Her godparents lived in a neighboring village, and they had told her to go ahead and have the baby and she could live with them if she was thrown out of her house. She seemed resigned to what was happening. When he said goodbye, Casimiro gave her a pair of low-heeled shoes and a flowered shawl, and she thanked him by kissing his hand.

The next time he passed through the village, Asunta no longer lived at home, and her family refused to talk to him about her. Her father was even more surly than he had been on the first visit and told him straight out not to come back. No one could or would say where her godparents lived. Casimiro told himself that he had done everything in his power for the girl, that he should not lose any more sleep over her. If he happened to run into Asunta again, he would help her.

But his life was never the same again. The roads, the mountains, the villages where he had spent so many years traveling, first with Don Pericles and then on his own, without ever feeling he faced any risk greater than having a blowout or being stranded on the bad roads—suddenly these places became increasingly violent. Casimiro began to see electric towers that had been dynamited and bridges that were blown up, roads blocked by boulders and tree trunks, threatening graffiti and red flags on the hillsides. And armed groups, to whom he invariably had to give some of what he was carrying: clothing, provisions, knives, machetes. And patrols of soldiers and the anti-insurgency forces called sinchis also began to appear along the roads, examining his papers and looting his van just as the rebels did. In the villages they complained of abuses, thefts, killings, and in certain regions a true exodus began. Families, entire communities, abandoned their lands, houses, and animals, and headed for the cities along the coast.

Soon his business barely provided enough for him to survive, until one day he realized he was losing money. Why did he go on traveling, buying and selling? Perhaps because he had gotten it into his head that this was the way to find Asunta. The idea had changed from a challenge and a diversion into an obsession. He asked for her so often, wherever he went, that people thought he had gone crazy and found it amusing to give him false clues or tell him lies.

He returned to her village twice, trying to learn from her family where she was. The first time, her father hurled stones and insults at him. But one of Asunta's sisters came out to the road and said the girl's godparents lived in Andahuaylas and were named Gallirgos. But no one in Andahuaylas knew anything about a family by that name. The second time he went to Asunta's house, her father had died, and her mother and all her brothers and sisters had gone to Ica with other families of comuneros. There had been a massacre in the region, and they were frightened.

Why did he look for Asunta with so much perseverance? He asked himself the question and could not find the answer. Was it because of his possible son or daughter, who would be about three years old now? As if it were a ritual, he continued to ask for her wherever he went, though he really did not have much hope of finding her and knew he would receive only negative replies. She

must have gone to Lima, like so many other girls from the sierra.
And was probably working as a maid, or doing manual labor, or
had married and given his child some brothers and sisters.

A good deal of time had passed, and Casimiro Huarcaya was
thinking less and less about Asunta, when he drove into Arcca,
south of Ayacucho, on a night when the whole village was
intoxicated—it was the start of the fiesta. As he left the café where
he had eaten, he found himself surrounded by a hostile crowd of
men and women who insulted him, pointed at his hair, and called
him nacaq and pishtaco. They were so drunk there was no point
in trying to reason with them, to explain that not every man unlucky
enough to have light hair wandered the world looking for human
victims so he could steal their fat, and Casimiro decided to get into
his van. But they would not allow him to leave. They were fearful
and angry, and they urged each other on.

They pulled him from the van and began to beat him, not
listening to his explanations. When he thought he would never
escape, he heard shots. He saw armed men and women, and the
hostile circle around him broke. From the ground where he had
fallen, stunned by the blows he had received, Casimiro heard the
voices of his saviors telling the mob from whose hands they had
rescued him that there was no such thing as pishtacos, that those
were superstitions, obscurantist beliefs foisted on the people by
their enemies.

Then he recognized Asunta. No question about it. Despite the
dim light and the confusion in his mind, he did not have a moment's
doubt. It was Asunta. She did not wear braids now but had her
hair cut short, like a man's. And instead of her wide skirt she was
dressed in jeans and sneakers. And held a rifle in her hands. She
had recognized him too, apparently. She did not respond when he
waved and smiled at her. She was explaining to the other armed
men and women around him that the albino, Casimiro Huarcaya,

had raped her five years before, taking advantage of the fiesta in another village. And left her pregnant. And when she told him, he had treated her worse than a prostitute. And later, like a man throwing a bone to a dog, he condescended to give her some money for an abortion. It was Asunta, but it wasn't Asunta. At least, it was difficult for Casimiro to see the timid girl who had kissed his hand in this cold, somber, didactic woman who spoke in public of intimate matters as if she were talking about someone else.

He tried to tell her that he had been looking for her all this while. He tried to ask her what had happened to the baby, and if it had been born albino like him. But his voice failed him. The men and women spoke for a long time, exchanged comments in Spanish and Quechua, asked him questions he could not answer. When he saw that they had come to a decision about him, he was overcome by a sense of unreality. So there she was, the woman he had spent so many years searching for. She approached him, her rifle aimed at his head. And Casimiro was sure her hand would not tremble when she fired.

•

"Civil Guard, a Civil Guard," said Mercedes. "It never entered my mind that you were one of those traffic cops."

"I know that with me you've come down in the world," replied the boy. "But don't worry, I'll get ahead with a woman like you at my side."

"If I ever saw you in a Civil Guard uniform, I'd die of embarrassment," she said.

"Why did she have such a low opinion of us?" Lituma grumbled.

"What else?" Tomasito sighed. "Because we make such lousy money."

They had left Huánuco at six, an hour behind schedule, and

were occupying the single seat next to the driver of the old Dodge. Four other passengers were crowded in back, among them a woman who moaned "Oh, Jesus" at every pothole. The driver wore a cap pulled down over his ears and a scarf covering his mouth, so that his face was almost completely hidden. He played the radio as loud as possible, and when Carreño and Mercedes talked into each other's ear the others could not hear what they were saying. As the vehicle climbed higher into the Cordillera, the reception grew worse, and whistles and humming drowned out the music.

"Squeezed together like that, you had a good chance to feel her up," Lituma observed.

"You're talking so you'll have an excuse to kiss me on the neck," she said, her mouth against his ear.

"Does it bother you?" he whispered, slowly brushing his lips around her earlobe.

"Necking like that in cars is fantastic," declared Lituma.

"You're tickling me," she said. "The driver must think I'm some kind of idiot who can't do anything but laugh."

"It's just that you don't take love seriously." Carreño continued to kiss her.

"Promise me you'll never put on a cop's uniform again," said Mercedes. "At least while we're together."

"I'll promise you anything you want," the boy said, carried away by love.

"You see," Lituma said, sighing. "You did put it on again, and up here you can't even take it off. You'll die with your boots on, Tomasito. Did you ever see that movie?"

Carreño had his arm around her shoulders, and when the Dodge gave a jolt he tried to soften the impact on Mercedes with his body. Night fell rapidly, and the weather turned cold. They put on the alpaca sweaters they had bought in Huánuco, but one of the car windows was broken and icy air filtered in through the crack. Finally, when there was nothing but static, the driver turned off the radio.

"It's not that I think anything's going to happen," he said, raising his voice behind the scarf. "But it's my duty to warn you. There've been a lot of assaults on this route lately."

None of the passengers said anything, but the atmosphere in the vehicle thickened like curdling milk. Carreño felt Mercedes stiffen.

"And we'll both probably go to our graves wearing the uniform, Tomasito. Don't you get tired sometimes of waiting for them? Don't you think sometimes: 'Just let them come, just let this damn war of nerves be over once and for all'?"

"And what does that mean?" the moaning woman in the back seat finally asked. "Does that mean we're in danger?"

"I hope not," replied the driver. "But it's my duty to warn you."

"And if they do attack, then what?" asked another passenger.

"Then the best thing is to keep your mouths shut," the driver recommended. "At least, that's my advice. They have weapons and itchy trigger fingers."

"In other words, just give them everything we have, like sheep," the woman said angrily. "Even the shirts off our backs. Damn, that's really great advice!"

"If you want to be a heroine, that's fine with me," said the driver. "I'm only giving my opinion."

"You're scaring the passengers," Carreño intervened. "Advice is one thing. Making people afraid is something else again."

The driver turned his head slightly and looked at him. "I don't want to scare anybody," he declared. "But I've been attacked three times, and the last time they split my knee with a sledgehammer."

There was a long silence, broken by the spasms and snorts of

the engine and the metallic clanking of the car as it jolted over ruts
and stones in the road.

"I don't know why you do such dangerous work," said one of
the passengers who had not spoken before.

"For the same reason you travel overland to Lima when you
know how dangerous it is," said the driver. "Because I have to."

"I should never have gone to Tingo María. I should never have
accepted an invitation from that imbecile," Mercedes whispered in
the boy's ear. "I was doing just fine, I could buy clothes, I liked
doing the show at the Vacilón, I was independent. And now they're
after me and here I am shacked up with a Civil Guard."

"It was your destiny." The boy kissed her again on the ear
and felt her shiver. "Maybe you don't believe it, but the best part
of your life is beginning now. Do you know why? Because we're
together. Want me to tell you something?"

"I'm always waiting for the good stuff, a little feeling up and
fucking around to take my mind off having to live like a monk, and
you always get romantic," Lituma complained. "You're hopeless,
Tomasito."

"What?" she whispered.

"We're together until death do us part." Carreño nibbled the
edge of her ear and Mercedes burst into laughter.

"Are you on your honeymoon, by any chance?" The driver
glanced at them.

"We just got married," Carreño replied immediately. "How'd
you guess?"

"I have a sixth sense." The driver laughed. "Besides, you
haven't stopped kissing."

Someone in the back seat laughed, and a passenger murmured:
"Congratulations to the happy couple."

Carreño pulled Mercedes even closer and whispered as he

kissed her: "Now the whole world knows you're my wife. Now you'll never be free."

"If you keep on tickling me, I'll change my seat," she whispered. "I'm peeing my pants, I'm laughing so hard."

"I'd give anything to see a nice little broad peeing," Lituma howled, shaking his cot. "It never occurred to me, damn it. And now it's making me hot and there's not a woman in sight."

"You'd have to go into the trunk," said Carreño. "Well, I'll give you some time off. Ten minutes with no kissing. You can rest on my shoulder, like in the truck. I'll wake you up if there's an attack."

"It was getting good with all that peepee, and you send her off to sleep," Lituma protested. "Just my luck."

"What a funny little cop you are," she said, making herself comfortable.

"Nobody can ruin our honeymoon," said the boy.

The highway was empty; from time to time they passed a huge truck that forced the Dodge to the side of the road. It wasn't raining, but the sky was overcast, and instead of stars, a faint glow softened the contours of leaden clouds and snow-covered peaks and crags on the horizon. Carreño began to doze.

"What woke me up was a light in my eyes and a voice saying, 'Papers,' " the guard continued. "I was still half asleep but I checked my belt and the revolver was where it belonged."

"Now we're back to cowboys again," observed Lituma. "How many did you kill this time?"

Mercedes rubbed her eyes and shook her head from side to side. The driver handed the passengers' voter identifications to a man who held a submachine gun and leaned his head halfway into the car. Carreño saw a sentry post illuminated by lanterns, a coat of arms, and another man, wrapped in a poncho, who was carrying a submachine gun over his shoulder and rubbing his hands together. A metal chain was stretched between two barrels, blocking the road. There were no lights or houses in view, only hills.

"Just a minute," the man said, and he walked to the post, holding the documents in his hand.

"I don't know what's eating them," the driver remarked, turning toward the passengers. "They never stop cars here, least of all at this time of night."

In the stale light of the lantern inside the post, the guard inspected each document, bringing it close to his eyes as if he were nearsighted. The other man continued to rub his hands.

"He must be freezing out there," murmured the woman in the back seat.

"Wait till we get to the barrens, then you'll find out what cold means," warned the driver.

They sat in silence and listened to the whistling of the wind. The police were talking to each other now, and the one who had collected the documents was showing the other a paper and pointing at the Dodge.

"If anything happens to me, you keep on going." The boy kissed Mercedes on the ear, watching the two men leave the post and approach the automobile, one behind the other.

"Mercedes Trelles," said the man, putting his head inside the car again.

"Was that your Piuran's last name?" said Lituma. "Then she must be related to somebody I know. Patojo Trelles. He had a shoe store near the Municipal Movie Theater and was always eating banana chips."

"That's me."

"Come with us a moment, we have to check something."

He gave the other documents to the driver so he could return them to the passengers, and waited while Carreño got out and then helped her from the car. The other guard now held the submachine gun in both hands and stood a meter away from the Dodge.

"Neither of them seemed to think it was very important," said Tomás. "They looked bored, like it was just routine. Maybe it was only a coincidence that they called her. But I couldn't take any chances when it came to her."

"Sure, of course not," Lituma joked. "You're one of those guys who shoot first and ask questions later."

Mercedes walked slowly toward the post, followed by the man who had inspected their documents. Carreño remained standing beside the open door of the car, and though it was unlikely the police officer watching the car could see in the darkness, Tomás gave him an exaggerated smile.

"I don't know how you don't die of cold up here, Chief," he said, making a show of rubbing his hands together, saying "Brrr." "How high are we?"

"Thirty-two hundred meters."

The boy took out a pack of cigarettes and placed one in his mouth. He was about to put it back, but as if he had just thought of it, he offered the pack to the man. "Care for a smoke?" At the same time, not waiting for an answer, he took two steps toward him. The policeman was in no way alarmed. He took a cigarette and set it between his lips without thanking him.

"That was one sloppy cop," Lituma declared. "I'm pretty sloppy myself, and even I would've suspected something."

"They were asleep on their feet, Corporal."

Carreño lit a match, but the wind blew it out. He lit a second, hunching over to protect the flame with his body, all his senses alert, like an animal ready to pounce; he heard the woman in the back ask the driver to close the door, and he brought his hand up to the mouth where the cigarette dangled. The policeman froze when, instead of a light, the barrel of a pistol knocked against his teeth.

"Don't shout, don't move," Tomás ordered. "I'm telling you for your own good."

With his eyes fixed on the man, whose mouth fell open—the cigarette rolled on the ground—Tomás gently took the submachine gun with his free hand but focused his ears on the car, waiting for the driver or one of the passengers to shout a warning to the guard inside the post.

"But he didn't hear a thing, and the passengers were half asleep and had no idea what was going on," Lituma intoned. "You see, I'm one step ahead of you. Know why? Because I've seen a lot of movies in my life, and I know all the tricks."

"Hands up," he ordered in a loud voice from the doorway. He aimed his revolver at the policeman sitting at a small table, and pointed the submachine gun at the head of the one he held in front of him as a shield. He heard Mercedes give a little cry, but he did not look at her, he did not take his eyes off the man at the table, who, after a stunned moment, raised his hands, staring and blinking in stupefaction.

" 'Take his gun,' I told Mercedes." Carreño recalled. "But she was scared to death and didn't move. I had to tell her again, shouting this time."

"Didn't she almost pee her pants then, too?"

Using both hands, she picked up the weapon the officer had left on the table.

"I made the two of them stand against the wall, with their hands on their heads," the boy went on. "You wouldn't believe how cooperative they were, Corporal. They let me search them, take their pistols, tie them together, and not a peep out of them."

It was only as Tomás and Mercedes were leaving that one had the courage to murmur: "You won't get very far, compadre."

"And you didn't," said Lituma. "I'm going to sleep, Tomasito. I'm tired, and your story is boring."

"I have enough guns to take care of myself," Carreño cut him off.

"What's going on here?" the driver said behind him.

"Nothing, nothing at all, we're leaving now."

"What do you mean, nothing?" he heard him exclaim. "Who are you? Why . . ."

"Take it easy, go on, it doesn't have anything to do with you, nothing's going to happen to you," said the boy, pushing him outside.

The passengers had climbed out of the Dodge and were standing around Mercedes, bombarding her with questions. She waved her hands and shook her head, almost hysterical: "I don't know, I don't know."

Carreño threw the guards' submachine guns and pistols into the front seat of the Dodge and motioned to the driver to get behind the wheel. Taking Mercedes by the arm, he forced her into the car.

"Are you going to leave us here?" The woman who had complained earlier was indignant.

"Somebody will pick you up, don't worry. You can't come with me, they'll think you're involved."

"Then leave me behind, too," protested the driver, who was already at the wheel.

"Why the hell did you take the driver?" Lituma yawned. "Wasn't Mercedes enough company for you?"

"I don't know how to drive, and neither does my wife," Carreño explained. "Just get us out of here, and step on it."

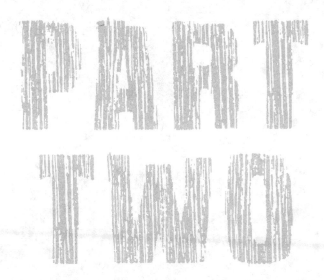

PART
TWO

6 / "WELL, I THINK I'm ready to go now," Corporal Lituma said, estimating that he would reach Naccos before dark if he left immediately.

"Absolutely not, my friend." The tall blond engineer, who had been so pleasant to him since his arrival in La Esperanza, interrupted, raising two cordial hands. "You might still be on the road at nightfall, and I don't recommend that. You'll have supper with us and sleep here, and first thing tomorrow Francisco López will take you back to Naccos in the jeep."

The dark-haired engineer, the one they called Shorty, also insisted, and Lituma did not need much urging to spend another night at the mine. First, because it was certainly imprudent to travel through these desolate places in the dark, and second, because it would allow him more time to see and listen to the gringo who was visiting La Esperanza, an explorer, or something like that. He had been fascinated from the first. Lituma had never seen such long hair, so wild a beard, except in pictures of the prophets and apostles, or on half-naked madmen or beggars wandering the streets of Lima. Yet there was nothing crazy about this man; he was a scholar. But unassuming and friendly, with the air of someone who lived in the clouds, had lost his way on earth, and was totally indifferent to, or unaware of, the danger he had faced when the terrucos attacked the mine. The engineers called him the Prof, and sometimes Red.

As he took statements, prepared an inventory of what the attackers had stolen, and filled out the necessary forms for the insurance company, Lituma heard the engineers, especially the blond one, tease the Prof unmercifully about the horrible things the terrucos would have done to him if they had learned that an agent of the C.I.A. was right there under their noses, hiding in the water tank. He, in turn, expanded on the theme. As far as horrible things were concerned, he could give a few lessons to the terrucos, mere novices who only knew how to kill people with bullets or knives, or by crushing their skulls, which was child's play compared to the techniques employed by the ancient Peruvians, who had achieved the heights of refinement. Even more than the ancient Mexicans, despite an international conspiracy of historians to conceal the Peruvian contribution to the art of human sacrifice. Everyone knew that Aztec priests stood at the top of the pyramids and tore out the hearts of the victims of the Flower Wars, but how many people had heard about the religious passion of the Chancas and Huancas for human viscera, about the delicate surgery in which they removed their victims' livers and brains and kidneys and ate them in their ceremonies, washing it all down with good corn chicha? The engineers joked and so did he, and Lituma pretended to concentrate on writing the documents but did not miss a word of their conversation. And he would have given anything to sit for a while and listen to the banter and have a chance to examine the man's outlandish appearance.

Was he a gringo? His light eyes and fair hair and beard streaked with abundant gray made him look like one. So did the rough red-and-white checked jacket he wore with his jeans and cowboy shirt and mountain climber's boots. No Peruvian dressed this way. But he spoke absolutely perfect Spanish and used many words that Lituma had not heard before although he was sure they existed in books. Son of a bitch, he was a real brain. Lituma would enjoy himself tonight.

In the good times, the engineers told him, La Esperanza had employed over a hundred miners, but now there were barely thirty working the tunnels. And at the rate things were going, what with all the troubles and falling metal prices, it might have to close down, like other mines in Cerro de Pasco and Junín. They kept it open out of defiance more than anything else, since it was no longer profitable. Their camp was like the one in Naccos: very small, with wooden barracks and a couple of more solidly built houses where the office was located and where the engineers slept when they were at the mine. The foreman lived in one wing (he was not there now because he had taken the wounded man to Huancayo), and they gave Lituma a room in that building. It had a bed, a kerosene lamp, and a washbasin. Through the window he could see the two water towers, located between the mine entrance and the barracks, two large tanks secured on stone pilings, each with an iron ladder. One had been emptied for an annual cleaning, and that was where the engineers and the professor had gone to hide when they heard the terrucos. They kept out of sight, trembling with cold and fear— or did they joke in whispers there, too?—for the three hours it had taken the attackers to shoot it out with the half-dozen security men, forcing them to run (the dead man and the wounded one had belonged to the group led by Francisco López); then they looted explosives, fuses, medicines, boots, and clothing from the storeroom and infirmary, and harangued the miners, whom they forced out of the barracks and assembled in the nearby open space lit by a few acetylene lamps.

"Do you know what I'll remember about this adventure, Corporal?" asked the blond engineer, whom Shorty called Bali. "It won't be how frightened I was, or everything they stole, or even the poor boy they killed, but the fact that none of the miners betrayed us."

They were sitting at a long table, beginning their meal. Appetizing aromas mingled with the smoke from their cigarettes.

"If even one had pointed a finger or nodded his head toward the water tank," Shorty agreed, "they'd have given us a revolutionary trial and we'd be in paradise by now, isn't that right, Bali?"

"You and I would be in hell, Shorty. But the Prof would certainly have gone straight to heaven. Because, believe it or not, Corporal, Red here hasn't committed his first sin yet."

"I wouldn't pull a dirty trick like that," said the professor, and Lituma tried to detect a single foreign-sounding syllable in his accent. "I would have gone with the two of you and shared your flames—the ones that burn, not the ones you used to be in love with."

He cooked while the two engineers, Francisco López, and the corporal each had a glass of aromatic Ican pisco that filled Lituma's veins with delicious warmth and his head with an excited sense of well-being. The professor had prepared a real banquet: a soup of dried potatoes and beans with chunks of chicken meat, and breaded steak with white rice. Delicious! With the food they had cold beer that made Lituma very happy. He hadn't eaten this well for months, not since he had been in Piura. He was having such a good time that from the moment he sat down at the table with them he almost forgot about the disappearances in Naccos and the nightly laments and romantic confessions of Tomasito, the two topics, he realized now, that had occupied all his thoughts lately.

"And do you know why I'll always remember the loyalty of those thirty miners, Corporal?" Bali insisted. "Because they taught Shorty and me a lesson. We thought they were in cahoots with the terrucos. And now, you see, we're here thanks to their silence."

"Alive and kicking and raring to go, with a damn good story to tell our friends," Shorty concluded.

"There's more to this than meets the eye," said the Prof, raising his glass of beer. "You think you owe your lives to the workers who didn't betray you. I say your debt is to the apus of these mountains. They were kind to you because of me. In other words, I'm the one who saved you."

"Because of you, Prof?" Shorty asked. "What did you give to the apus?"

"Thirty years of study." The professor sighed. "Five books. A hundred articles. Oh, and even a linguistic-archaeological map of the central sierra."

"What are apus, Doctor?" Lituma finally dared to ask.

"The ancestral gods, the tutelary spirits of the hills and mountains in the Cordillera," replied the professor, delighted to speak about the thing he seemed to love best. "Every peak in the Andes, no matter how small, has its own protective god. When the Spaniards came and destroyed the idols and the burial grounds and baptized the Indians and prohibited pagan cults, they thought they had put an end to idolatry. But in fact it still lives, mixed in with Christian ritual. The apus decide life and death in these regions. They're the reason we're here now, my friends. Let's drink to the apus of La Esperanza!"

Emboldened by the pisco, the beer, and the cordial atmosphere, Lituma intervened again: "In Naccos there's a woman who's part witch and knows a lot about these things, Doctor. Señora Adriana. And like you say, according to her the hills are full of spirits, and she says she communicates with them. She swears they're evil, that they have a taste for human flesh."

"Adriana? The wife of Dionisio the pisco seller?" asked the professor. "I know her very well. And her drunken husband, too. They used to go from village to village with a troupe of musicians and dancers, and he dressed up like an ukuko, a bear. Good informants, both of them. Haven't the Senderistas killed them yet for being antisocial types?"

Lituma was stunned. This man was like God: he knew everything and everybody. How could he, especially being a foreigner?

"Instead of Doctor, call me Paul, Paul Stirmsson, or just Pablo, or Red, which is what my students call me in Odense." He had taken a pipe from one of the pockets of his red-checked jacket, filled it with black tobacco from a couple of cigarettes, then tamped it down with his fingers. "In my country we call physicians 'doctor,' not humanists."

"Go on, Red, tell Corporal Lituma how you became a Peruvophile," Shorty urged.

When he was still a boy in short pants, back in Denmark, his native country, his father had given him a book by a man named Prescott about the Spanish discovery and conquest of Peru. Reading it had decided his fate. From that time on, he was filled with curiosity about the people and events, the story of this country. He had dedicated his whole life to studying and teaching Peruvian customs, mythology, and history, first in Copenhagen and then in Odense. And for the past thirty years he had spent every vacation in the Peruvian sierra. The Andes were like home to him.

"Now I understand why you speak Spanish so well," Lituma said softly, in awe.

"You should hear him speak Quechua," Shorty interjected. "He has endless conversations with the miners, just as if he were a full-blooded Indian."

"You mean you speak Quechua, too?" Lituma exclaimed, thunderstruck.

"The Cuzco and Ayacucho variants," the Prof specified, making no effort to hide his pleasure at the police officer's astonishment. "And a little Aymara, too."

However, he added, the Peruvian tongue he would like to have learned was the language of the Huancas, the ancient central Andean culture that had been conquered by the Incas.

"That is to say, wiped out by the Incas," he corrected himself. "They acquired a good reputation, and since the eighteenth century everyone has spoken of the Incas as tolerant conquerors who adopted the gods of the vanquished. A great myth. Like every empire, the Incas were brutal to the peoples who did not docilely submit to them. They practically eradicated the Huancas and the Chancas from history. They destroyed their cities and drove them out, dispersed them all over the Tahuantisuyo through their system of mitimaes—the massive displacements of populations. And as a result there is almost no trace of their beliefs or customs. Not even their language. The Quechua dialect that survives in this zone is not the language of the Huancas."

He added that modern historians did not have much sympathy for them because they had helped the Spaniards against the Incan armies. Weren't they right to do so? They were following an ancient principle: the enemy of our enemy is our friend. They had helped the Conquistadors in the belief that they, in turn, would help the Huancas gain their freedom from those who had enslaved them. They were wrong, of course, since the Spaniards imposed a servitude even harsher than that of the Incas. History had committed an injustice against the Huancas: they were barely mentioned in the books about ancient Peru, and generally were recalled only as a savage people who had collaborated with the invaders.

The tall blond engineer—was Bali his name or his nickname?—got to his feet and brought back the bottle of intensely aromatic Ican pisco that they had enjoyed before the meal.

"Let's inoculate ourselves against the cold," he said, filling their glasses. "And if the Senderistas come back, they'll find us so drunk we won't even care."

The wind howled at the windows and roof and shook the building. Lituma felt intoxicated. It was incredible that Red knew Dionisio and Doña Adriana. He had even seen the cantinero in the days when he roamed the countryside, dancing at fairs, dressed like an ukuko with his little mirrors, his chain and mask. How great it would be to listen to the three of them talk about apus and pishtacos. Son of a bitch, that would be something. Did the professor really believe in apus, or was he being a wise-ass? Lituma thought about Naccos. Tomasito must be in bed by now, gazing at the ceiling in the darkness, lost in the thoughts that ate at him every night and made him cry in his sleep. What a woman that Mercedes must be. She'd left the boy half crazed. Dionisio and Doña Adriana's place would be full of melancholy drunks, and the cantinero would cheer them up with his songs and his mincing around, urging them to dance with each other, touching their bodies as if by accident. A raging faggot, what else could you say? He thought about the laborers asleep in their barracks, holding on to the secret of what had happened to those three men, a secret he would never know. The corporal felt another attack of nostalgia for distant Piura, for its hot weather, its outgoing people who could never keep a secret, its deserts and mountains without apus or pishtacos, a place that had lived in his memory like a lost paradise ever since they'd sent him to these savage highlands. Would he ever set foot in Piura again? He made an effort to follow the conversation.

"The Huancas were animals, Red," declared Shorty, examining his glass against the light as if he feared that some insect had fallen inside. "And the Chancas, too. You're the one who told us about the barbaric things they did to keep their apus happy. Sacrificing children, men, women to the river they were going to divert, the road they were going to open, the temple or fortress they were building—that's not what we call civilized."

"In Odense, not far from the district where I live, a sect of

Satanists killed an old man by sticking him with pins, as an offering to Beelzebub." Professor Stirmsson shrugged. "Of course they were animals. Can any ancient people pass the test? Which of them was not cruel and intolerant when judged from a contemporary perspective?"

Francisco López, who had gone out to see if everything was in order, came back, and with him an icy blast blew into the room where they sat talking around the table.

"Everything's quiet," he said, taking off his poncho. "But the temperature's really fallen and it's beginning to hail. Touch wood, let's hope a huayco doesn't come down tonight as an added bonus."

"Warm up with a little drink." The dark-haired engineer filled his glass again. "That's all we need. First the terrorists, then a huayco."

"I wonder," murmured the blond engineer, completely lost in thought, talking to himself, "if what's going on in Peru isn't a resurrection of all that buried violence. As if it had been hidden somewhere, and suddenly, for some reason, it all surfaced again."

"If you say another word about that ecologist, I'm going to sleep," said Shorty in an effort to silence him. And, pointing at his friend, he explained to Lituma, who was looking at him in surprise: "He knew Señora d'Harcourt, the woman they killed last month in Huancavelica. He takes one drink and philosophizes about her. And there's a big difference between a miner and a philosopher, Bali."

But the blond engineer did not respond. He was self-absorbed, his eyes shining with drink, a lock of hair falling over his forehead.

"I tell you the truth, if there's one death that's difficult to understand, it's Hortensia's." The professor's face grew somber. "But, of course, we make a mistake when we try to understand these killings with our minds. They have no rational explanation."

"She knew the risk she was taking," said Bali, his eyes very wide. "And she went on. Like you, Red. You know the risk, too. If they had caught us last night, maybe Shorty and I could have negotiated with them. But they would have smashed your head in with stones, just like they did to Hortensia. And still you come back here. I take my hat off to you, my friend."

"Well, you both come back here, too." The professor returned the compliment.

"We earn our living from this mine," said Shorty. "We used to, at any rate."

"What is it about Peru that stirs such passion in certain foreigners?" said Bali in amazement. "We don't deserve it."

"It's a country nobody can understand." Red laughed. "And for people from clear, transparent countries like mine, nothing is more attractive than an indecipherable mystery."

"I don't think I'll ever come back to La Esperanza," Bali said, changing the subject. "I don't feel like playing the hero, least of all for a mine that's losing money. I swear, I was shitting with fear last night."

"The Prof and I sensed it, up there in the tank," said Shorty. "I mean, we smelled it."

Bali laughed, the professor laughed, and López laughed, too. But Lituma remained very serious, barely listening to them, numb with profound uneasiness. Later, when they had finished the bottle of pisco, said good night, and gone to their rooms, the corporal stopped at the door of Professor Stirmsson's room, which was next to his.

"I'm still curious about one thing, Doctor." He spoke respectfully, stumbling somewhat over his words. "Did you say that the Chancas and the Huancas sacrificed people when they were going to build a new road?"

The professor was bending over to take off his boots, and the acetylene lamp distorted his features, giving him a phantasmagoric appearance. It occurred to Lituma that a golden halo, like the ones in religious pictures, might suddenly appear around his white hair.

"They didn't do it out of cruelty, but because they were very devout," he explained. "It was their way of showing respect for the spirits of the mountains, of the earth, whom they were going to disturb. They did it to avoid reprisals and to assure their own survival. So there would be no landslides, no huaycos, so that lightning wouldn't strike them dead and their ponds wouldn't flood. You have to understand their thinking. For them, there were no natural catastrophes. Everything was decided by a higher power that had to be won over with sacrifices."

"I once heard Doña Adriana say exactly what you're saying, Doctor."

"Give my regards to her and Dionisio," said the Prof. "The last time we were together was at the Huancayo fair. Adriana was very attractive when she was young. Then she lost her looks, the way we all do. I see you're interested in history, Corporal."

"A little," Lituma agreed. "Sleep well, Doctor."

.

They've been scared ever since they heard about the pishtaco invasion, heard that in the neighborhoods of Ayacucho the people have been organizing patrols to fight them. "We have to do the same thing," they say. "We can't let the throat-slashers have their way in Naccos, too." They want to light bonfires at night around the barracks so they can spot them as soon as they show up. They always attack where times are getting hard. It was the same story when things began to go bad in Naccos. Because this used to be a very prosperous mining town. That's why Timoteo and I came here when we ran away from Quenka.

I was young then, and the Naccos mine hadn't been abandoned yet; it was full of miners from all over the region, even from places as far away as Pampas, Acobamba, Izcuchaca, and Lircay. They were always opening new tunnels to mine the silver, the zinc. And the contractors had to go farther and farther away to find people to come to the mine. It was called the Santa Rita. They built barracks and put up tents all over the slopes; a lot of miners even slept in the hollows under the boulders, wrapped in their ponchos. Until one day the engineers said the high-quality ore had run out, all that was left was worthless junk.

When they started to let workers go and the Santa Rita began to give out and a lot of people left Naccos, that was when the strange things happened that nobody could explain. And the town was filled with the same kind of suspicion, the fear that the highway laborers are feeling now. A little fat man from Huasicancha who was a watchman at the warehouse began to lose weight and say he felt strange, like he had been emptied out inside and his body was nothing but skin and bones, a balloon you could burst with a pin, and he said his head was drained of ideas and memories. When he died a couple of weeks later, he was so shriveled and thin he looked like a sickly ten-year-old. He couldn't remember where he came from or what his name was, and when people came to visit him he was confused and would ask them in a feeble little voice if he was a man or an animal, because he wasn't even sure about that. Nobody told me this story, Timoteo and I saw it with our own eyes.

The watchman's name was Juan Apaza. It wasn't until they buried him at the bottom of the ravine that the Santa Rita miners and their families began to suspect that Apaza's mysterious sickness wasn't a sickness at all but that a pishtaco had crossed his path. Just like now, everybody in Naccos got very nervous. "Is there any remedy?" they said. "Is there anything we can do against the pishtacos?" They came to me because word got around that I knew which hills were male and which ones female and also which rocks gave birth. Sure there are remedies, of course there's something you can do. Be careful and take precautions. Put a pan of water at the entrance to the house so the magic powder the pishtaco throws at his victims has no effect—that works. A drop of urine on shirts and sweaters before you put them on—that helps. Wear something made of wool, and women should wear a sash and carry scissors, a sliver of soap, a clove of garlic or a little salt—that's good, too. They didn't do a thing, and that's why it all turned out the way it did. They didn't accept the truth; people now are starting to. Because there's too much proof for them not to believe. Isn't that right?

By the time they realized what was going on in Naccos, the pishtaco that killed Juan Apaza had dried out a few more victims. Back then, they used human fat in ointments, and mixed it in with the metal to make the bells ring true. Now, since the pishtaco invasion, a lot of people in Ayacucho are sure they send the fat out of the country, or to Lima, where there are factories that only run with grease from a man or a woman.

I knew that pishtaco at the Santa Rita. After he dried out Juan Apaza, he dried out Sebastián, Timoteo's friend. Everybody in Naccos followed his story, step by step, because he told the miners about it as soon as he started to feel strange. I mean, beginning with the night he was outside the village in the meadows, tending a herd of llamas, and suddenly he ran into a man he knew, one of the Santa Rita contractors. He was wrapped in a poncho, with his hat pulled over his ears, and he was leaning against a boulder and smoking. Sebastián recognized him right away. He'd seen him in the hamlets and communities in the region, talking to the campesinos, telling them they should go to work in Naccos and advancing them a few soles to convince them.

Sebastián went over to him to say hello, and the contractor offered him a cigarette. He was white, an outsider with a little cockroach-colored beard and light eyes; in Naccos they called him

Stud because he was such a womanizer (he chased me a few times, but Timoteo never found out). They were smoking and talking about the bad luck that had come to the Santa Rita, about the ore running out, when all of a sudden Stud blew a puff of smoke in Sebastián's face, and it made him sneeze. Right then and there he felt dizzy and sleepy. Of course it wasn't cigarette smoke but the powder the pishtaco uses to confuse his victims so they won't know he's taking their fat. What kind of powder? Almost always a powder made from crushed llama or alpaca bones. When you inhale it you don't feel anything, you don't know what's going on. The pishtaco can cut out your insides and you won't even notice or feel any pain. That's what Stud did, and starting that night Sebastián began to lose weight, and he got smaller and forgot everything he knew. Just like Juan Apaza. And finally he died too.

That's what happened back when Naccos made its living from the Santa Rita mine, and that's what's happening now, when Naccos makes its living from the highway. Misfortune won't come from the terrucos who are executing so many people or taking them away to be in their militia. Or from the pishtacos that are wandering around. Sure, they always come when times are hard, the Ayacucho invasion proves that. There must be a few around here, in the caves in those hills, collecting their supply of human fat. They must need it down in Lima, or in the United States, to grease the new machines, the rockets they send to the moon. They say no gasoline or oil can make all those scientific inventions work like the fat of a serrano. That must be why they sent their throat-slitters, they have machetes with a curved blade that can stretch out like gum all the way to the victim's neck. They do harm too, nobody can say they don't.

But the worst misfortunes always come from the spirits who turn away their faces. The ones who ask for more than people can give. They're up there, stone with the stones, waiting until misfortune makes the laborers open their minds to them. But you like to get angry when I explain it to you. What's the point of asking if you cover your ears and don't want to understand? You should follow my husband's advice instead: keep drinking till you're drunk, when you're drunk everything becomes better than it really is, and then the terrucos disappear, and the pishtacos, and everything that makes you angry and scared.

·

"But why me?" Mercedes suddenly asked again.

"I'm sorry, Tomasito," Lituma interrupted in the darkness. "That article in the Lima newspaper about people stealing children's eyes really got to me. I'm not up to hearing about your love life tonight. Let's talk about the eye-thieves instead. Or about Dionisio and the witch. I can't get them out of my head, either."

"No way, Corporal," Tomás replied from his cot. "The nights belong to Mercedes and nobody else, unless I'm on duty. I spend enough time during the day worrying myself sick about everything that's going on. You can have the pishtacos, and I'll stick to my sweetie."

"Why didn't they stop you, too, or both of us at least?" Mercedes repeated.

The question had been on her lips ever since their escape from the police. Carreño had given her all the answers: maybe there was a record of her name because they connected her with Hog, who had been in the police files for a long time; maybe they found some mistake or a suspicious mark on her voter's identification; or maybe they called her for the same reason they could have called any other passenger, just to get some money out of her. Why worry about it anymore? The worst was over. Wasn't she free? Hadn't they crossed half the sierra with no problems? They'd get to Lima safe and sound in just a couple of hours. As if to emphasize Carreño's words, the engineer sounded the train whistle, and the strident blast rebounded and echoed along the bare hills around them.

"The paper didn't talk about pishtacos but eye-cutters, or eye-robbers," Lituma said. "But you're right, Tomasito, they're like the serrucho pishtacos. What I can't get through my head is that even in Lima people are beginning to believe this stuff. How can that be? It's the capital of Peru!"

"You think I'm listening, but I'm not here," whispered Tomasito. "I'm in the sierra train, going down, down to Desamparados, with my arms around my sweetheart."

"Convince me," she said softly, huddling against him. "Convince me it was just a coincidence that they called me. I don't want to go to jail. A woman I know was sent to Chorrillos. I went to visit her. I'll kill myself before I go to jail."

The boy held her tight and soothed her. They were sitting very close together on a seat meant for one passenger. The car was crowded, people were standing, carrying bundles, packages, even chickens, and at each station more passengers got on. Soon you wouldn't be able to breathe. Just as well they were coming into the Matucana station.

Tomás pressed his mouth against Mercedes's thick hair. "I swear nothing will ever happen to you," he promised. "I'll always save you, like I did last night."

He kissed her and saw that she was closing her eyes. Through the window he could see occasional villages on the hilltops and slopes, and painted advertisements began to appear on the stones along the tracks. It was a leaden afternoon, with low clouds threatening a rain that never fell. Well, typical Lima weather.

"Something serious is happening in this country, Tomasito," Lituma interrupted again. "How can a whole district in Lima get so crazy they believe a story like that? Gringos putting five-year-old kids in luxury cars and cutting out their eyes with ultrasonic scalpels. Sure, maybe a few crazy women say those things. Lima has its Doña Adrianas, too. But a whole district believing it and people keeping their children home from school and looking for foreigners to lynch: it's incredible, isn't it?"

"The only eyes I care about belong to my Mercedes," whispered the guard. "As big as stars and the color of brown sugar."

He felt no misgivings now. He had while they were crossing the Andes at the mercy of the man behind the wheel, and to keep him from turning them in, Carreño let him see the pistol from time to time. But they had gotten along pretty well on the trip. The driver swallowed, or pretended to swallow, the story that Carreño and Mercedes were running away from a jealous husband who had reported her to the police. He had stopped twice to buy food and drinks, and suggested they take the train in Cerro de Pasco. As payment for his services, Carreño left the two submachine guns with him.

"If you want, you can return them, like a good citizen. Or sell them. You'll get a pile of money for those toys."

"I'll toss a coin and decide," said the driver, and he wished them a happy honeymoon. "I'll wait a couple of hours before I go to the police."

"The paper said that last month people went crazy like this in Chiclayo, and in Ferrañafe, too," Lituma continued. "They said a woman saw four gringos in white robes taking a boy away; they found the body of another boy in a ditch, and his eyes were missing and the eye-robbers had left fifty dollars in his pocket. They formed patrols, just like in Ayacucho when there were rumors about the pishtaco invasion. Lima, Chiclayo, Ferrenafe, they're all catching the serrucho superstition. No different from Naccos. It's like an epidemic, isn't it?"

"To tell you the truth, Corporal, I don't give a damn. Because right now I'm happy."

Death in the Andes

The train pulled into the Desamparados station at about six. It was growing dark, but the lights had not been turned on yet and the waiting room on the upper level was in shadow when Carreño and Mercedes walked through. There were no police in sight, and none at the exit except for the ones standing guard at the iron fence around the Government Palace.

"We'd better go our separate ways now, Carreñito," said Mercedes when they were on the street.

"You plan to go home? They'll be watching it, just like they'll be watching my place. We'd better hide a few days at my mother's house."

They took a taxi, and after giving an address in Breña, the boy leaned over and whispered in Mercedes's ear: "So, you want to get rid of me?"

"I want things to be very clear," she said in a low voice, so the driver could not hear. "I can't change what happened, that's water under the bridge. But I fought hard for my independence. So don't get any ideas. I'm not going to give it all up for a Civil Guard."

"An ex-Civil Guard," the boy interrupted.

"We'll only stay together until we're out of the mess you got us into. Okay, Carreñito?"

"I can't help seeing Dionisio and the witch in all this," said Lituma. "It's like those two savages were turning out to be right, not civilized people. Knowing how to read and write, wearing a tie and a jacket, finishing school, living in the city—it's not enough anymore. Only witches can understand what's going on. Do you know what Dionisio said this afternoon in the cantina? That to be a wise man you have to be the child of incest. Every time that pervert opens his mouth he gives me the shivers. How about you?"

"Right now I have the shivers, too, but a different kind, Corporal. Because I'm about to start my roller-coaster honeymoon."

As they were driving down Avenida Arica in Breña, the dim streetlights came on. The taxi circled La Salle Academy, went along a narrow alley, and was about to turn where the boy had indicated when Carreño said: "Just keep going straight. I changed my mind. Take us to Barrios Altos instead."

Mercedes turned, looking at him in surprise, and saw that Carreño was holding the revolver.

"Peru is being overrun by devils and lunatics, and all you can do is go on and on about that woman. What they say is true, Tomasito: nobody's as self-centered as a man in love."

"Some guy was under the streetlight in front of the house, and I didn't like it," the boy explained. "Maybe I'm just on edge, but we can't take any chances."

In Barrios Altos, he had the driver stop at the old-age home, and he waited for the taxi to drive away before taking Mercedes by the arm, pulling her along for a few blocks until they reached a shack, with bars at the doors and windows, built out from the ground floor of a faded three-story building. The door opened right away. A woman in bathrobe and slippers, with a scarf tied around her head, looked them up and down, showing no joy.

"Things must be pretty bad for you to come around," she said to Carreño by way of greeting. "You haven't been here in a dog's age."

"Yes, Aunt Alicia, they're pretty bad right now," Tomás acknowledged as he kissed the woman on the forehead. "That little room you rent out, is it empty by any chance?"

The woman examined Mercedes from head to toe and responded with a grudging nod.

"Can you rent it to me for a few days, Aunt Alicia?"

She moved aside to let them in.

"It was vacated yesterday," she said. Mercedes murmured "Good evening" as she passed, and the woman mumbled something in reply.

She preceded them down a narrow hallway with photographs on the walls, opened a door, and turned on the light. The room had a single bed covered with a pink spread, and a trunk that took up half the space. There was a small bare window, and a wooden crucifix hung on the wall at the head of the bed.

"There's no supper, and it's too late for me to go out and buy anything," the woman declared. "Tomorrow I can fix you lunch. Yes, even though it's a single and there are two of you . . ."

"I'll pay for a double," the boy agreed. "What's fair is fair."

She nodded and closed the door behind her as she left.

"That's some story about what a little saint you were," Mercedes commented. "You brought women here, didn't you? That bitch didn't even blink when she saw me."

"Anybody would think you were jealous," he teased.

"Jealous?"

"I know you're not," said Carreño. "I just wanted to see if a joke would get rid of that scared look on your face. I never brought anybody here. Alicia isn't even my aunt. Everybody calls her that. This used to be my neighborhood. Come on, we'll wash up and go out to eat."

"In other words, according to that pervert, wise men are the children of a brother and sister, or a father and daughter, something barbaric like that," Lituma rambled on. "I hear things in Naccos that I never heard in Piura. Dionisio must be a child of incest. I don't know why I'm so interested in him and the witch. They're the ones who really run things here. You and I don't even count. I try to find out about them from the laborers and the foremen and the comuneros, but I can't shake anything loose. Besides, I don't know if they're pulling my leg. Do you know what the Huancayan who drives the steamroller said about Dionisio? That his last name in Quechua was—"

"Eater of Raw Meat," his adjutant interrupted. "Damn it, Corporal, now are you going to tell me that his mother was killed by lightning?"

"These things are important, Tomasito," Lituma grumbled. "For understanding his idiosyncrasies."

Mercedes had sat down on the bed and was looking at Carreño in a way that seemed kindly to the boy.

"I don't want to deceive you," she told him again, in a friendly voice, trying not to hurt him. "I don't feel about you the way you feel about me. It's better for me to tell you, isn't it? I'm not going to live with you, I'm not going to be your wife. Get that into your head, Carreñito. We'll only stay together until we're out of this mess."

"That's plenty of time for you to fall in love with me," he purred, stroking her hair. "Anyway, you couldn't leave now even if you wanted to. Who else besides me can get you out of this? I mean, who else besides my godfather can get us out of this?"

They washed in a bathroom so tiny it seemed like a toy, and then went out. Carreño took her arm and with a sure step led her along shadowy streets filled with gangs of boys smoking on every corner, until they came to a Chinese restaurant that had private booths behind grease-stained screens. The place was full of smoke, the smell of frying, and rock music blaring on the radio. They sat down near the street door, and to go with several dishes they would share, Carreñito ordered cold beer. Over the music they could hear curses and an African drum rhythm.

"They once gambled for me in a dice game. I want you to know that, Carreñito." Mercedes stared at him, not smiling. She had deep circles under her eyes and looked haggard: her eyes did not sparkle the way they had in Tingo María and Huánuco. "I've had rotten luck since the day I was born, and there's not a damn thing I can do about it."

"They gambled for her in a crap game?" Lituma showed interest for the first time that night. "Tell me about that, Tomasito."

"Just what I said," she replied grimly. "The worst kind of drunks and tramps. Shooting dice. That's what I got away from, that's where I come from. I pulled myself up on my own, nobody helped me. And I was doing okay until you came along. You pushed me back into the hole, Carreñito."

"Well, Corporal, I finally made you forget about pishtacos and eye-robbers, Doña Adriana and Dionisio."

"You know, years ago I saw the same kind of thing, and I never forgot it," Lituma replied. "Did they gamble for her back in Piura?"

"She didn't say where or how. Just that it happened, and it really pissed me off. Gambling for her, like she was a thing! My sweetheart!"

"Didn't she say if it was in a little bar owned by a babe they called La Chunga, over by the Piura Stadium?"

"She wouldn't tell me anything else. Just that, just to show me how much she'd come up in the world compared to where she started out. And how I pushed her down again when I killed Hog."

"It's really funny," said Lituma. "In that bar I saw one of my friends, one of the Invincibles I told you about, sell the girl he was with to La Chunga so he could go on playing poker. Suppose the Piuran in both our stories is the same woman? Are you sure the love of your life is named Mercedes and not Meche?"

"Well, Meche can be a nickname for Mercedes, Corporal."

"And that's another reason I have a hard time with the idea of hiding out," she said. "I got away from all that. I want to go home. Take a bath in my own bathroom, I always keep it nice and clean. Change my clothes, get rid of this grime, it's been on me for five days."

She was about to say something else, but just then the waiter came with their food and Mercedes stopped talking. When he asked if they wanted forks or chopsticks, Carreño said chopsticks.

"I'll teach you to eat like the Chinese, sweetheart. It's real easy. When you learn how, you can use the sticks just like a knife and fork."

"Everything was going fine for me," she said as they ate. "I was saving up to go to the United States. A friend of mine in Miami said she'd find me a job. And now I'm back where I started, without a pot to piss in."

"Meche, Mercedes, you're right, that's a real coincidence," said Tomasito. "They could be the same person, why not. It's enough to make you believe in miracles. Or pishtacos. Only now you have to tell me . . ."

"Don't worry, I never fucked Meche, Tomasito. Unfortunately. She was the best-looking broad in Piura, I swear."

"If you want to go to the United States, we'll go," the boy promised. "I know how to get in without a visa, through Mexico. A guy I know is making a fortune doing that."

"So how much does a Civil Guard earn?" she said with a commiserating look. "Not much more than what I pay my cleaning girl, I bet."

"Maybe even less." He laughed. "Why do you think I have to do my little extras and take care of hogs while they live like kings with their women in Tingo María?"

For a time they ate in silence, and finished the bottle of beer. Then they ordered ice cream, and the boy lit a cigarette. He blew smoke rings toward the ceiling.

"The funny thing is, you seem happy," she said.

"I am happy," he said, blowing her a kiss. "Want to know why?"

Mercedes smiled in spite of herself. "I know what you're going to say." And she looked at him with that expression—Carreño couldn't tell if it was pity or disdain—and added, "Even if you have fucked up my life, I can't stay mad at you."

"That's something," he said joyfully. "It starts off like that, and you end up falling in love."

She laughed, more willingly now.

"Have you been in love before?"

"Never like now," the boy stated unequivocally. "Nobody ever made me feel like this. Well, I never met a woman as beautiful as you, either."

"It could be Mechita, life is full of coincidences. Do you have a picture of her?"

"We didn't even have time to have our picture taken together," the guard lamented. "You don't know how sorry I am about that. It would've been terrific to look at her, too, not just remember her."

"I only met him a couple of weeks before I went away with him. At a club in Barranco. He came to see me in the show. He took me back to his house, in Chacarilla del Estanque. What a house! He gave me presents. He wanted to set me up in an apartment. Everything. Anything I wanted if I didn't see other men. That's how I got to make the damn trip to Pucallpa. Come spend the weekend with me, you'll get to see the jungle. And I went. And, just my luck, I went to Tingo María, too."

The boy became very serious. "And did Hog hit you every time you went to bed with him?"

He immediately regretted his words.

"Are you checking up on me?" she said angrily. "Do you really think you're my boyfriend, or my husband?"

"I guess we're having our first quarrel," said the boy, trying to smooth things over. "It happens to every couple. We won't talk about it anymore. Are you happy now?"

They said nothing for a while, and Carreño ordered two cups of tea.

While they were drinking, Mercedes spoke again. Not with anger, but firmly: "Even though I saw you kill a man, you seem like a good person. And that's why I'm telling you this for the last time, Carreñito. I'm sorry you fell in love with me. But I can't love you back. It's the way I am. I decided a long time ago not to let anybody tie me down. Why else do you think I'm not married? That's why. I only have friends, with no commitments, like Hog. That's how it's always been with me. And that's how it's always—"

"Until we go to the United States," he interrupted.

Mercedes finally smiled. "Don't you ever get mad?"

"I'll never get mad at you. You can keep telling me the most awful things."

"The truth is, you're racking up points," she acknowledged.

The boy paid the bill.

As they were leaving, Mercedes said she wanted to call her apartment. "I lent it to a girlfriend while I was in the jungle."

"Don't tell her where you're calling from, and don't say anything about when you'll be back."

The phone was next to the register, and Mercedes had to squeeze behind the counter to use it. As she spoke, although he was not listening to what she said, Carreño knew she was hearing bad news. She came back visibly upset, her chin trembling.

"Two men were asking for me at my house, and they insisted that my friend tell them where I was. They were cops, they showed her their papers."

"What did you say?"

"I told her I was calling from Tingo María and would explain everything later," said Mercedes. "My God, what am I going to do now?"

"And what happened to the Meche your friend sold to the dyke so he could go on playing poker?" asked Tomás.

"She just vanished into thin air, nobody ever knew where," replied Lituma. "A mystery nobody in Piura could solve."

"Now you'll go to sleep and forget all about it," said the boy. "Nobody will come looking for us at Aunt Alicia's. Don't worry, sweetheart."

"And La Chunga never would tell us what happened to Mechita."

"The missing men seem to be haunting you, Corporal. Don't blame Dionisio or Doña Adriana so much, or the terrucos or the pishtacos. From what I can see, you might be the one responsible for the disappearances."

7 / IT WAS STILL DARK when Francisco López shook a startled Corporal Lituma awake. They ought to leave right away because López had to be back in La Esperanza before nightfall. He had made coffee and toasted some bread on the portable burner. The engineers and the professor were still asleep when they set out for Naccos.

It had been a three-hour drive to La Esperanza, but the trip back took almost twice as long. It had rained heavily the night before in the uplands of the Cordillera, and the road was flooded and blocked by landslides. The corporal and the driver were obliged to stop and roll boulders out of the way so the jeep could drive through. When it sank into mud, they had to push the vehicle or lay boards or flat stones under the wheels to free it.

At first, Francisco López's attempts to make conversation with Lituma failed. When he spoke, all he got in return were grunts, monosyllables, or nods. But after an hour or so, the corporal suddenly broke the silence, murmuring behind his scarf: "That has to be it, the damn serruchos sacrificed them to the apus."

"Are you talking about the disappearances in Naccos?" Francisco López shot him a disconcerted glance.

"It may be hard to believe, but that's what those motherfuckers are like." Lituma nodded. "And no question that Dionisio and the witch put the idea in their heads."

"That Dionisio is capable of anything." Francisco López laughed. "I guess it isn't true that alcohol kills. If it did, how could that drunk still be alive?"

"Have you known him a long time?"

"I've been running into him all over the sierra ever since I was a kid. He was always showing up at the mines where I worked. I was a contractor before I went into security. In those days, Dionisio didn't have his own place, he was an itinerant cantinero who went from mine to mine, village to village, selling pisco, chicha, aguardiente, and putting on shows with a troupe of performers. The priests finally got the damn cops to run them out. Sorry, I forgot you were one, too."

Lituma kept his head buried in his scarf, his kepi pulled down low on his forehead: all the driver could see were cheekbones, a flat nose, and dark eyes that scrutinized him through half-closed lids.

"Was he already married to Doña Adriana?"

"No, he met her later, in Naccos. Didn't you hear the story? It's one of the great scandals in the Andes. They say that to get her he knocked off the miner she was married to. And then ran away with her."

"It never fails," exclaimed Lituma. "Wherever that guy goes, everything turns degenerate and bloody."

"That's all we needed now," said the driver. "Noah's flood."

The rain had begun to pour down with real fury. The sky darkened quickly and filled with thunder that rumbled across the mountains. A heavy curtain fell against the windshield, and the wipers did not provide enough visibility for them to avoid potholes and flooded stretches of roadway. They advanced very slowly, the jeep bucking like a skittish horse.

"What was Dionisio like back then?" Lituma's eyes were glued to the driver. "Did you spend much time with him?"

"I got drunk with him sometimes, that's about it," said Francisco López. "He always showed up at fairs and festivals with his musicians and some Indian girls who were pretty much whores; they did some wild dances. Once at the carnival in Jauja I saw him go crazy doing the Jalapato. Have you ever seen that Jaujan dance? They dance and dance and then, while they're still moving, they pull the head off a live duck. Dionisio pulled the heads off every one, he wouldn't give the others a chance. They finally kicked him out."

The jeep moved at a snail's pace through a landscape devoid of trees and animals, crawled past rocks, ravines, peaks, and meanders shaken by the violent downpour. But not even the storm could distract Lituma from his obsession. His brow was creased into a deep frown, and to withstand the jolting he clutched at the door and roof of the jeep.

"That guy gives me nightmares," he confessed. "He's the one responsible for everything that's happening in Naccos."

"It's funny the terrucos haven't killed him yet. They execute faggots, pimps, whores, every kind of degenerate. Dionisio is all those things and more."

Francisco López shot a rapid glance at Lituma. "You seem to believe Red's stories, Corporal. You shouldn't, that gringo has an active imagination. Do you really think they'd sacrifice those three men? Well, why not? Around here they kill anybody for anything. They're always finding graves, like that one outside Huanta with the ten Protestant missionaries. Why shouldn't there be human sacrifices too."

He laughed, but Lituma did not find his joke funny.

"It's no laughing matter," he said. A succession of thunderclaps cut off the rest of what he had to say.

"I don't know how we'll get all the way to Naccos," Francisco López shouted when he could make himself heard. "If it's raining there like it is here, the road down will be a mudslide. Why don't you come back to the mine with me?"

"No way," Lituma said quietly. "I have to straighten this out once and for all."

"Why do you care so much about the missing men, Corporal? After all, what difference can it make to you if there are three poor bastards more or less in the world?"

"I knew one of them. A little mute who cleaned up the post for us. A very decent guy."

"You want to be another John Wayne, Corporal. Another Lone Ranger."

A couple of hours later, when they reached the spot where the jeep had to turn, the rain had stopped. But the sky was still overcast, and in the distance the storm's thunder rumbled like the unrhythmic beating of a drum.

"I don't know, I don't like leaving you here alone," said Francisco López. "Maybe we should wait awhile until the road dries."

"No, I'd better do it now," said the corporal, climbing out of the jeep. "Before the rain starts again."

They shook hands, and he barely listened as the head of security at La Esperanza thanked him for making the trip and writing up the reports. When he began to climb down the slope, the engine engaged and the jeep drove away.

"You motherfuckers!" he bellowed then at the top of his lungs. "Fucking serruchos! Goddamn Indians, you superstitious pagan sons of bitches!"

He heard his voice repeated in echoes that rebounded along

the high walls of the mountains invisible in the fog. The explosion of insults made him feel better. He sat down on a rock, cupped his hands to protect the flame from the wind, and lit a cigarette. That's what had happened, it was obvious. The mystery had been solved by that Prof who was so crazy about Peru. So that's what history was good for. He remembered the course at San Miguel Academy in Piura taught by Professor Néstor Martos. He had a good time in that class because Professor Martos, who showed up in the strangest outfits, wrapped in a shawl, bearded, high on chicha, explained everything like a Technicolor movie. But it had never occurred to Lituma that studying the customs of the ancient Peruvians might help him understand what was going on now in Naccos. Thank you, Red, for clearing up the mystery. But he felt more discouraged and confused than ever, because although his head told him there could be no doubt, that all the pieces had fallen into place, his heart did not want to accept it. How could a normal person with even a shred of intelligence believe that Pedrito Tinoco and the two laborers had been sacrificed to the spirits of the mountains the highway would disturb? And that poor bastard of a mayor, coming here to hide and changing his name to escape the terrucos, only to end up smashed to pieces at the bottom of a mine.

He tossed away his cigarette and watched the wind whirl it through the air. He started walking again. It was all downhill, but the rain had washed away the trail, the ground was as slippery as soap, and he had to step very carefully in order not to fall flat on his back. Two days ago the walk had taken him and Francisco López an hour and a half, but it would be three times longer now. But better go slow and not break a leg in this barren place where there wasn't even a bird to make you feel less of an orphan. What would Tomasito say? He imagined his adjutant's face, the disbelief in his eyes, how he would want to throw up. Or maybe not; thinking about his Piuran girlfriend had inoculated him against feeling discouraged. Doña Adriana had convinced them; if they wanted to avoid a catastrophe at the construction site—a huayco, an earth-quake, a massacre—there was only one thing to do: find human blood for the apus. And to soften them up and make them accept her advice, that faggot got them drunk. I can't believe it, Corporal. That's what happened, Tomasito. That's why they all say those two were behind it. But one thing wasn't clear. If this was an offering to the apus, wasn't one enough? Why three? Who knows, Tomasito. Maybe a whole tribe of apus had to be placated. A highway has to cross a lot of mountains, doesn't it?

He slipped and found himself sitting in the mud. He stood and fell again, this time on his side. He laughed at his own clum-siness but really felt like crying. For the disastrous condition of his uniform and the gashes on his hands, but most of all because the world, his life, had become unbearable. He wiped his palms on the seat of his trousers and continued on his way, holding on to the rocks at every step. How was it possible that the laborers, many of whom had adopted modern ways and at least completed primary school, who had seen the cities, listened to the radio, went to the movies, dressed like civilized men—how could they behave like naked, savage cannibals? You could understand if they were Indians from the barrens who had never set foot in a school and still lived like their great-great-grandfathers, but with guys like these who played cards, who had been baptized: how could it be?

The sky had cleared slightly, and far below, through the gray-ness of the day, Lituma could make out the lights of the camp. That was when he realized that for some time, along with the distant thunder, he had been hearing a deep rumble, a constant shuddering of the earth. What the hell was it? Another storm coming up behind him? Even the weather betrayed you in the goddamn Andes. What the fuck was happening? A tremor? An earthquake? No question now: the ground was trembling beneath his feet and there was a turpentine smell. All around him a hoarse, deep sound came from the heart of the mountain. On every side, between his feet, pushed or chased by invisible hands, pebbles and rocks were rolling down the slope, and then he realized that in an unconscious effort to find shelter, he had crouched down on his hands and knees beneath a high, pointed ledge covered with patches of yellow-green moss.

"Oh my God, what is it, what's happening?" he shouted, crossing himself, and this time there was no echo because the dense, complex, unending noise, the granitic rumble that came rolling down the mountainside, had swallowed up every other sound. They said that Dionisio's mother had been struck by lightning. Was another lightning bolt going to kill him now? He trembled from head to foot, his hands sweating with fear. "Dear God, I don't want to die, please, by all that's holy," he called out again, and his throat felt cracked and dry.

The sky had turned even blacker, and although it was early afternoon it seemed as dark as night. As if he were dreaming, he saw a vizcacha as big as a rabbit jump out from among the stones and race past him down the hill, its ears rigid with terror, leaping blindly, stumbling till finally it disappeared from view. Lituma tried to pray but couldn't. Was it an earthquake? Was he going to die, flattened by the boulders bouncing past him, crashing into each other, splitting and shattering in all directions with a maddening din? Animals had a sixth sense, they could smell catastrophes, that's why the vizcacha had fled its hole, running for its life: it could smell the end of the world. "Forgive my sins," he bellowed. "I don't want to end this way, damn it." He huddled on all fours against the rock, and on either side, and over his head, he saw stones, chunks of earth, every imaginable kind of rock hurtle past him, and he felt the ledge shudder with the impact as they broke against it or careened away. How much could it withstand? He had a presentiment of an enormous boulder rolling down from the very top of the Cordillera, heading straight for the ledge that pro-tected him, crashing into it and, in a matter of seconds, pulverizing the rock and him along with it. He closed his eyes and pictured his body turned into a glob, a stinking, bloody mush of bones, blood, hair, pieces of clothing and shoes, all mixed together, buried in the mud, dragged down the mountain, down, down, and only then did it occur to him that this avalanche, this collapsing, crum-bling mountain, was carrying its load of missiles straight for the camp. "It's a huayco," he managed to think, keeping his eyes closed, trembling as if he had tertian fever. "It'll flatten me first and then everybody down below."

When he opened his eyes, he thought he was dreaming. To his right, in an immense cloud of dust, and scattering snow in every direction, a boulder as big as a truck came crashing down the slope, taking everything in its path, opening a furrow as wide as the bed of a great river. It was followed by a dizzying whirlwind of more boulders, rocks, pebbles, tree branches, clumps of ice and earth, and Lituma thought he could see animals, beaks, feathers, bones in the midst of that tumultuous confusion. The noise was deafening, and the dust grew thicker and covered everything, in-cluding him. He coughed and choked, and his hands were bloody from clutching at the muddy soil. "It's the huayco, that's what it is, Lituma," he repeated to himself, feeling his heart pound in his chest. "It's killing you little by little." Then he felt a blow on the head and recalled in a flash the time when he was a kid and had been knocked out in a brawl with Camarón Panizo under the Old Bridge in Piura, and saw stars, moons, suns, just like now, as he went under and everything turned black.

He was still shivering when he came to, but now it was from the cold that made his bones creak. Night had fallen, and the pain when he tried to move made him feel as if he had been run over by a car that had ground everything under his skin to a pulp. But he was alive, and it was wonderful that instead of the clamoring torrent of dirt, stone, and rock, a peaceful, icy calm now reigned on earth. And even more so in the sky. For a few moments he was so bewitched by the sight that he forgot his body: thousands, millions of stars of every magnitude glittering all around a yellow circle that seemed to shine only for him. He had never seen a moon so big, not even in Paita. He had never seen a night so filled with stars, so quiet, so sweet. How long had he been unconscious? Hours? Days? But he was alive, and he had to move. If not, you'll freeze to death, compadre.

He rolled slowly from side to side and spat, for his mouth was clogged with dirt. The silence was incredible after that terrifying noise. A silence you could see and hear and touch. Sensation was returning to his limbs, and he managed to sit up. When had he lost his left boot? No bones seemed to be broken. Everything hurt, but nothing was especially painful. He had survived, that was the fantastic thing. Wasn't it a miracle? Nothing less than a huayco had passed over him. Or beside him. And here he was, worse for wear but alive. "We Piurans are hard nuts to crack," he thought. And he was filled with anticipatory vanity as he imagined the day when he would be back in Piura, sitting in La Chunga's bar, telling the Invincibles about this great adventure.

He was on his feet, and all around him in the pale moonlight he could see the devastation caused by the avalanche. The gash the immense stone had opened. Rocks and mire everywhere. Patches of snow here and there in the mud. But no wind, no sign of rain. He looked into the darkness down below, toward where the camp should be. He could not see any lights. Had the cataract of earth, mud, and rock buried it all—barracks, people, machines?

He crouched down, felt around, and finally located his boot. It was full of dirt. He cleaned it the best he could and put it on. He decided to go down now and not wait for daylight. With this moon, if he took his time, he'd get there. He was serene and happy. As if he had passed a test, he thought, as if these damn mountains, this damn sierra, had finally accepted him. Before starting out, he pressed his mouth against the rock that had sheltered him, and whispered, like a serrucho: "Thank you for saving my life, mamay, apu, pachamama, or whoever the fuck you are."

.

"Tell us the story about you and the pishtaco, Doña Adriana," that's what they say as soon as they have their first drink, because there's nothing they like as much as the death of a throat-slitter. "The one you helped to kill, was he the same one who dried out your cousin Sebastián?" No, it was another one. It happened much earlier. I still had all my teeth then, and no wrinkles. I know there are a lot of versions, I've heard them all, and since it happened so long ago I've forgotten a few details. I was young then and hadn't left my village yet. I must be very old now.

Quenka is far away, on the other side of the Mantaro, near Parcasbamba. When the river swelled with the rains and swallowed up the land, the village turned into an island, hugging the top of the hill, the flooded fields all around it. A pretty village, Quenka, prosperous, and the crops grew on the plain and along the slopes. Everything grew there: potatoes, beans, barley, corn, chilis. Pepper trees, eucalyptus, and willows protected us from whirlwinds. Even the poorest campesinos had a few hens, a pig, some sheep, a flock of llamas that they grazed in the uplands. I had a quiet, easy life. I was the most popular of my sisters, and my father, who was the most important man in Quenka, rented out three of his fields and worked two of them, and he owned the general store that sold liquor, medicines, tools, and the mill where everybody came to grind their grain. Lots of times my father was in charge of the fiestas, and then he went all out and brought in a priest and hired bands of musicians and dancers from Huancayo. Until the pishtaco came.

How did we know he had come? Because of the change in the peddler Salcedo. For years he had brought remedies, clothes, and tools for my father's store. He was from the coast. He drove around in a noisy truck that was covered with dents; the motor and the clanking let us know he was coming long before any of us in Quenka could see him. Everybody knew him, but this time we hardly recognized him. He had grown taller and huskier, until he was like a giant. Now he had a beard the color of a cockroach and bloodshot, bulging eyes. People gathered round to greet him and he looked at us like he wanted to devour us with those eyes. Men and women both. And me, too. A look I'll never forget, it made everybody suspicious.

He was dressed in black, with knee-high boots and a poncho so big that when it fluttered in the wind it looked like Salcedo was going to fly. He unloaded the truck, and went to sleep, like he did all the other times, in the back room of our store. He wasn't a talker anymore, telling us news from outside and being friendly with people. He was quiet, inside himself, and hardly said a word. He looked at us with those sharp eyes that made the men uneasy and scared the girls.

He left one morning at dawn after spending two or three days in Quenka and getting my father's order. The next day, one of the boys who tended flocks in the uplands came down to the village to tell us that the truck had gone off the highway, that it went over the side on a curve on the road to Parcasbamba. You could see it from the edge of the cliff, smashed to pieces at the bottom of the ravine.

With my father leading them, a group of neighbors made their way down there. They spread out in a circle and found the four tires, the springs, the dented metal sides, the chassis, parts of the motor. But not a sign of Salcedo's corpse. They searched the canyon wall, thinking he had fallen out when the truck went over the side. Not a trace. And no blood on the wreckage or on the rocks nearby. Could he have jumped clear when he realized he was going off the road? "That must be it," they said. "He jumped out and another truck picked him up and he's probably in Parcasbamba or in Huancayo now, getting over his scare."

But the truth was that he'd stayed in Quenka, he'd gone to live in some old caves on the same mountain where his truck went over the side, those caves that are like a wasps' nest and have paintings by the ancient ones on the walls. That was when he began to do his pishtaco evil. He would lurk at night on the roads, on a bridge, behind a tree, appear to a lone shepherd, or travelers, or mule drivers, or migrants, or people taking their crops to market or coming back from a fair. He would come out of nowhere, with no warning, in the dark, eyes flashing. His enormous body was wrapped in the flying poncho, and it paralyzed them with terror. Then it was no problem for him to take them back to his cave with its dark, freezing tunnels, where he kept his surgical instruments. He slit them from ass to mouth and hung them up and roasted them alive over pans that collected their fat. He skinned them and made masks out of their faces and cut them into little pieces and crushed their bones to make his hypnotic powder. Several people disappeared.

Then, one day, he showed himself to Don Santiago Calancha, a cattle seller who was coming back to Quenka from a wedding in Parcasbamba. Instead of taking him to his cave, he talked to him. If Calancha wanted to save his own life and the rest of his family, he had to give him one of his daughters to be his cook. And Salcedo told him exactly the entrance to the cave where he should leave the girl.

It goes without saying that Calancha swore he would obey but didn't follow the pishtaco's instructions. He barricaded himself inside his shack with his machete and a pile of stones, ready to face Salcedo if he came to steal his daughter. Nothing happened the first day, or the second, or for the first two weeks. But during the third week, in the middle of a rainstorm, lightning struck Calancha's roof and the house caught fire. He and his wife and his three daughters were all burned to a crisp. I saw their skeletons. Yes, Dionisio's mother died exactly the same way. I didn't see that, maybe it's just talk. The people of Quenka went out to watch the fire, and drenched and sad, they heard laughter along with the whistling of the wind and the boom of thunder. It came from the caves where Salcedo lived.

And so the next time the pishtaco asked for a girl to be his cook, the Quenkans held a meeting and decided to do what he asked. The first one who went to work for him in his cave was my oldest sister. My family, and many other families, walked with her to the entrance the pishtaco had said she should come to. They sang to her and prayed for her and a lot of people were crying when they said goodbye.

He didn't dry her like he did my cousin Sebastián, though my father used to say maybe it would've been better if he had cut out her fat. He kept her alive but turned her into a pishtaco's slut. First he abused her, throwing her down on the damp ground in the cave and drilling her with his tool. My sister's howling on her wedding night could be heard in every house in Quenka. Then she lost her will and only lived to serve her lord and master. She loved to cook the potato mush he liked, and she dried and salted the strips of flesh from his victims for the dishes of charqui they ate with corn, and helped him hang his victims from hooks that Salcedo had fastened into the stone so the fat would drip into copper pans.

Death in the Andes

My sister was the first of several girls who went into the cave to cook for him and be his helpers. From that time on, Quenka submitted to his authority. We brought him offerings of food and left them at the entrance to the cave, and sometimes we left a girl he had asked for. We resigned ourselves to having neighbors disappear every once in a while when the pishtaco Salcedo carried them off to renew his supply of fat.

And then did a brave prince come? No prince, but a dark-skinned horse trainer. Anybody who knows the story can cover his ears or leave. Does it seem like you're living through it yourselves? Does it give you courage? Does it make you see that for great evils there are always great remedies?

Big-nosed Timoteo heard what was happening in Quenka and made a special trip from Ayacucho to go into the caves and face the pishtaco. Timoteo Fajardo, that was his name. I knew him. He was my first husband, though we never did get married. "Can an ordinary mortal face a creature of the devil?" people would ask him. My father also tried to talk him out of it, when Timoteo respectfully told him about his plan to go into the pishtaco's cave and tear off his head and free us from his tyranny. But Timoteo stood firm. I've never known anybody so fearless. He was a good-looking man, even though he had such a big nose. He could make his nostrils flare like two mouths. That was his good fortune. "I can do it," he said, full of confidence. "I know the recipe for sneaking up on him: a clove of garlic, a pinch of salt, a crust of dry bread, a little ball of burro shit. And, just before I go into the cave, a virgin peeing over my heart."

I was the right one. I was young, intact, and when I listened to him, he seemed so brave, so sure of himself, that without asking my father's permission I offered to help him. But there was one problem. How would he find his way out of the tunnels after he killed Salcedo? The caves were so big, so complicated, that nobody had ever explored all of them. They turned, went up, went down, wound around, spreading out and twisting together like the roots of a eucalyptus tree. And, besides the bats, some had poison gases that no human could breathe and survive.

How would Timoteo Fajardo get out after he killed the pishtaco? His huge nose gave me the idea. I fixed a thick stew, nice and spicy, with that green chili that loosens the most stubborn bowels. He ate the whole pot and held everything in until his belly almost burst. And then he went into the cave. It was late afternoon and the sun was still shining, but after he took a few steps, Timoteo found himself in darkness. Every so often he would stop, pull down his trousers, squat, and leave a pile. At first he walked just trusting to luck, covering his eyes with his arm because the bats swooped down from the roof and beat at his face with their heavy wings. He felt the threads of spiderwebs on his skin. And for a long time he kept walking, stopping to empty his belly, then walking some more. Until he saw a light, and he followed that until he came to the pishtaco's home.

The giant was sleeping, lying on the ground with the three girls who cooked for him. In the light of some lamps that burned human fat, and almost fainting from the stink, he saw human remains hanging from bloody hooks, the fat dripping into bubbling pots. He didn't waste any time, but lifted his machete and with one blow cut off the head of the throat-slitter and shook his whores awake. When they opened their eyes and saw their master with his head cut off, they went wild and started screaming. Timoteo calmed them down and brought them to their senses: he had rescued them from slavery and now they could live a normal life again. Then the four of them started back, guided by the stinking trail he had left on the way in; his hunting dog's nose could follow it without any hesitation.

That's the story of the giant Salcedo. A tale of blood, corpses, and shit, like every story about the pishtacos.

·

"Go on, enjoy yourself, tell me about your trials and tribulations, Tomasito," Lituma urged. "You're lucky; lately I have trouble sleeping because of those damn disappearances."

"Those two weeks in Lima were my honeymoon," said his adjutant. "And nothing but one scare after another; every calamity you can think of happened to us. We even thought they were trying to kill us. But the fear added a little spice to our love, and we did it every night, two, even three times in a row. It was wonderful, fantastic, Corporal."

"Mercedes finally started to love you?"

"At night, I was sure of it. My beautiful Piuran was pure honey in bed. But in the light of day her mood changed. She was always reminding me that I had fucked up her life, that she would never be my wife."

Two days after they rented the room at Aunt Alicia's in Barrios Altos, Mercedes decided to withdraw her savings from the Banco Popular branch on Plaza de la Victoria where she had her account. She went in alone. Carreño waited for her on the corner and had his shoes shined. She took a long time. When she finally appeared in the doorway of the bank, a short man whose scarred face revealed his black and Indian ancestry dropped the paper he was reading as he leaned against a lamppost, took a few calm steps, and suddenly rushed her. They struggled, and he tried to grab the handbag that Mercedes held on to with both hands as she kicked at him and screamed. Some passersby stopped and watched but did not dare intervene. When Carreño raced over to them, revolver in hand, the thief let her go and ran off as if the devil were after him. They hurried down Manco Capac Avenue and hailed a taxi. Mercedes was more angry than frightened; although the man did not get her money, he had torn her voter's identification.

"And why do you think the guy wasn't just an ordinary thief? Isn't Lima full of muggers?"

"Because of what happened afterward," said the boy. "This was our first piece of bad luck. There were two more, and they were even worse. I began to see Hog's hand rising from the grave to take his revenge. 'Don't you feel that the danger is bringing us even closer, sweetheart?' I would say to her."

"How can you talk about love at a time like this, you little fool." Mercedes was furious. "Can't you see I've lost the only ID I have? Talk to your godfather once and for all and get him to help us."

But Carreño's efforts to get in touch with him were useless. He was not permitted to call him at the office, and his home phone was always busy. The operator said it was not out of order, so perhaps it was off the hook intentionally. Iscariote's wife told him that Fats was not back from the jungle yet. And Carreño's mother, whom he asked to go to his room in Rímac, gave him more bad news.

"The door was kicked in, everything was pulled out and thrown around, my bed was burned and had a pile of shit on it; what a scare for my old lady. Like they were planning to set fire to my room and for some reason didn't and decided to shit on my bed instead," said Tomás. "Could that be another coincidence, Corporal?"

"The pile of shit proves they were thieves," replied Lituma. "A lot of them think that if they want to stay out of the slammer, after they clean out a house they have to take a shit in it. Didn't you know that?"

"When I told her about my room, Mercedes began to cry." Tomasito sighed. "I could feel her trembling in my arms, and I was more in love with her than ever, Corporal. Don't worry, sweetheart, please don't cry."

"They're after us, they're looking for us," Mercedes wailed, the tears running down her cheeks. "It can't be a coincidence, first the bank and now your room. It's Hog's men, they're looking for us, they're going to kill us."

But the vandals and arsonists had not discovered the hiding place, under some bricks behind the toilet, where Carreño kept his dollars.

"Dollars?" Lituma said in surprise. "You had money saved?"

"Believe it or not, almost four thousand dollars. Not from my Civil Guard salary, of course. From the little jobs my godfather gave me to do. Bodyguard for a couple of days, taking a package somewhere, watching a house, simple stuff like that. Every sol I made I changed into dollars over on Ocoña Boulevard and put in my hiding place. Thinking about my future. Now Mercedes was my future."

"Damn, that godfather of yours is like God, Tomasito. If we ever get out of Naccos alive, introduce me to him, please. I'd like to see a big shot's face before I die. I've only seen them in movies or in the papers."

"Quit dreaming, this won't get us to the States," said Mercedes, making calculations.

"I'll get all the money we need, honey. Believe me. I'll get you out of this safe and sound and take you to Miami, you'll see. And when we're there, looking at the skyscrapers and the blue beaches and the latest cars, will you say: 'Carreñito, I love you with all my heart'?"

"This is no time for jokes. Don't be such an idiot! Can't you see they're looking for us, that they want revenge?"

"At least I made you laugh." And the boy laughed, too. "I like it when you laugh, you have dimples that make my heart beat faster. As soon as my old lady brings us the money, we'll buy you a dress, okay?"

"You can't fuck for the first time at the age of twenty-three, Tomasito, it's too late," Lituma philosophized. "Excuse me for saying so. Having a woman is what scrambled your brains and made you softheaded."

"You never met her, you never held my Mercedes naked in your arms." Carreño sighed. "I just waited for night to come to be in paradise with my sweetheart."

"When you say things like that, I have an idea you don't really feel them, that you're kidding around or making a joke," said Mercedes. "Do you really feel that way?"

"What do I have to do to make you believe me?"

"I don't know, Carreñito. I don't know what to make of it, telling me those things all the time. When you're excited and become so affectionate, that's one thing. But you go on and on, all day."

"Boy, you sure were crazy about her," remarked Lituma.

Carreño and his mother arranged to meet at nightfall on the Alameda de los Descalzos. Tomás took Mercedes with him. He had the taxi drop them off across from the Plaza de Acho, and they walked toward the Alameda. They circled the block several times before approaching the church where she was waiting for them. She was small and bent and wore the habit of Our Lord of Miracles. She embraced and kissed her son for a long while in silence, and when he introduced Mercedes, she extended a small, cold hand. They went to a broken bench on the avenue to talk, and sat in near-darkness, since the closest streetlight was shattered. From among her skirts the woman removed a packet wrapped in newspaper containing the dollars he had saved, and handed it to Carreño. She did not ask Mercedes any questions or look at her even once. The boy took out a handful of bills and put them in his mother's pocket, not saying anything. Her face showed neither fear nor surprise.

"Did you hear anything from my godfather?" Tomás asked her.

She nodded. And leaned her head forward slightly to look into his eyes. She spoke in a kind of murmur, in Spanish that was fluent but had a strong mountain accent.

"I went to leave him the message and he came in person to my house," she said. "He was very worried. I thought he was going to tell me that something bad had happened to you, that they had killed you. He says you should get in touch with him right away."

"I've been calling him a few times a day, and his home phone is always busy."

"He doesn't want you to call him at home. You should try his office, before ten, and say it's the Chinaman."

"That made me feel better," said the boy. "If he went to see my mother, if he wanted me to call him, he couldn't be that angry with me. But it took me ten more days to get in touch with him. That upset Mercedes, but not me. Because it meant I could go on enjoying our honeymoon. Even with all the worry and the scares we had, I'll never be that happy again, Corporal."

When they said goodbye to his mother and returned to the pensión in Barrios Altos, Mercedes plagued Carreño with questions:

"How can your mother take all this without even batting an eye? She's not surprised that you're hiding out, that you're with me, that they ransacked your room. Do things like this always happen to you?"

"She knows that life in Peru has its dangers, honey. She may not look very strong, but she's made of iron. She went through hell just to feed me. In Sicuani, in Cuzco, in Lima."

Carreño was happy to have his money back, and laughed at Mercedes for putting her savings in the bank.

"This country is too dangerous to trust the banks; the best safe is your mattress. You saw what happened, that guy on La Victoria almost left you flat broke. But I'm glad he tore your voter's ID because now you have to depend on me. And to celebrate I'll take you dancing. Will you do some of the steps for me that you did in the show at the Vacilón?"

"How can you think about having a good time with everything that's happening to us!" Mercedes protested in horror. "You're an irresponsible half-wit."

"I'm just a man in love, sweetheart, and I'm dying to dance with you, cheek to cheek."

Mercedes finally gave in, and they went to Memory Lane, on the Paseo de la República. Nobody would see their faces there. It was a dark, romantic place where they played old Gardel tangos and the boleros of Leo Marini, Agustín Lara, and Los Panchos. Tomás and Mercedes drank Cuba libres, and the rum quickly went to Carreño's head. He chattered endlessly about the life they would lead in Miami. He would set up an armored-car business, he would be rich, they would get married and have children. He held Mercedes very close while they danced, and kissed her neck and face passionately.

"As long as you're with me, nothing will happen to you, word of honor. Wait till I talk to my godfather, wait till Iscariote gets back. Life will start to smile on us. It's already smiling on me, thanks to you."

"Memory Lane is a nice name." Lituma sighed. "Listening to you makes me nostalgic, Tomasito. A dark place, a few drinks, some romantic music, a nice loving broad dancing real close. Do those things still exist?"

"It was a beautiful night, Corporal, for as long as we were in the club," said the boy. "And she kissed me, too, on her own. 'She's falling in love with me,' I thought, and I was full of hope."

"You got me excited with all that kissing and smooching, Ca-rreñito," Mercedes said into his ear, nibbling his lobe. "Let's go to bed, come on, it was crazy for us to be out where everybody can see us."

When they left the club at about three in the morning, they were both tight. But the effects of the Cuba libres disappeared immediately when they saw fire trucks, a police car, and a crowd of people at the corner not far from Señora Alicia's pensión. The neighbors had rushed to the street when they heard the explosion.

"They got out of a van and just put the bomb in front of a wooden house about twenty meters from Aunt Alicia's pensión," the adjutant explained. "That was the third bad thing that happened to us. Another coincidence, Corporal?"

"Tomasito, I can't believe anything you're saying. I don't buy all this about a bomb. Don't screw around with me: if the dealers wanted to kill you, they would've killed you."

The explosion shattered the windows in many nearby houses and set fire to the trash in a vacant lot. Señora Alicia, wrapped in a blanket, was in the crowd. She pretended not to know Carreño and Mercedes as they mingled with the onlookers. They waited in the entryway to a block of houses until it grew light. They came back when the patrol cars and fire trucks had gone. Aunt Alicia hurried them inside. Nothing had happened to her house and she did not seem frightened; it did not occur to her that the bomb had anything to do with Carreño. She supposed, as the other neighbors did, that it was an attempt on the life of an official at the Prefecture who lived on the street. The van had stopped in front of his house, and Aunt Alicia, sitting at her window for a breath of fresh air, saw it and could even hear them whispering inside. It drove to the corner, and the men got out and placed the bomb. They were so careless they put it outside a vacant house. Or maybe it wasn't carelessness, maybe they didn't mean to kill anybody but just wanted to send a message to that guy at the Prefecture.

"Mercedes didn't believe the story about the official for a minute," said Tomasito. "She swore the thing was meant for us. She held up the best she could in front of Aunt Alicia, and then when we were alone she went to pieces."

"Who else was the bomb for but you and me? Forget all that shit about some official at the Prefecture. We're the ones hiding out, aren't we? And now they caught up with us. And let us know it. And while they're trying to kill us, we're out dancing at Memory Lane. Are you happy now, you damn fool?"

Her voice broke, and she was trembling and wringing her hands so hard that the boy forced them apart, afraid she would do herself harm. He could not calm her. She cried and repeated hysterically that she didn't want them to kill her; she berated him or huddled on the bed, sobbing and tossing from side to side, giving in to despair.

"I thought she would die, that she'd have an attack or something, she was so scared," said Tomasito. "Nothing scares me, but seeing her like that really threw me. I couldn't do a damn thing, I didn't know what to say to make her stop crying. I had run out of promises. I couldn't think of anything else to swear to, Corporal."

"What did you do?" Lituma asked.

He went to the tile he had loosened to hide the packet of dollars and, sitting on the edge of the bed, forced Mercedes to take the bills while he kissed her, smoothed her hair, dried her brow with his lips, and said:

"It's yours, sweetheart, whether you stay with me or not, it's yours. I'm giving it to you. You keep it, hide it from me if you want to. So you can feel safe until I talk to my godfather, so you don't feel like the ground's opening up in front of you. So you're not tied down and can leave whenever you want. Don't cry anymore, please."

"You did that, Tomasito? You gave her all your dollars?"

"On the condition she wouldn't cry anymore, Corporal," said the boy.

"That's even worse than killing Hog because he hit her, you prick!" Lituma jumped up from his cot.

8 / "A HUAYCO ROLLED over you and here you are, alive and kicking." The cantinero patted Lituma on the shoulder. "Congratulations, Corporal!"

Dionisio was the only one who seemed to be in good spirits in the funereal atmosphere of the cantina. It was crowded, but the laborers had the faces of condemned men. They were in small groups, holding their glasses, smoking endlessly, buzzing like wasps. Uncertainty distorted their features, and Lituma could see in their eyes the animal fear that gnawed inside them. After the devastation of the avalanche, nothing could save them from losing their jobs now. Son of a bitch, the serruchos had good reason for being so gloomy.

"I was given a new lease on life up there," the corporal acknowledged. "But I don't recommend the experience to anyone. I can still hear the awful noise those motherfucking boulders made coming down all around me."

"What about it, boys, a toast to the corporal," Dionisio proposed, raising his glass. "Our thanks to the apus of Naccos for saving a lawman's life!"

"On top of everything else, that faggot is making fun of me," thought the corporal. But he raised his glass and thanked him with a half smile, and nodded to the laborers who had raised theirs. Tomás Carreño, who had gone outside to urinate, came back in, rubbing his hands.

"What happened to you never happened to anybody else," he exclaimed, with the same expression of joy and astonishment he had shown while listening to the corporal tell him about his adventure. "They ought to put it in the papers."

"That's a fact," said a laborer with a pockmarked face. "Nothing like that's happened around here since Casimiro Huarcaya. A huayco rolls over you and you walk away!"

"Casimiro Huarcaya the albino?" asked Lituma. "The one who disappeared? The one who said he was a pishtaco?"

The albino came in late, when everybody in the cantina was already good and drunk, the way they always got on Saturday night. He was, too; his eyes were red and agitated beneath the pale lashes that made everyone so uneasy. Drunk and ready to fight, he announced his arrival at the door in his usual way: "Here he is, here comes the throat-slitter, the nacaq, the pishtaco! And if you don't believe me, damn it, just look at this." He took a small knife from his back pocket and displayed it, raising his right foot and bursting into reassuring laughter. Then, grimacing like a clown, he staggered to the bar, where Doña Adriana and her husband were busy serving their patrons, and leaned his elbows on the counter. He banged on the wood and demanded a glass of the strong stuff. At that moment Lituma knew what was going to happen to him.

"Who else would I be talking about?" the pockmarked man nodded. "Didn't you know the terrucos executed him and then he was resurrected, like Jesus Christ?"

"I didn't know anything, I'm the last person around here to find things out." Lituma sighed. "They executed him and he came back to life?"

"Well, Pichincho's exaggerating," a small, dark man, his hair like a porcupine's quills, stepped forward. "I think it was a fake execution. If it wasn't, how could he be shot and then wake up without a scratch?"

"It looks to me like now you all know Casimiro Huarcaya's life story by heart," said Carreño. "So why'd you tell the corporal and me you didn't know anything about the albino when he disappeared?"

"That's something I'd like to hear, too," Lituma said in a soft voice.

There was a charged silence, and all around them the sharp-angled faces with their flat noses, thick swollen lips, and narrow, suspicious eyes took refuge behind the stellar impenetrability that made the corporal feel like a Martian in Naccos. Until, after a moment, the serrano with the pockmarked face displayed a row of large white teeth in a huge smile: "It's just that we didn't know the corporal back then."

There were some approving murmurs, and the cantinero hurried to serve the albino, looking at him with the brittle, mocking smile that never left him. His face was puffier than usual, and through the cigarette smoke, his fat cheeks had a rosy glow beneath the stubble of his beard. He looked bigger and softer than at other times, and his limbs, his shoulders, his bones, seemed disconnected from their sockets. But he was very strong. Lituma had seen him pick up drunks and throw them out the door; not because they were looking for trouble, but because they had started to cry. Dionisio allowed the ones who turned belligerent with drink and wanted to fight to stay in the cantina, and even encouraged the other men to exchange blows with them, as if these drunken disputes amused him no end. The albino sipped at his glass, and Lituma, burning with apprehension, waited tensely for him to speak again. He did, facing the small gathering of men wrapped in their shawls and sweaters: "Isn't there a smoke for the throat-slitter? Tight-fisted bastards!"

No one turned to look at him, no one paid attention to him, and his face twisted as if he were overcome by a violent stomach cramp or a sudden attack of rage. His hair, eyebrows, and lashes were very light, but the most disconcerting thing about this brawny man was his white body hair and the white stubble on his face. He wore overalls and a hooded oilskin jacket that was open and displayed the white growth in the middle of his chest.

"Here you go, Casimiro." The cantinero handed him a cigarette. "The music's going to start again soon and then you can dance."

"That's good," said Lituma. "That means you're finally going to treat me like a serrano instead of a vulture up on the barrens. That deserves a drink. Take down a nice bottle for my friends, Dionisio: the drinks are on me."

There were grunted thanks, and while Dionisio opened the bottle and Doña Adriana handed out glasses to those who didn't have them, the corporal and his adjutant mingled with the other patrons. They had all crowded up to the bar in a tight knot, as if they were watching the end of a dice game with fistfuls of bills at stake.

"Are you saying the terrucos shot Huarcaya and he wasn't even hurt?" asked Lituma. "Tell me what happened."

"He used to talk about it when he was paying a visit to his animal, you know, when the booze went to his head," said the man with porcupine hair. "He went all over the sierra looking for a girl who'd had his baby. And one night he came to a village in the province of La Mar, where they almost lynched him because they thought he was a pishtaco. The terrucos attacked just then and saved him. And who do you think the terruco leader was? The girl he'd been looking for!"

"What do you mean, they saved him?" Carreño intervened. "Didn't you say they executed him?"

"Be quiet," ordered Lituma. "Don't interrupt."

"They saved him from the villagers who wanted to lynch him for being a pishtaco, but then the terrucos held one of their people's trials and sentenced him to death," said the porcupine, concluding the story. "The girl was in charge of the execution. And just like that, she put a bullet in him."

"I'll be damned," Lituma said. "How'd he get to Naccos after he was killed?"

The albino did not reply and spent some time trying to light the cigarette, but he was so drunk his hand could not bring the match flame up to the right place. Lituma could see an indefinable expression on Dionisio's glowing yet sooty face; it was the sarcastic, delighted look of a man who knows what is going to happen, who looks forward to it, enjoying it in advance. He knew what was going to happen, too, and he shuddered. But the other patrons did not appear to be aware of anything; some sat on the crates, but most remained standing, gathered in groups of two or three, holding bottles of beer, pisco, or anisette, or passing them around. The radio, high above the bar, blared through frequent static, playing the alternating tropical and Andean songs that Radio Junín always broadcast on Saturday night. As if his pride had been wounded by their lack of response, the albino challenged them again, turning his back on the cantinero and looking at the crowd with the eyes of a fish just pulled from the water:

"Did you hear that I'm the throat-slitter? The pishtaco, what they call a nacaq in Ayacucho. This is how I slice up my victims."

He made more passes in the air with his knife and repeated the clown grimaces, as if begging them to notice him, celebrate him, laugh at him, applaud him. Nobody seemed to notice his presence this time, either. But Lituma knew. All their senses were focused on Casimiro Huarcaya.

"At least, that's what he said happened, isn't it?" asked the pockmarked one, and several laborers nodded. "The terruca executed him, stood a meter away from him and fired her rifle. And Huarcaya died."

"He felt like he died, Pichincho," the porcupine corrected him. "He really just passed out. Sure, from fear. And when he came to, there was no bullet wound, just bruises where the people who thought he was a pishtaco had kicked him. The terruca only wanted to scare him."

"Huarcaya said he saw the bullet shoot out of the rifle and come right for his head," the pockmarked one insisted. "She killed him and he came back to life."

"I'll be damned," Lituma repeated, surreptitiously checking the reactions of various laborers in the crowd. "He survived one execution and came to Naccos so he could disappear. Do you think he survived that, too?"

They continued drinking their shots of pisco or anisette, passing the bottle, the glass of beer with a brief toast: "Here's to you, brother." They smoked, talked, hummed to the music on the radio. One who was drunker than the rest put his arms around an invisible girl, closed his eyes, and took a few clumsy dance steps, moving counter to his shadow on the wall. As always, Dionisio, in the state of exhilaration that came over him at night, encouraged them: "Go on, dance, have a good time, what's the difference if there's no women, everybody looks the same in the dark." They acted as if Casimiro Huarcaya weren't here, the hypocrites. But Lituma knew very well that no matter how they pretended, every one of the laborers was watching the albino out of the corner of his eye.

"I'm the one who comes out from under the bridges, from behind the rocks. I'm the one who lives in caves. I'm just like the one Doña Adriana killed, that's who I am," he thundered. "I appear on the road and blow magic dust in your face. You know what I'm talking about, don't you, Doña Adriana? Go on, kill me too, if you can, the way you and big-nose killed Salcedo. They killed me once, but not even the terrucos could finish me off. Damn it, I'm immortal!"

He hunched over a second time, and his pale face contorted as if his gut had suddenly cramped again, but a moment later he recovered, straightened up, and brought his glass greedily to his lips. Not realizing it was empty, he went on sipping and licking it with delight. Until it slipped from his fingers and rolled off the counter to the floor. Then Casimiro Huarcaya stood quiet, sulking, his hands to his face, peering obsessively with bulging eyes at the cracks, inscriptions, stains, cigarette burns on the wood of the bar. "Don't leave now, whatever you do," whispered Lituma, knowing the albino could not hear him. "Don't even think about leaving the cantina now. Wait till the others have gone, wait till they're so drunk they forget all about you." But as he offered this advice, he could hear Dionisio's viperish laugh. He looked around for him, and in fact, though he seemed to be watching the groups of men who filled the cantina, urging them with gestures to dance, his great fat face was laughing, his mouth stretched wide. Lituma knew beyond the shadow of a doubt that he was mocking his efforts to change what was bound to happen.

"Maybe he did survive," said Pichincho, kneading his smallpox scars as if they itched. "Huarcaya went off his head after what happened with the terruca. Didn't you hear that he used to brag about being a pishtaco? It was all he could talk about. He'd do his number here every night. Maybe he didn't disappear, maybe it was just a wild hair that made him leave Naccos and not say goodbye."

He spoke with so much insincerity that Lituma wanted to ask if he thought he and his adjutant were as fucking stupid as he was.

But it was Tomasito who said: "Made him leave without collecting his pay? That's the best proof the albino didn't leave because he wanted to: he didn't collect for seven days' work. Nobody makes a present of a week's wages to the company."

"Nobody who isn't out of his mind," Pichincho responded with absolutely no conviction, resigned to going on with the game. "Huarcaya had a screw loose ever since the terruca."

"When you come right down to it, what difference does it make if he disappeared?" said a man who had not spoken before, a hunchback with hollow eyes and teeth stained green from chewing coca. "We're all going to disappear when we die, aren't we?"

"And sooner than you think after this motherfucking huayco," a guttural voice exclaimed; Lituma could not tell which man had spoken.

Just then he saw the albino staggering toward the door. People stepped aside to let him pass, not looking at him, pretending that Casimiro Huarcaya was not there, that he did not exist.

Before he stepped through the door and was lost from view in the cold and dark, the albino challenged them one last time, his voice breaking with rage, or fatigue: "I'm going out to slit some throats. Whoosh! I'll fry the meat in its own fat and then I'll eat it. These are good nights for a throat-slitter. You can all drop dead, you shits!"

"Don't complain; after all, the huayco didn't kill anybody," said Doña Adriana from the other end of the bar. "Nobody was even hurt. Not even the corporal, who got in the way of the stones. You should give thanks! You should be dancing for joy instead of complaining, instead of being ungrateful!"

He walked out and headed straight for the barracks, dimly lit by yellow lightbulbs that the company kept burning on Saturdays until eleven, one hour later than the rest of the week. But after a few steps Huarcaya tripped and fell heavily to the ground. He lay there for a while, cursing, groaning, making strenuous efforts to get up. Gradually he succeeded, first a foot, then the knee of the opposite leg, then both feet, then a great push with his hands until he was standing again. To avoid another fall, he moved like an ape, bending over and swinging his arms to keep his balance. Was he headed for the barracks? The little yellow lights flickered like fireflies, but he knew they weren't because in the sierra, this high up in the Cordillera, there weren't any fireflies, were there? It was the lights in the barracks, moving up and down, moving left and right, coming toward him, then moving back. Casimiro giggled and tried to brush them away. Seeing his clownish behavior, Lituma laughed, too, but he was sweating ice and shivering. Would Casimiro ever reach the barracks and the wooden bunk that was waiting for him with its straw mattress and blanket? He turned, walked forward, moved back, spun around, trying to stay on the path marked by those elusive lights that grew more crazed by the second. He was so exhausted he didn't even have the strength to curse them. But suddenly he was inside the barracks, down on all fours, struggling to climb into his bunk. He finally succeeded, banging his face against the crossbar and feeling scratches on his forehead and arms. Huddling there, face down, with his eyes closed, he began to retch and tried to vomit, with no success. Then he attempted to cross himself and pray, but he was so tired he couldn't lift his arm, and besides, he couldn't remember the Our Father or Hail Mary. He lay in an acidic half sleep, trembling, belching, feeling a pain that moved through his belly and chest before tormenting him under the arms, on his neck, along his thighs. Did he know they would be coming for him soon?

"What good does it do us to survive if the huayco left us without work, mamay," the hunchback said to Doña Adriana. "Can't you see how it smashed the shovels, the tractors, the steamroller?"

"Is that any reason to dance for joy, Doña Adriana?" asked

the porcupine. "Somebody better explain it to me, because I don't get it."

"Didn't it leave us without a roof over our heads? Didn't it bury a hundred meters that were ready for paving?" called another laborer from among the groups of men. "Now they have the excuse they wanted to stop the project. No more money! That's it! Tighten your belts and to hell with you!"

"It could've been the apocalypse, so stop your sniveling," replied Doña Adriana. "You could've lost your legs and hands and eyes, it could've broken every bone in your bodies, and you'd have to spend the rest of your lives crawling around like worms. And still these dirty ingrates are crying!"

"*Ay, ay, ay, ay, Sing and don't cryyyyy,*" Dionisio interrupted in a husky voice. "In other words, gentlemen, we should drown our sorrows and dance a nice little huayno in the Sapallanga style."

He was in the center of the cantina, pushing first one man, then another, trying to form a line that would turn and turn again to the beat of the muliza on the radio. But Lituma could see that not even the drunkest patrons wanted to follow him. This time the alcohol, instead of helping them forget the sinister future, made it even darker. The cantinero's hopping and crooning produced a slight vertigo in Lituma.

"Are you all right, Corporal?" Tomasito took his arm.

"The drink went to my head," Lituma stammered. "I'll feel better in a minute."

The camp generator had been turned off, and dawn would be breaking in a few hours. But they carried lanterns and moved freely through a darkness cut by yellow cylinders. There were so many they barely fit into the narrow space, but they did not push or interfere with one another, or hurry, or appear to be afraid or angry, much less nervous or uncertain. They seemed serene and confident and, strangest of all, thought Lituma, there was no smell of alcohol in the cold air they brought in from outside. They moved with calm determination, they knew what they were doing, what they were going to do.

"Do you want me to help you puke?" asked Tomasito.

"Not yet," answered the corporal. "But listen, if I start dancing like these perverts, grab me and don't let me do it."

The one who woke the albino did so by shaking his shoulder, with no ill will, even with a certain delicacy.

"Come on, Huarcaya, come on. It's time to get up."

"It's still dark," the albino protested in a faint voice. And, in his confusion, he added something that seemed very stupid to Lituma: "It's Sunday, only the watchmen work today."

No one laughed at him. They remained motionless and quiet, and in the immense silence it seemed to the corporal that they were all listening to the fierce pounding of his heart.

"Come on, Huarcaya," ordered the porcupine? the pockmarked one? the hunchback? "Don't be lazy, get up."

In the darkness, hands reached out toward the bunk and helped the albino sit up, then get to his feet. He could barely stand; without so many arms holding him, he would have collapsed like a rag doll.

"I can't even stand," he complained. And with no trace of hatred, as if he didn't really want to, as if it were a matter of principle, he tried again to curse them: "You shits!"

"It's just the booze, Huarcaya," someone consoled him in a kindly way.

"You feel like this because you're not yourself anymore."

"I can't even walk, damn it," the albino protested sadly. His voice was very different from what it had been when he boasted in the cantina that he was the throat-slitter. Now it was resigned, Lituma thought, the voice of a man who knows and accepts his fate.

"It's just the booze," repeated another, encouraging him. "Don't worry, Huarcaya, we'll help you."

"I'm pretty high, too, Corporal," declared Tomasito, not letting go of his arm. "Only you can't tell with me, it all stays inside. Well, it's no wonder, we must've had five piscos at least, don't you think?"

"You see? I was right." Lituma turned to look at him and saw his adjutant at a great distance even though he felt his hand holding tight to his arm. "These serruchos knew all about the albino, they made damn fools of us. I bet you they know where the body is, too."

"I'm so high I won't be able to think about you tonight," said Tomás. "It's not that I'm with anybody, it's because the corporal had a huayco go right over him and it didn't kill him. Just think, Mercedes baby! Just think what it would've been like to be all by myself at the Naccos post and not be able to talk about you. That's why I got drunk, sweetheart."

They held him by the arms and supported his weight, walking him to the door of the barracks, not mistreating him, not forcing him to hurry. The press of so many bodies in the narrow space made the double row of wooden bunks shift and creak. For an instant the cones of light from the lanterns illuminated their faces half hidden by shawls or hard hats or wool sweaters pulled up to their ears. Lituma recognized and forgot them.

"What kind of poison anisette did that motherfucker Dionisio give me?" the albino complained weakly, trying in vain to be angry. "What kind of potion did that witch Doña Adriana pour in my drink? They're the ones who made me talk so crazy."

No one said anything, but the ominous silence spoke volumes to Lituma. The corporal was panting, his tongue protruding. That's what it was. The albino's threats and crazy boasts didn't come from him but from the filthy stuff he had been given to drink in the cantina, who knows with what plan in mind. That's why he said those stupid things, that's why he was so agitated. That's why nobody paid attention when he challenged them. No wonder, no wonder: why would anybody take offense if they were the ones responsible for the condition he was in? They had already half killed Casimiro Huarcaya.

"It must be damn cold outside," lamented Tomasito.

"No, it's not so bad," replied someone in the crowd. "I just went out to piss and it wasn't too bad."

"The drink keeps you warm so you don't feel it, compadre."

"With the booze you won't feel cold or anything, Huarcaya."

They held him, they led him, they supported him, passing him from hand to hand, and for a moment Lituma lost sight of him in the great patch of animated shadows waiting outside the barracks. They were moving and murmuring, but when the albino was among them, when they saw him, heard him, or guessed he was there, they grew silent and still, like at the door of the church, Lituma thought, when Christ, the Virgin, the patron saint appears, carried on the shoulders of the religious fraternity, and the procession begins. In the icy darkness of night, under millions of reverent stars, between the looming hills and the barracks, there now reigned the intense solemnity and expectant devotion of the Holy Week Masses that Lituma remembered from his childhood. As remote as Tomás's flushed face. He listened carefully, and he heard Casimiro Huarcaya, who had already been moved a considerable distance by the dense crowd: "I'm not anybody's enemy, I don't want to be anybody's enemy. It was the poison Dionisio gave me! The potion his wife fixed for me! They made me say all that shit I said before."

"We know, Huarcaya," they reassured him, they patted him. "Don't worry about it. Nobody's your enemy, compadre."

"We're all grateful to you, brother," said a voice, so soft it might have been a woman's.

"Right, that's right," several of them repeated, and Lituma imagined dozens of heads nodding, silently conferring on the albino their recognition and affection. With no need for orders, knowing what each was to do, the mass of men began to move, and although no one spoke, or even whispered, the crowd could be heard advancing, compact, in step, stirred to the bone, tremulous, on the way to the hills. "The abandoned mine, the old Santa Rita," thought Lituma. "That's where they're going." He was listening to the sound of many feet treading on the stones, splashing in the puddles, the soft movement of bodies, the sound as they brushed against each other, and when he calculated that it had been a long while since he had heard the albino complain, he quietly asked the man next to him: "Is Casimiro Huarcaya dead yet?"

"Don't try to talk."

But the man on his left took pity on his ignorance and informed him, in a barely audible voice: "To be acceptable, he has to be alive when he gets down there."

They were going to throw him down the water intake of the abandoned mine while he was still conscious. They would climb up there in a procession, silent, absorbed, overcome by emotion, holding him by the arms, picking him up each time he tripped, soothing him, encouraging him, letting him know they did not hate him, that they held him in esteem, that they were grateful for what he was going to do for them, and when they reached the great opening that their lanterns would illuminate, the place where the wind would be whistling, they would say goodbye and push him and hear him fall with a long shriek and land with a distant, dull thud, and they would imagine him broken on the rocks at the bottom of the shaft where he had gone to meet his destiny.

"He can't hear, he doesn't feel a thing," someone said behind him, as if reading his mind. "Corporal Lituma is out cold."

.

Timoteo Fajardo wasn't really my husband, my only real husband was Dionisio. I never married Timoteo, we just lived together. My family wasn't good to him, and the people in Quenka were even worse. Even though he freed us from the pishtaco Salcedo, nobody helped him persuade my father to give him permission to marry me. Instead, they turned him against Timoteo, they said: "How can you give your daughter to a dark-skinned big-nose? Everybody knows they're rustlers." That's why we ran away and came to Naccos. As we were leaving, when we were in the clearing where you can see the village, we cursed them for being ungrateful. I never went back to Quenka and I never will.

I don't deny anything and I don't admit anything, and if I sit staring at the hills and pucker my lips, it's not because questions make me uneasy. But because a lot of time has gone by. I'm not sure anymore if we were happy or unhappy. Probably happy in the early days, when I thought that boredom and routine were happiness. Timoteo found a job at the Santa Rita mine, and I cooked for him and washed his clothes and everybody took us for man and wife. Back then, there were a lot of women in Naccos, not like now. And when Dionisio came with his dancers and his wild girls, the women here went wild, too. Husbands and fathers whipped their backsides raw to keep them in line, but they ran after him just the same.

What was it about him? Why did they fall so hard for a fat drunk? Reputation, legend, mystery, joy, a prophetic gift, bottles of aromatic pisco from Ica, and a formidable prick. What more do you want? He was famous all over the sierra, no fair or fiesta or important wake in the villages of Junín, Ayacucho, Huancavelica, or Apurímac took place without him. I mean, without them. Because Dionisio traveled with a troupe of musicians and dancers from Huancaya and Jauja who wouldn't leave him for anything. And with those wild girls who cooked during the day and at night went crazy and did outrageous things.

The fiesta didn't begin until Dionisio's company showed up at the entrance to the village, beating their drums, blowing their quenas, strumming their charangos, making the ground shake with their dancing. Even if they'd already set off the fireworks and the priest had said his prayers, there was no fiesta without Dionisio. They worked everywhere, they were always coming and going from one place to the other, even though they had a bad name. A bad name for what? For doing dirty things, for being the spawn of Satan. For burning churches, knocking the heads off saints and virgins, stealing babies. It was priests' gossip more than anything else. They were jealous of Dionisio for being so popular, and their revenge was to slander him.

The first time I saw him, chills ran down my spine. He was right there, where the company office is now—it used to be the Naccos square—selling pisco from big clay jars that he brought in on muleback. He had set planks across two sawhorses and put up a sign: *This is the cantina.* "Don't gulp down beer and cane liquor, boys. Learn how to drink!" he preached to the miners. "Just taste this fine grape pisco from Ica, it makes you forget your troubles, it brings out the happy man you have inside." "Pay a visit to your animal!" It was the Patriotic Festival, and there were bands of musicians, costume contests, magicians, tijeras dancers. But I couldn't enjoy any of the entertainments; even though I didn't want to, my feet and head took me to him. He was younger then, but not too different from what he is now. A little fat, sort of flabby, pitch-black eyes, curly hair, and that way of walking, half skipping, half stumbling, that he still has. He waited on the customers and

came out to dance and infected everybody with joy. "Now a muliza," and they followed him, "The pasillo," and they did what he
said, "It's time for the huaynito," and they stamped the ground
with their feet, "The trencito," and they formed a long line behind
him. He sang, he jumped, he skipped, he played the charango,
blew on the quena, raised his glass, shouted, crashed the cymbals,
banged the drum. For hours and hours, and he never got tired.
Hours and hours, putting on the Jauja Carnival masks and taking
them off, until all Naccos was a whirlwind of drunk, happy people.
Nobody knew who was who anymore, where one person began
and the other ended, who was man, who was animal, who was
human, who was woman. When it was my turn to dance with him
he squeezed me and put his hands all over me, made me feel his
cock hard against my belly, put his tongue down my throat where
it sizzled like something frying in a pan. That night Timoteo Fajardo kicked me till I bled and said: "You'd go with him if he asked,
wouldn't you, you whore?"

He didn't ask, but maybe I would have gone with him if he
had, been one more woman in Dionisio's band, one more wild girl
following him to all the hamlets and districts in the sierra, traveling
every road in the Andes, up to the cold barrens, down to the hot
valleys, in the rain, in the sun, cooking for him, washing his clothes,
doing whatever he said, performing at the Saturday fairs, even
whoring if that's what he wanted. People said that when they went
down to the coast for a new supply of pisco, on the nights there
was a full moon, the wild girls and the dancers would dance stark
naked on the sandy ground near the ocean, and Dionisio would put
on woman's clothes and call up the devil.

They said everything you could think of about him, and they
said it with fear and awe. But nobody really knew much about his
life, it was just talk. They said that his mother had been burned
by lightning during a storm, for example. That he had been raised

in the Huanta uplands by the women in an Iquichan community where they still worshipped idols. That when he was young he went crazy in a mission run by the Dominican fathers, and the devil made a pact with him and gave him back his reason. That he had lived in the jungle with Indian cannibals. That he learned about pisco when he was traveling through the deserts along the coast, and that was when he began to sell it all over the sierra. That he had women and children everywhere, that he had died and come back to life, that he was a pishtaco, a muki, a healer, a witch, an astrologer, a diviner. There was no mysterious or savage thing they didn't say about him. He liked having a bad name.

Sure, he was more than just an itinerant pisco peddler, everybody knew that; more than the leader of some folk musicians and dancers, more than a performer, more than the owner of a traveling whorehouse. Yes, sure, that much was clear, but what else was he? A devil? An angel? God? Timoteo Fajardo could see in my eyes that I was thinking about Dionisio, and he would go into a rage and beat me. The men were jealous of him, but they all admitted: "Without him, there's no fiesta." As soon as he came and set up his bar, they'd run to buy their shots of pisco and drink with him. "I educated you," Dionisio would tell them. "You used to get drunk on chicha, or beer, or cane liquor, but now you do it with pisco, the drink of thrones and seraphim."

I learned a little more about him from an Ayacuchan woman from Huancasancos. She had been one of his wild girls, then she left and came here as the wife of a crew chief at the Santa Rita mine, just about the time that pishtaco dried out Juan Apaza. We became friends, we would go to the gully together to wash clothes, and one day I asked her why she had so many scars. Then she told me. She traveled with Dionisio's troupe a pretty long time, sleeping outdoors wherever they happened to be when it grew dark, huddled together against the cold, going from fair to fair and market

to market, living on the money that people at the fiestas gave them.
When they had a good time on their own, far from other people's
eyes, the troupe went wild. Or, as Dionisio says, they paid a visit
to their animal. The wild girls moved from loving each other to
attacking each other. From petting to scratching, from kissing to
biting, from hugging to shoving, without ever stopping the dance.
"Didn't it hurt, mamita?" "It hurt afterward, mamay; with the
music and the dancing and the drinking, it was wonderful. You
forgot your worries, your heart pounded, you thought you were a
hawk, a pepper tree, a hill, a condor, a river. We got all the way
up to the stars dancing, loving each other, attacking each other.
"Why did you leave if you liked it so much?" Because her feet
swelled and she couldn't keep up with them on the road. There
were a lot of them in the troupe and they couldn't always get a ride
on a truck. So they would go on foot, walking for days, for weeks.
You could do that back then, there were no terrucos or sinchis in
the Andes. And that's why the Huancasancos woman finally resigned herself to marrying the crew chief and settling down here
in Naccos. But she always dreamed about her old adventures and
missed the travel and the vices. She would hum sad huaynitos,
remembering, and sigh, "Ay, I was happy once." And touch her
scars with nostalgia.

And so I became very curious. I had been restless ever since
I danced with him and he put his hands on me at the Patriotic
Festival, and the next time Dionisio came to Naccos and asked me
if I wanted to marry him, I said all right. The mine was failing.
The ore had run out in the Santa Rita, and Padrillo had people
scared to death after he dried out Sebastián, Timoteo's friend.
Dionisio didn't ask me to be one of the wild girls, to be just another
woman in his troupe. He asked me to marry him. He had been in
love with me ever since he found out how I helped Timoteo hunt
down the pishtaco Salcedo in the Quenka caves. "You're fated to

be with me," he said. Later on, the stars and the cards told me it was true.

We got married in the Muquiyauyo community, where they had a lot of respect for him because he cured all their young men of an epidemic of hard-ons. Yes, swollen pricks. They came down with it one rainy summer. It's funny, sure, but they were crying, they were desperate. From the moment they opened their eyes when the rooster crowed it was swollen and red, and burned like an ají pepper. They didn't know what to do. They washed in cold water and nothing, it would start to swell and stand up again like a jack-in-the-box. And while they were milking or planting or pruning, while they were doing what they had to do, it hung fat and heavy between their legs like a spur or the clapper of a bell. They brought in a priest from the San Antonio de Ocopa monastery. He said Mass and exorcised them with incense. But that didn't help: their cocks just kept pushing and growing until they broke through their trousers and came out to see the sun. Then Dionisio came to town. They told him what had happened, and he organized a fiesta procession with dancing and music. Instead of a saint on a platform, they carried a clay prick made by the best potter in Muquiyauyo. The band played a military march for it, and the girls decorated it with wreaths of flowers. Then they followed his instructions and threw it into the Mantaro. The young men who had the disease jumped into the river, too. When they came out they were normal again, their cocks were little and wrinkled and sleeping again.

At first the priest in Muquiyauyo didn't want to marry us. "He's no Catholic, he's a pagan, a savage," he said, shooing Dionisio away with his hand. But after a few drinks he gave in, and we were married. The fiesta lasted for three days, and there was dancing and eating, dancing and drinking, dancing and dancing, enough to drive you crazy. At nightfall on the second day, Dionisio took me by the hand, led me up a hill, and pointed to the sky. "Do you see that little group of stars over there, in the shape of a crown?" They stood out from all the rest. "Yes, I see them." "That's my wedding gift to you."

But he couldn't take me yet, he had to keep a promise first. Far from Muquiyauyo, on the other side of the Mantaro, high in the Jauja mountains, in the hamlet of Yanacoto, where Dionisio had been a boy. When his mother died, after she was burned by lightning, he wouldn't accept her death. And he went looking for her, sure he'd find her somewhere. He took to the road, wandered like a lost soul, traveled everywhere until he discovered pisco on the ranches of Ica and began to sell it and promote it. One day he saw her in a dream: his mother said she would meet him, at midnight on Carnival Sunday, in the Yanacoto cemetery. He went there, full of excitement. But the caretaker, a cripple named Yaranga whose nose was eaten away by ulcers, didn't want to let him in unless he pulled down his trousers first. They talked it over and came to an agreement: Yaranga would let him in to keep his appointment if he would come back and bend over for him before his wedding night. Dionisio went in, talked to his mother, said goodbye to her, and now, at his wedding fiesta fifteen years later, I had to go with him so he could keep his promise.

It took us two days to get up to Yanacoto, the first day by truck, the second day by mule. There was snow on the barrens, and the people's lips were purple and their faces were cracked with the cold. The cemetery didn't have the wall around it anymore that Dionisio remembered, and no caretaker either. We asked and they said that Yaranga had gone crazy and died years ago. Dionisio didn't stop asking questions until finally they showed him his grave. Then, that night, when the family who put us up had gone to sleep, he took me by the hand and led me to the place where Yaranga was buried. All day I had seen him carving something with his knife from a willow branch. An erect prick, that's what it was. He greased it with candle wax, set it on Yaranga's grave, pulled down his trousers and sat on it, howling. Then, in spite of all the ice, he pulled off my underpants and fucked me. More than once, in front and from behind. I wasn't a virgin but I think I howled more than he did, until I passed out. That was our wedding night.

The next morning he began to teach me the lore. I had a talent for telling the winds apart, for hearing the sounds inside the earth, for speaking with people's hearts by touching their faces. I thought I knew how to dance, but he taught me to get inside the music and get the music inside me and let it dance me instead of me dancing it. I thought I knew how to sing, but he taught me to let the singing take control, to be the servant of the songs I sang. Little by little I learned to read the lines on palms, to interpret the shapes the coca leaves make when they fall on the ground after you toss them in the air, to find where the trouble is by passing a live guinea pig over the sick person's body. We kept traveling, going down to the coast to stock up on pisco, livening up a lot of fiestas. Until the roads started to be dangerous with so much killing, and the villages began to empty out, to shut themselves inside an angry suspicion of outsiders. The wild girls left, the musicians abandoned us, the dancers vanished like smoke. "It's time for you and me to put down roots, too," Dionisio said to me one day. It seems we had grown old.

I don't know what happened to Timoteo Fajardo. I never heard. But I did hear the gossip. For years it followed me everywhere, like my shadow. Did you poison his potatoes and kill him so you could run away with that fat lush? Did he kill him with a muki's tricks? Did you make a present of him to the pishtaco? Did you take him up to your witches' Sabbaths at the top of the hill, and did the drunken wild girls tear big-nose to pieces? Did you all eat him afterward, you witch? By this time they were calling me witch, and Doña, too.

·

"I made you suffer on purpose, I didn't answer your calls or give you the appointment you kept asking for," the commander lashed out at Carreño by way of greeting. "To make you squirm. And I wanted to plan something really special for your punishment, you fucking son of a bitch."

"Well, the famous godfather at last," exclaimed Lituma. "I've been waiting for him, I'm more interested in him than anybody else in your story. Let's see if this helps me get over that damn huayco. Go on, go on, Tomasito."

"Yes, Godfather," Carreño agreed humbly. "Whatever you say."

Fats Iscariote, to avoid looking him in the eye, kept his face buried in his breaded steak with fried eggs, fried potatoes, and white rice. He chewed furiously and took long swallows of beer between mouthfuls. The commander was in civilian clothes and wore a silk ascot around his neck, and dark glasses. His bald skull gleamed in the semidarkness cut by regularly spaced fluorescent lights. A lit cigarette dangled from his lips, and his right hand swirled a glass of whiskey back and forth.

"When you killed Hog you showed disrespect for me because I sent you to Tingo María to be his bodyguard," said the commander. "But that isn't what really pisses me off about the dumbass thing you did. Do you know what does? The reason you did what you did. Go on, asshole, tell me why you did it."

"You know why, Godfather," the boy answered quietly, lowering his eyes in humility. "Didn't Iscariote tell you?"

"Were you in a whorehouse?" asked Lituma. "With music, and girls around the table? Was your godfather like the king there?"

"A discotheque and bar, and sort of a cathouse," explained Tomasito. "It didn't have rooms. The guys had to take the hookers to the hotel across the way. My godfather was one of the owners, I think. I wasn't noticing anything, Corporal, my balls were up under my tonsils."

"I want to hear it from your own lips, you fucking son of a bitch," the commander ordered with an imperial gesture.

"I killed Hog because he was hitting her for fun," the boy said in a faint voice, keeping his head lowered. "You knew that, Iscariote already told you."

The commander did not laugh. He sat very still, looking at him from behind his dark glasses, nodding slightly. He tapped his glass of whiskey against the table in time to the salsa music. Until finally, without turning around, he grabbed the arm of a woman in an iridescent blouse who was walking past the table. He pulled her to him, made her lean over, and asked point-blank: "Do you like it when the guys you fuck hit you, yes or no?"

"I like everything you do to me, baby." The woman laughed, tugging gently at his mustache. "Want to dance?"

The commander sent her back to the dance floor with a good-humored little shove. And craned his head toward Carreño, who sat rigid in his chair.

"Women like it a little rough in bed, you prick, and you didn't even know it." He made a gesture of disgust. "What really pisses me off is that I trusted a jerk who doesn't know his ass from a hole in the ground. I ought to kill you, not for knocking off Hog but for being so damn stupid. Are you sorry, at least?"

"I'm sorry I offended you, my mother and I owe you so much," the boy stammered. And mustering his courage, he added, "But forgive me, Godfather, I'm not sorry about Hog. I'd kill him again if he came back to life."

"Is that so?" exclaimed the commander in surprise. "Do you

hear what he's saying, Iscariote? Do you think he's turned into an even bigger asshole than he was when he came in? Do you hear how mad he is at poor Hog just because he slapped his whore around a little?"

"She wasn't his whore, just his girlfriend, Godfather," Carreño interrupted in a pleading tone. "Please don't call her that. I beg you, she's my wife now. I mean, she will be soon. Mercedes and I are going to get married."

The commander stared at him for a moment and finally burst out laughing.

"My soul came back to my body, Corporal," said Tomasito. "That laugh meant he was beginning to forgive me even though I pissed him off so damn much."

"Was he something more than a godfather, Tomasito?" asked Lituma. "Was he your father, by any chance?"

"I wondered about it too, lots of times, Corporal. I've asked myself that question since I was a kid. But I don't think so. My mother was a maid in my godfather's house for more than twenty years, in Sicuani, in Cuzco, in Lima. His mother was an invalid, and she dressed and bathed and fed her. Well, I don't know, maybe he is my father. My old lady would never tell me who got her pregnant."

"Sure he is," said Lituma. "After what you did to Hog, you didn't deserve his forgiveness. You could have gotten your godfather into real trouble, fucked him up with the drug dealers. If he forgave you, he must be your father. The only people you can forgive for things like that are your children."

"Well, I offended him, but I did him a favor, too," said Tomasito. "Because of me his service record improved, and they even pinned a medal on his chest. He became famous for getting rid of that dealer."

"If you fell for her so hard, this Mercedes must be some piece of ass," said the commander, still laughing a little. "Did you ever try her, Iscariote?"

"No, boss, no. But I don't think she's as great as Carreñito says. He's crazy about her, so he thinks she's perfect. She's a little brunette with nice legs, that's all."

"Maybe you know a lot about food but not about women, Fats, so just eat your steak and shut up," said Carreñito. "Don't listen to him, Godfather. Mercedes is the most beautiful woman in Peru. You understand, you must have been in love some time."

"I don't fall in love, I just fuck, and that's why I'm a happy man," declared the commander. "Killing for love in this day and age! Damn! They ought to exhibit you in a cage at the circus. Would you let me give her a try so I'll know if her ass was worth the shit you pulled?"

"I don't lend my wife to anybody, Godfather. Not even you, no matter how much I respect you."

"Don't think you're forgiven just because I cracked a few jokes with you," said the commander. "The little trick you played on Hog may cost me the beautiful pair of balls God gave me."

"But you even got a medal for knocking off a dealer," Carreño protested feebly. "You're a national hero in the war against drugs. Don't say I did you harm. Admit it was a favor, Godfather."

"I've had to find the good in something bad, you shit," replied the commander. "Whatever, you put me in a touchy situation, and it can cause me problems. If Hog's people want revenge, who will they go after? Who will they fuck with? A little jerk like you, or me? Will you be sorry at least if they send me to the graveyard?"

"I'd never forgive myself, Godfather. And I swear I'd go to the ends of the earth to hunt down anybody who hurt a hair on your head."

"Shit, your feeling for me brings tears to my eyes," said the commander, taking a drink of whiskey and clucking his tongue.

And with no transition, and in a way that permitted no reply, he ordered: "Before you say another word, to help me decide what your penance will be, go get this Mercedes and bring her here. Right now. I want to see for myself if her ass is worth all the inconvenience."

"Damn," exclaimed Lituma. "I could see it coming, the tricky bastard."

"I was scared to death, Corporal," Tomasito confessed. "What would I do, what could I do if my godfather went too far with Mercedes?"

"Pull out your pistol and shoot him, too," said the corporal.

"What could I do?" his adjutant repeated, tossing and turning on his cot in despair. "We needed him for everything. For Mercedes's voter's ID, for taking care of my situation. You understand, technically I was a deserter from the Civil Guard. It was a bitter pill for me, I can tell you."

"Do you think I'm afraid of him?" Mercedes laughed.

"It's a sacrifice we have to make to get out of this, sweetheart. It'll be a bad half hour, that's all. He's calming down, he even started to kid around with me. Now he's curious and wants to meet you. I won't let him treat you with disrespect, I swear."

"I can take care of myself, Carreñito," said Mercedes, smoothing her hair, her skirt. "Not even commanders or generals treat me with disrespect. How do I look? Do I pass the test, my dear sir?"

"With top grades," the commander said hoarsely. "I approve, I approve. I can see you know the score, kid. Good, I like broads with a little spirit."

"So this means we call each other *tú?*" said Mercedes. "I thought I'd have to call you Godfather, like him. Well, all right, let's call each other *tú*, pussycat."

"Granted, you have a nice face, nice body, nice legs," said the commander. "But that's not enough to turn a boy into a killer. You must have something else that knocked my godson flat on his back. So tell me, what did you do to him?"

"The trouble is, I didn't do a thing," said Mercedes. "I was more surprised than anybody when he went out of control. Didn't he tell you about it? First he shot him, then he told me he did it for me, that he was in love with me. I couldn't believe it, I still can't. Isn't that how it happened, Carreñito?"

"Yes, Godfather, that's exactly how it happened," said the boy. "Mercedes wasn't to blame for anything. I got her into this mess. Are you going to help us? Will you get Mercedes a new voter's ID? We want to go to the States and make a new start."

"You must have done something very special to the boy to make him this crazy about you," said the commander, bringing his face close to Mercedes and taking her by the chin. "How'd you do it, kid, with a love potion?"

"I beg you not to be disrespectful to Mercedes," said the boy. "Please, Godfather, I can't let you do that. Not even you."

"Did your godfather know that Mercedes was the first woman you slept with?" asked Lituma.

"No, he didn't, nobody did," his adjutant replied. "If anybody told him I would've beaten him to a pulp. Only you and Mercedes know, Corporal."

"Thanks for your confidence, Tomasito."

"But that wasn't the worst moment of the night. The worst was when my godfather danced with her. I could feel the anger rush to my head, like it was going to explode any second."

"Calm down, calm down, don't be an asshole, Carreñito." Iscariote patted his arm. "What difference does it make if he dances with her and squeezes her a little? He's making you pay, he's making you jealous. Basically he's already forgiven you, he's going to take care of your problems. It's all working out like I said it would in Huánuco. Don't think about anything else."

"But I was thinking that he was holding her too tight and feeling her up." Tomasito's indignant voice quivered in the dark. "I don't care what happens to me, he's going too far. I'm going to teach him a lesson."

But just then the commander brought Mercedes back to the table, laughing for all he was worth.

"She can really dish it out, I have to congratulate you, boy," he said, giving Tomás an amiable slap on the head. "I made her a damn good proposition, but she wouldn't take it."

"I knew you were testing me again, that's why I turned you down, pussycat," said Mercedes. "Besides, you're the last person in the world I'd cheat on Carreñito with. So, are you going to help us?"

"It's better to have a woman like you for a friend, not an enemy," said the commander. "That's some dame you've taken on, boy."

"And he helped us." Tomasito sighed. "The next day Mercedes had a new ID. And that same night she took off."

"You mean as soon as she got her papers she left you, Tomasito?"

"With the four thousand dollars I gave her," his adjutant murmured very slowly. "They were hers. I had given them to her. She left me a note saying what she said so many times. That she wasn't the woman for me, that I'd get over it, the same old thing."

"So that's how the damn thing ended," said Lituma. "Shit, Tomasito."

"Yes, Corporal," said his adjutant. "That's how the damn thing ended."

9 / "HIS NAME IS PAUL, and he has a funny last name, Stirmsson or Stirmesson," said Lituma. "But everybody calls him Red. He was one of the guys who made that incredible escape when the terrucos came into La Esperanza. He told me he knew you both. Do you remember that gringo?"

"A busybody, he wanted to know everything about everything." Doña Adriana nodded, grimacing with dislike. "He always had a notebook, he was always writing. He hasn't been around here for a long time. So, he was one of the men hiding in the water tank?"

"He was a snoop, he studied us like we were plants or animals." Dionisio spat. "He followed me all over the Andes. He didn't care about us, he only wanted to put us in his books. I can't believe that gringo bastard Red is still alive."

"He was surprised to hear you were alive, too," Lituma replied. "He thought the terrucos must've executed you by now for being antisocial types."

They were talking at the door of the cantina, under a vertical white sun that reverberated on the tin roofs of the barracks that had remained standing. Groups of laborers were using planks, pulleys, ropes, picks, and shovels to remove some of the boulders brought down by the huayco, trying to open a road so they could bring out whatever machinery the avalanche had not flattened or made inoperative. Despite the activity in the shack that had been set up as an office to replace the one destroyed by the rockslide, Naccos seemed empty. Fewer than a third of the laborers remained in the village, and more were leaving; there, for example, on the trail up to the Huancayo road, Lituma could see three figures climbing in single file, with bundles on their backs. They walked quickly and in step, as if they did not feel the weight they were carrying.

"This time they've just resigned themselves to leaving," he said, pointing at the three men. "No strikes, no protests."

"They know it wouldn't do any good," Dionisio said without a trace of emotion. "The huayco did the company a favor. They've been wanting to stop work for a long time. Now they have an excuse."

"It's not an excuse," said the corporal. "Don't you see how things are? How can they build a highway now that a mountain's fallen on Naccos? It's a miracle nobody died in a catastrophe like that."

"That's what I've been trying to get into their hard heads," grumbled Doña Adriana, with an ill-tempered gesture toward the men moving boulders. "We could all be dead, squashed like cockroaches. And instead of giving thanks for being safe, all these Indians do is complain."

"Well, they escaped the huayco, but now they know they'll die a slow death from no work and starvation," Dionisio murmured with a little laugh. "Or worse things. At least let them kick up a little fuss."

"Do you believe the avalanche didn't kill us because that was what the apus of these mountains wanted?" the corporal asked, trying to look into Doña Adriana's eyes. "Am I supposed to give thanks to them, too, for still being alive?"

He expected Dionisio's wife to say something nasty about him being like a lunatic, always harping on the same thing, but this time the witch said nothing and did not turn toward him. She was frowning, absorbed, her gaze lost in the craggy peaks that surrounded the settlement.

"We talked about the apus with Red, over in La Esperanza," the corporal went on after a moment. "He thinks the mountains have their spirits, Doña Adriana, just like you. The apus. Blood-thirsty spirits, or so it seems. If a scholar who knows as much as that gringo does says so, it must be true. Thank you for saving my life, señores apus of Junín."

"You can't call them señores apus," Dionisio corrected him. "Because apu means señor in Quechua. And repetition is an insult, Corporal, sir, as the song says."

"You shouldn't say Corporal, sir, either," replied Lituma. "Corporal, or sir, but the two of them together is just pulling my leg. Though you're always pulling somebody's leg."

"I try to keep a sense of humor," Dionisio acknowledged. "But the things that are going on make it hard not to become bitter like everybody else."

And he began to whistle one of the melodies he danced to at night, when the whole cantina was drunk. With an aching heart, Lituma listened to the melancholy tune. It seemed to come from the beginning of time, to carry a challenge from another race, from a world buried in these huge mountains. He half closed his eyes, and in front of him he could see the docile little dancing figure of Pedrito Tinoco taking shape, faint in the white brilliance of the day.

"It makes me dizzy to climb all the way up to the post in this sun," he said softly, taking off his cap and wiping the sweat from his forehead. "Can I sit with you awhile?"

Neither of them replied. Lituma sat on one corner of the bench occupied by Doña Adriana. Dionisio remained standing, smoking and leaning against the scarred wood of the cantina door. The shouts and exclamations of the laborers moving the rock reached them sporadically, sounding close or distant depending on the shifting direction of the wind.

"The company radio was finally working this morning, and I was able to send my report to headquarters in Huancayo," the corporal remarked. "I hope they answer soon. I don't know what my adjutant and I can do here anymore except wait for them to kill us or disappear us, like they did the mute. What about you? What will you do now? Leave Naccos, too?"

"What else can we do?" said Dionisio. "Not even the Indians in the community want to live in Naccos anymore. Most of the young people have gone down to the coast or to Huancayo. Just a few old people are still here, and they're dying off."

"Then only the apus will be left," Lituma declared. "And the pishtacos and mukis. And they'll have to feast on each other's blood. Right, Doña Adriana? Don't make that face, it was a joke. I know you're in no mood for jokes. Neither am I. I'm talking about it because no matter how hard I try not to think about you know what, I can't help it. Those three men are poisoning my life."

"Why do you care so much about those poor bastards?" Dionisio exhaled a mouthful of smoke. "So many people disappear or die every day, why do you only worry about them? What about the man they killed in La Esperanza? You just like mysteries, I already told you that once."

"The disappearances aren't a mystery anymore," the corporal asserted, turning again to look at Doña Adriana, but she would not return his glance this time, either. "The other night, thanks to Red,

I finally got it straight. I swear, I wish I didn't know. Because what happened to them is the most stupid and perverse of all the stupid and perverse things that happen up here. And nobody's ever going to make me change my mind about you two being responsible. Especially you, Doña Adriana."

But not even this got a reaction out of Dionisio's wife. She continued to frown, to look at the hills, as if she had not heard, or as if she had things on her mind too important for her to listen to such trifles.

"Have a smoke and forget those dumb ideas." Dionisio handed him a pack of black-tobacco cigarettes. "Think about how you'll be leaving soon, maybe going back home, how your life will be easier than it was in Naccos."

Lituma took a cigarette and put it in his mouth. The cantinero lit it with an old long-wick lighter whose flame warmed the corporal's mouth and nose. He inhaled deeply and exhaled energetically, watching the smoke spiral upward in the clean golden air of burning midday.

"If I get out of here alive, I'll have those three with me wherever I go," he said. "Especially the little mute, who disappeared the night he came down here to buy beer. Understand?"

"Of course he understands, Corporal." His adjutant laughed. "Some nice Cuzco beer, ice-cold, and on the double. You understood perfectly, didn't you, Pedrito?"

Pedrito Tinoco nodded several times with those rapid, identical bows that made Lituma think of a chicken pecking kernels of corn, took the bills the corporal handed him, bowed one last time, turned, and walked out of the post, disappearing into the moonless night.

"We shouldn't have sent him when it was so dark, so late," said Lituma, exhaling smoke from his mouth and nose. "When it took so long, we should have gone down to see what had happened, why he didn't come back. But it started to rain and we got lazy. Tomasito and I started talking, and we lost track of time."

In spite of the rain, the mute hurried down the slope as if he had the eyes of a fox or knew by heart where to step and where to jump. He clenched the bills tightly so he would not drop them. Pedrito was soaked when he reached the cantina door. He knocked several times, pushed it open, went in, and was greeted by a mass of shapes partially dissolved in clouds of smoke. He smelled a dizzying stink of sweat, alcohol, tobacco, urine, excrement, semen, and foul-smelling vomit. But it was not the odors or the tomb-like silence caused by his arrival that put him on the defensive, making him alert and suspicious of imminent danger, but the fear that his instincts sensed everywhere, a thick, quivering fear that troubled the eyes of all the laborers and seemed to fill the air, to drip from the walls, the bar, above all from the tense faces contorted into grimaces and expressions caused by more than drunkenness. No one moved. Everyone turned to look at him. Pedrito Tinoco was intimidated, and he bowed several times.

"There he is, he's the one you want, there's nobody better than him." Doña Adriana's hoarse, spectral voice burst from behind the bar. "They sent him, they have sent him. It must be him. It is him. The mute, nobody better."

"Of course they must have argued about it," Lituma added. "Of course there must have been some who said 'Right, let it be him,' and others who said 'No, the poor half-wit, not him.' I guess there must have been one or two at least who weren't so drunk, who felt sorry for him. And all the while, instead of going down to see why he didn't come back, Tomasito and I went to sleep. Or talked about the woman who had left him. We were accomplices, too. Not the planners, not the instigators, like you two. But accomplices all the same, accomplices by omission, in a way."

They were all very drunk; some were staggering, leaning against the walls or holding on to each other to keep from falling down. Their glazed, brilliant eyes pierced the clouds of smoke to examine Pedrito Tinoco. Confused at feeling himself the center of that collective attention, fearful because of the dark, nameless threat he could sense, he did not dare approach the bar. Until Dionisio came to him, took him by the arm, kissed him on the cheek, something that at first disconcerted the little mute and then made him giggle nervously, and put a glass of pisco in his hand.

"Your health, your health," he urged him to drink. "Join the crowd, my friend."

"He's innocent, he's pure, he's an outsider, he's been marked since Pampa Galeras," Señora Adriana recited, prayed, intoned. "Sooner or later the terrucos would have executed him. If he's going to die anyway, it should be for something worthwhile. Aren't all of you worthwhile? Out cold, sleeping there in those barracks, dead tired after breaking your backs on the highway, isn't that worth it? Figure it out and decide."

As the sharp warmth went down to his chest and tickled his stomach, Pedrito Tinoco began to realize that beneath the rubber-tire soles of his muddy sandals, his feet covered with scabs, the ground was softening, spinning. Like a top. Some time, some place, he had known how to make tops dance by winding a string around them and tossing them with a deft snap of his arm: spinning in air until their colors blurred, until they looked like motionless hummingbirds beating their wings in the air, a little ball flying to the sun, then falling. The sharp tip would land on the stone in the ditch, skip along the edge of the stall, come to rest on the stone bench of the house, wherever his eye had looked before his hand gave the order to the string. And it danced there a long time, jumping and humming, happy little top. Doña Adriana talked and heads nodded in agreement. Some of them elbowed their way through the crowd and approached the mute and touched him. They had not lost their fear, not at all. Pedrito Tinoco no longer felt as embarrassed as he had when he first arrived. He was still clenching the bills in his hand, and in sudden obscure flashes he would give a start, telling himself, 'I have to go back.' But he did not know how to leave. Each time he took a sip of pisco the cantinero applauded him, patted him on the back, and, in an occasional outburst of enthusiasm, kissed him on the cheek.

"The kiss of Judas is what you gave him," said Lituma. "And all the while I'm snoring or listening to Tomasito talk about his troubles with that girl of his. Dionisio, Doña Adriana, you were lucky. If I'd come down to the cantina and caught you red-handed, I don't know what would've happened to you, I swear."

He spoke without anger, with fatalism and resignation. Doña Adriana was still lost in thought, uninterested in him, watching the laborers remove the debris. But Dionisio burst into laughter, opening his mouth wide. He had squatted down on his heels, and the wool scarf grotesquely exaggerated the size of his neck. He looked at Lituma in amusement, opening and closing his prominent eyes, which were less bloodshot than usual.

"You would've made a good storyteller," he declared with great conviction. "I had a few in my troupe when I was young. We traveled from village to village, fair to fair. Dancers, musicians, acrobats, freaks, magicians, everything. Storytellers too. They had a lot of success, kids and grownups used to hang on every word and protest when the story was over. 'More, more, please.' 'Another one, tell us another one.' With that imagination of yours you would've been one of my stars. Almost as good as Adriana, Corporal, sir."

"He can't drink any more, he's groggy. He can't take another drop," someone crooned.

"Force it down his throat, and if he vomits let him vomit," a frightened voice pleaded. "He's not supposed to feel anything, he's supposed to forget who he is, where he comes from."

"Speaking of mutes, in some villages in La Mar province, in Ayacucho, they feed parrot tongues to people who can't talk," said Dionisio. "And that cures them. I bet you didn't know that, Corporal, sir."

"You'll forgive us, won't you, Little Father?" a man whispered hoarsely in Quechua, transfixed with grief, barely getting the words out. "You'll be our saint, you'll be remembered at the fiesta as the savior of Naccos."

"Give him more booze, you bastards, quit fucking around," ordered one of the tough ones. "If you're going to do something, do it right."

Instead of the quena or flute he played on other occasions, this time Dionisio began to play the harmonica. Its sharp little metallic voice irritated Pedrito's nerves; many hands supported his arms and back, kept him from falling. His legs were rags, his shoulders straw, his stomach a lake with ducks, his head a whirlwind of phosphorescent fireflies. The stars twinkled, and quick-moving rainbows colored the night. If he'd had the strength, he could have reached out his hand and touched a star in the sky. It would be soft and tender, warm and friendly, like the neck of a vicuña. From time to time he was shaken by retching, but there was nothing left to throw up. He knew that if he focused his eyes and wiped away the tears that clouded them, there, floating in the immensity of the sky, he would see the joyful flock of vicuñas trotting over the snow-covered mountains to the moon.

"Those were different times, better times than now for lots of reasons," Dionisio added with an air of sadness. "Especially because people wanted to enjoy themselves, knew how to enjoy themselves. They were as poor as they are now, and there were troubles then, too, in a lot of places. But here in the Andes, people still had what

they've lost now: an enthusiasm for enjoying themselves. A desire
to live. Now they move and talk and get drunk, but they all seem
half dead. Haven't you noticed that, Corporal, sir?"

If there were stars, he was no longer in Dionisio's cantina.
They had taken him outside, and that was why, even though tiny
fires blazed inside his body, warming his blood, he could feel the
icy night on his face, the tip of his nose, his hands, his feet, which
had lost their sandals. Was it hailing? Instead of foul smells, his
nostrils breathed in a clean aroma of eucalyptus, toasted corn, the
bubbling cool water of a spring. Were they carrying him? Was he
on a throne? Was he the patron saint of the fiesta? Was a good
father there at his feet, praying to him, or was it the prayer of the
woman who sold religious pictures and slept in the doorway of
the slaughterhouse in Abancay? No. It was the voice of Señora
Adriana. There must be an altar boy, too, hemmed in by the
crowd, ringing the little silver bell and swinging the censer whose
fragrance flooded the night. Pedrito Tinoco knew how to do that,
he had done it in the Church of Our Lady of the Rosary, in the
days when his skillful hands made the tops dance. He could spread
the incense around so that it went straight up to the faces of all the
saints on the altar.

"They even had a good time at wakes, drinking, eating, telling
stories," Dionisio continued. "We went to a lot of funerals with
the troupe. The wakes lasted for days and nights, and the demijohns
were emptied. Now, when people leave this world, their relatives
say goodbye without ceremony, as if they were dogs. That's a kind
of decadence, too, don't you think, Corporal, sir?"

A cry, or a sob, abruptly shattered the reverent silence of the
procession carrying him up the hill. What were they afraid of? Why
were they crying? Where were they going? His heart began to
pound, and suddenly the sick feeling left him. They were taking
him to be with his friends again, of course. Of course. They were

there waiting for him, up in the place they were carrying him to. He was overcome by an intense emotion. If he'd had the strength he would have started howling, leaping, thanking them with bows down to the ground. His joy was overflowing. They would stiffen when they heard him approach, and stretch their long necks, their damp snouts would quiver, their huge eyes would look at him in surprise, and when they recognized his smell the entire flock would be happy the way he was happy now, looking forward to their meeting. They would touch and embrace, their limbs would entwine, and he and they would forget the world, playing and rejoicing because they were together.

"Let's finish it, you motherfuckers," pleaded the tough one, who had lost his earlier certainty; he, too, was beginning to doubt, to feel frightened. "The air's sobering him up, he'll know what's going on. No, damn it."

"If you believed even a tenth of that story, you would've arrested us and taken us to Huancayo," Doña Adriana interrupted, coming out of her self-absorption. She gave Lituma a pitying look. "So don't try to trick us, Corporal."

"You and these ignorant serruchos sacrificed him to the apus," said the corporal, getting to his feet. He was overcome by fatigue. He continued speaking as he put on his kepi. "I know it the way I know my name is Lituma. But I can't prove it, and even if I could, nobody would believe me, least of all my superiors. So I'll have to stick my tongue up my ass and keep the secret to myself. Nobody believes in human sacrifice nowadays, right?"

"I do," said Doña Adriana, wrinkling her nose and waving goodbye.

.

I know it seems strange, us staying in Naccos instead of some other village in the sierra. But when our traveling days were over and old age caught up with us, Naccos wasn't the ruin it turned into later. It didn't seem like it was dying minute by minute. The Santa Rita mine closed, but it was still a busy place, it had a strong campesino community and one of the best fairs in Junín. On Sundays this street was full of traders, they came from all over, Indians, mestizos, even white señores, buying and selling llamas, alpacas, sheep, pigs, looms, wool that was sheared or ready for shearing, corn, barley, quinoa, coca, skirts, hats, jackets, shoes, tools, lamps. Anything men and women needed was bought and sold here. Back then there were more women than men, go on and drool, you lechers. Our place had ten times more business than now. Dionisio went down to the coast once a month to stock up on demijohns. We earned enough to pay two drovers to drive the mules and load and unload the merchandise.

We both liked Naccos, liked the people passing through. Strangers coming and going, climbing up to the barrens in the Cordillera, or going down to the jungle, or on their way to Huancayo and the coast. This is where we met, where Dionisio fell in love with me, where our connection to each other began. There's always been talk of a highway to replace the mule trail. They talked about it for years and years before they decided to build it. It's a shame, when they finally started work and all of you came with your picks and shovels and drills, it was too late. Death had won its battle with life. It was written that the highway would never be finished, that's why I don't even pay attention to those rumors that keep you awake at night, that make you get drunk. Stopping the work, firing all of you, those are things I saw a long time ago in a trance. I hear them, too, in the heart beating inside the tree, inside the stone, and I read them in the kestrel's innards, and the guinea pig's. The death of Naccos has been settled. The spirits decided and it will happen. Unless . . . I've said it before and I'll say it again: Great troubles need great remedies. That's the history of man, says Dionisio. He always had the gift of prophecy, and with him I got it, too, he passed it on to me.

Besides, thanks to these hills, Naccos had an aura, a magic power. That suits Dionisio and me. Danger always attracted us. Doesn't it represent true life, life that's worthwhile? But security is boredom, it's stupidity, it's death. It was no accident pishtacos came here, like the one who dried Juan Apaza and Sebastián. That's right. El Padrillo. The decay of Naccos attracted them, and the hidden life in the burial mounds. These mountains are full of ancient tombs. Without those presences there wouldn't be so many spirits in this part of the Andes. It was a real struggle for us to get in touch with them. Thanks to them we learned a lot, even Dionisio, who already knew so much. A lot happened, a great effort was needed for them to show themselves. To know when the condor flying overhead was a messenger and when it was an ordinary hungry animal hunting its prey. Now I never make a mistake, one glance and I can tell the difference, and if you doubt it you can test me. Only the spirits of the tallest, strongest hills, the ones that have snow all year round, the ones that pierce the clouds, only they take on the bodies of condors; the small ones, they're kestrels or falcons, and some of the puny little hills are thrushes. Those are weak spirits, they can't make catastrophes happen. The worst they can do is harm, like bringing misfortune to a family. They're satisfied with the offerings of liquor and food the Indians make when they cross the gorges.

So many things happened here in the past. Long before they opened the Santa Rita, I mean. The gift of prophecy allows you to see behind as well as ahead, and I've seen what Naccos was like before it was called Naccos, before decay won its victory over the desire to live. There was a lot of life here because there was a lot of death. Plenty of suffering and plenty of joy, the way it should be; the bad thing is how it is now in Naccos, in the whole sierra, maybe in the whole world, when there's only suffering and nobody remembers what joy was like. In the old days people had the courage to face great troubles by making sacrifices. That's how they maintained the balance. Life and death like a scale with two equal weights, like two rams of equal strength that lock horns and neither one can advance or retreat.

What did they do to keep death from defeating life? Hold your stomachs, you might want to vomit. These truths aren't for weak trousers but for strong skirts. Women took on the responsibility. Women, that's right. And they did what they had to do. But the man the people chose in council to be lord of the fiestas for the coming year, that man trembled. He knew he would be a leader and authority only until then; after that, the sacrifice. He didn't run, he didn't try to escape after he presided over the fiesta, after the procession, the dances, the feasting and the drinking. No, none of that. He stayed to the end, willing and proud to do good for his people. He died a hero, loved and revered. And that's what he was: a hero. He did some hard drinking, he played the charango or the quena or the harp or the tijeras or whatever instrument he knew, and he danced, stamping his heels and singing, day and night, until he drove out sorrow, until he could forget and not feel anything and give his life willingly and without fear. Only the women went out to hunt him down on the last night of the fiesta. They were drunk, too, wild like the wild girls in Dionisio's troupe, just like them. But back then the husbands and fathers didn't try to hold those women down. They sharpened knives and machetes for them, and urged them on: "Look for him, find him, hunt him down, bite him, make him bleed, so we'll have a year of peace and good harvests." They hunted him in a chako, just the way the Indians in the community used to hunt the puma and the stag when there were still pumas and stags in this sierra. The hunt for the lord of the fiesta was just like that. They formed a circle and closed him inside, singing, always singing, dancing, always dancing, shrieking to encourage each other when they felt him near, knowing that the lord of the fiesta was surrounded, that he could not escape. The circle got smaller and smaller until they caught him. His rule ended in blood. And the next week, in a great council, they elected the lord for the following year. The happiness and prosperity in Naccos, that's how they paid for it. They knew it, and none of them lost their nerve. Only decay, what we have nowadays, is given away for nothing. You men don't have to pay anybody anything to live in uncertainty and fear, to be the wrecks you are. That's free of charge. Work on the highway will stop and you won't have jobs, the terrucos will come and there'll be a slaughter, the huayco will come down and wipe us off the map. The evil spirits will come out of the mountains to celebrate, they'll dance a farewell cacharpari to life, and so many condors will be circling overhead they'll blot out the sky. Unless . . .

It's not true that Timoteo Fajardo left me because he lost his courage. False that the big-nose found me the morning after the saint's fiesta, at the mouth of the Santa Rita mine, holding the lord's manhood in my hand, and was afraid he'd be chosen lord for the following year and ran away from Naccos. That's just talk, like the story that Dionisio killed him so he could be with me. When those things I'm telling you about happened in Naccos, I was still floating among the stars, pure spirit without a body, waiting my turn to take the form of a woman.

Like pisco, music helps us understand bitter truths. Dionisio has spent his life teaching them to people, but it hasn't done much good, most cover their ears so they won't hear. I learned everything I know about music from him. Singing a huaynito with feeling, giving yourself over to it, letting yourself go, losing yourself in the song until you feel that you're the song, that the music is singing you instead of you singing the music, this is the path to wisdom. Stamping your feet, stamping and spinning, adorning the figure, making and unmaking it without losing the rhythm, forgetting yourself, leaving yourself, until you feel that the dance is dancing you, that it's deep inside you, that it commands and you obey, this is the path to wisdom. You are no longer yourself, I am no longer myself but all the others. That's how we leave the prison of the body and enter the world of the spirits. By singing. Dancing. Drinking, too, naturally. You travel when you're drunk, Dionisio says, you pay a visit to your animal, you shake off worry, you discover your secret, you become who you really are. The rest of the time you're in prison, like the corpses in the ancient tombs or the cemeteries we have today. You're somebody's slave or servant, always. When we're dancing and drinking, there are no Indians, no mestizos, no white señores, no rich or poor, no men or women. The differences are wiped away and we become like spirits: Indians, mestizos, señores, rich and poor, women and men. Not everybody travels when they dance or sing or drink, only the best ones. You have to have a will for it and lose your pride and shame and come down from the pedestal where people have put themselves. The man who doesn't put his thoughts to sleep, who doesn't forget himself, or throw off his vanity and pride, or become the music when he sings and the dance when he dances and drunkenness when he drinks—that man does not leave his prison, does not travel, does not pay a visit to his animal or rise up to become spirit. That man does not live: he is decay, he is the living dead. And he cannot nourish the spirits of the mountains, either. They want first-rate creatures who have freed themselves from their slavery. Many people, no matter how drunk they get, do not become drunkenness. Or the song or the dance, even though they yell and shout and stamp the ground until it gives off sparks. But that little mute who works for the cops, he does. Even though he's mute, even though he's a half-wit, he feels the music. He knows. And I've seen him dance, all alone, going up or coming down the hill, running his errands. He closes his eyes, he concentrates, he begins to walk in rhythm, to take little steps on tiptoe, to move his hands, to jump. He's hearing a huayno that only he can hear, that they sing only to him, that he sings without making a sound from deep inside his heart. He loses himself, he goes away, he travels, he leaves, he approaches the spirits. The terrucos didn't kill him that time in Pampa Galeras, because the spirits of the mountains were protecting him. Or maybe they had marked him for something greater. They'd receive him with open arms, like those lords in the old days who were offered up by the women, the ones who sleep now in the tombs. But you, in spite of your trousers and the balls you're so proud of, you're shitting with fear. You prefer to have no work, to be dried and sliced by the pishtacos, to let the terrucos take you into their militia, let them stone you to death, anything before you'd shoulder a responsibility. It's no wonder there are no women left in Naccos. They withstood the attack of the evil spirits, they maintained the life and prosperity of the village. It began to go down when they left, and you men don't have the courage to stop it. You let life slip away, you let death fill the empty places. Unless . . .

.

"I didn't care about the dollars, they were hers," Tomasito declared with absolute conviction. "But her leaving, the thought that I'd never see Mercedes again, that she'd be with another man, or other men, and never be mine again—that was a terrible blow. It tore me apart, Corporal. I even thought about killing myself, I swear. But I didn't even have the heart to do that."

"Now I get it," Lituma observed. "Now I understand you better, Tomasito. Like crying in your sleep. Now I understand. And why you can talk about only one thing and never talk about anything else. But what I have a hard time figuring out is how after a dirty trick like that, after Mercedes took off in spite of everything you did for her, you still love her. You ought to hate her guts."

"I'm a serrucho, don't forget," the boy joked. "Don't they say that for us there's no love without a beating? 'The more you hit me, the more you love me'—don't they say we say that? In my case, the proverb came true."

"Turnabout is fair play," Lituma encouraged him. "Instead of crying so much over an ungrateful woman, you should've gotten your dick into another broad. That's how you would've forgotten all about the Piuran."

"That's the remedy my godfather prescribed," said Tomasito.

"Nothing lasts forever, not even cunt trouble," the commander assured him. And gave him an order: "You go over to the Dominó right now and fuck that skinny Lira, she's hot, or Celestina with the big tits. And if you have the dick for it, fuck the two of them together. I'll call and tell them to give you a discount. If that pair of asses moving on top of you doesn't get Mercedes out of your head, they can have my stripes."

"I tried to do what he said, I went," the boy recalled, with a little forced laugh. "I had lost my will. I was like a rag, I did whatever anybody told me to. I went, I took a hooker to the little hotel across from the Dominó to see if that would make me start to forget her. And it was even worse. While the hooker was sweet-talking me, I was thinking about Mercedes, comparing my honey's sweet little body to the one I had in front of me. I didn't even get hard, Corporal."

"You confess things that are so personal I don't know what to say." Lituma became confused. "Doesn't it embarrass you to talk about things like that, Tomasito?"

"I wouldn't tell just anybody," his adjutant explained. "But I trust you even more than Iscariote. To me, you're like the father I never knew, Corporal."

"That Mercedes was a lot of woman for you, boy," declared the commander. "You would've gone through hell with her. She's a broad who aims high, even Hog wasn't big enough for her. Didn't you see the airs she put on the night you introduced us? She called me pussycat, the stupid bitch."

"If I could always have her with me, I'd steal for her, I'd kill for her again." Carreño's voice broke. "Anything. Want to hear something even more private? I'll never fuck another woman. They don't interest me, they don't exist. If I can't have Mercedes, I don't want any of them."

"Son of a bitch," Lituma commented.

"To be honest with you, I would've liked to fuck her brains out and that's the truth," the commander said hoarsely. "I propositioned her when I danced with her in the Dominó. Kind of testing her, too, like I told you. Do you know what she did, Godson? She grabbed my fly as bold as brass and said: 'I wouldn't do you for all the money in the world, not even if you put a pistol to my chest. You're not my type, pussycat.' "

He was in uniform, sitting at the small desk in his office on the first floor of the Ministry. A small Peruvian flag and a fan that was turned off were among the stacks of folders. Carreño wore civilian clothes and remained standing, facing a photograph of the President of the Republic, who seemed to look at him sardonically from the wall. The commander was wearing his eternal dark glasses; he toyed with a pencil and a letter opener.

"Don't tell me those things, Godfather. It makes me feel even worse."

"I'm telling you so you'll know that woman wasn't right for you," the commander said encouragingly. "She would've gone to bed even with priests and faggots. She was a libber, and that's the most dangerous thing a woman can be. You're lucky to be rid of her, even if it wasn't your choice. Okay, let's not waste any more time. We have to think about your situation. You haven't forgotten you're in one hell of a mess because of Tingo María, have you?"

"He must be your father, Tomasito," Lituma whispered. "He must be."

The commander searched his desk and picked up a file from the stack of folders. He waved it at Carreño.

"It won't be easy to straighten things out and clean up your service record. But if we don't, the black mark will follow you the rest of your life. I've found a way, thanks to a buddy of mine, a smart lawyer who's connected to the service. Do you know what you are? A repentant deserter, that's what. You took off, you realized your mistake, you thought things over, and now you've come back to ask forgiveness. As proof of your sincerity, you've volunteered to go to the emergency zone. You're going to hunt down subversive criminals, boy. Sign here."

"I really would like to have known your godfather," Lituma interrupted, filled with admiration. "What a guy, Tomasito."

"Your application has been accepted and you already have your assignment," the commander continued, blowing on the ink where Carreño had signed. "Andahuaylas, under the command of an officer with a lot of balls. Lieutenant Pancorvo. He owes me some favors, he'll treat you fine. You'll be in the sierra for a few months, less than a year. That'll get you out of circulation until they forget about you and your record is clean. When you're blessed and forgiven, I'll find you a better post. Aren't you going to thank me?"

"Iscariote was very good to me, too," said Tomás. "He was like my shadow until I took the bus to Andahuaylas. I think he was afraid I'd kill myself. He says food is the cure for a broken heart. Like I told you before, he lives to eat."

"Tamales, barbecue, roast pork with sweet potato, seviche of corvina fish, stuffed green peppers, scallops a la parmigiana, Lima potatoes, and ice-cold beer," the fat man enumerated with a magnificent gesture. "That's for starters. Then, spicy chicken fricassee with white rice, and stewed kid. And to top off the evening, Doña Pepa's blue-corn pudding with nougat. So cheer up, Carreñito."

"If we eat just half of that, it'll kill us, Fats."

"Maybe it'll kill you," said Iscariote. "But as far as I'm concerned, a full belly makes me feel brand-new. This is the life. You'll forget all about Mercedes before we get to the kid."

"I'll never forget her," the boy declared. "I mean, I don't want to forget her. I never imagined I could be so happy, Corporal. Maybe it's better that things worked out the way they did. That it didn't last too long. Because if we'd gotten married and stayed together, the things that poison other couples would've happened to us too. But now all my memories of her are good ones."

"She took off with your four thousand dollars after you killed a guy for her and got her a new voter's ID, and you just think she's wonderful." Lituma was appalled. "You're a masochist, Tomasito."

"I know you won't give a damn what I say," Iscariote exclaimed suddenly. He was sweating and breathing heavily and his great mass of flesh quivered with gluttony; he held a forkful of rice in the air and moved it in time to his words. "But let me give you some friendly advice. Do you know what I'd do if I was in your shoes?"

"What would you do?"

"Get revenge." Iscariote carried the fork to his mouth, chewed with his eyes half closed, as if he were in ecstasy, then swallowed, drank some beer, licked his heavy lips with his tongue, and continued: "I'd make that cow pay."

"How?" asked the boy. "Even though I feel awful and have indigestion, you make me laugh, Fats."

"Fucking her up where it'll hurt her the most." Iscariote panted. He had taken a large white handkerchief with a blue border from his pocket and was wiping away the sweat with both hands. "Sending her to jail as Hog's accomplice. It's easy, all you have to do is file a charge against her. And while they're investigating and there's all that red tape with the judge, she'll be in the women's prison at Chorrillos. Wasn't she scared to death to go to jail? She'd do a little time there for being so ungrateful."

"Then I could go there at night with ladders and ropes and rescue her. This is getting interesting, Fats."

"At Chorillos I can fix it so they put her in the cell block with the half-breed dykes." Iscariote spoke quickly, as if he had thought the plan out carefully. "They'd make her see stars and the moon, Carreñito. And half of them have syphilis, so they'd infect her, too."

"I don't like that so much, Fats. My sweetheart with syphilis? I'd tear every one of those dykes apart with my bare hands."

"There's another possibility. We look for her, we find her, we take her to the station at Tacora, where I have a compadre. She spends the night in a cell with all the crazies, the dope addicts and degenerates. The next morning she won't even remember her name."

"I'd go and find her in her cell and fall down on my knees and worship her." The boy laughed. "She's my Saint Rose of Lima."

"That's why she left you." Iscariote had begun his attack on the desserts and spoke with his mouth full, in a choked voice. "Women don't like so much consideration, Carreñito. They get bored. If you treated her the way Hog did, she'd be tame by now, she'd still be with you."

"I like her just the way she is," said the boy. "Vain, forward, lots of experience. She has a lousy character, and I like it just fine. Everything she is and does I like. Even if you don't believe me, Corporal."

"Why shouldn't I believe you're crazy?" said Lituma. "Everybody's crazy here. Aren't the terrucos crazy? Aren't Dionisio and the witch out of their minds? Wasn't that Lieutenant Pancorvo stark raving mad when he burned a mute to make him talk? Is there anything more insane than these serruchos scared to death of mukis and throat-slitters? Don't people have more than one screw loose when they make people disappear just to keep the apus in the hills quiet? At least when you're crazy in love, you don't hurt anybody except yourself."

"But you manage to keep a cool head in this madhouse, Corporal," said his adjutant.

"That must be why I feel so out of place in Naccos, Tomasito."

"Well, I give up, we won't take our revenge, and Mercedes can go on planting the world with dead boyfriends and bruised lovers," said Iscariote. "At least I cheered you up. I'm going to miss you, Carreñito. I was getting used to us doing jobs together. I hope things go well for you in the emergency zone. Don't let the terrucos bust your balls. Take care of yourself, and drop me a line."

"That must be why I can't imagine them taking me out of here," added Lituma. "Well, let's get some sleep, it must be close to dawn. Do you know something, Tomasito? You've told me your whole life story. I know the rest. You went to Andahuaylas, you were with Pancorvo, they transferred you here, you brought Pedrito Tinoco with you, we got to know each other. What the hell else are we going to talk about at night?"

"About Mercedes, what else?" his adjutant decreed categorically. "I'll tell you about my sweetheart all over again, from the beginning."

"Son of a bitch." Lituma yawned, making his cot creak. "All over again from the beginning?"

EPI-
LOGUE

THE FIGURE EMERGED suddenly from the eucalyptus trees on the slope facing the post, as Lituma was taking down the clothes he had hung to dry on a rope stretched between the door of the shack and the protective wall of sacks and rocks surrounding it. He saw the figure from the side and from the front, interposing itself between him and the red ball beginning to sink behind the mountains. The setting sun dissolved it, swallowed it up. But in spite of distance and the glare that made his eyes water, he knew it was a woman.

"That's it, they've come," he thought. He was paralyzed, feeling his fingers clench at damp undershorts. But no, it couldn't be the terrucos, the woman was alone, she carried no weapons, and besides, she seemed confused, unsure of which direction to take. She looked to the right and the left, searching, she went back and forth among the eucalyptus trees, hesitating, deciding on a path and then changing her mind. Until, as if he were just what she had been looking for, the woman caught sight of Lituma. She stood still, and although she was too far away for him to see her features, the corporal was certain that as soon as she spotted him in the doorway of the shack, with the clothes on the line, wearing his gaiters and his green drill trousers, his unbuttoned tunic and his kepi, with his Smith & Wesson in its holster, her face brightened. Because now she was waving at him with both hands in the air, as if they knew each other and were very good friends and had arranged to meet. Who was she? Where did she come from? Where was she going? What could a woman who was not an Indian be doing at the top of that hill in the middle of the barrens? Because Lituma also knew that immediately: she was not an Indian, she did not have braids, she was not wearing a full skirt or a hat or a blanket but slacks and a sweater and over that a topcoat or a jacket, and what she held in her right hand was not a bundle tied with a rope but a handbag or small valise. She continued waving, almost angrily, as if shocked at his lack of response. Then the corporal raised his hand and returned her greeting.

For the half hour or forty-five minutes that it took the woman to climb down the slope with the eucalyptus trees and up the slope to the post, Lituma focused all his senses on the operation, guiding her. He indicated with energetic movements of his arm which path she should take, the one that was most clearly marked, the least slippery, where she ran the smallest risk of rolling down the hill, for he was afraid the stranger would end up sliding, stumbling, falling to the bottom of the ravine, a possibility that made each step a test of balance. It was obvious she had never walked the hills. She was as much an outsider in Naccos as he had been a few months ago when he would stagger, twist, fall, and get up again, just as she was doing now, whenever he went back and forth between the post and the camp.

When she began to climb the hill to the shack and was close enough to hear him, the corporal called out his instructions: "That way, between those big rocks." "Just grab on to the plants, they'll hold you." "Not that way, it's all mud." When she was fifty meters from the post, the corporal walked down to meet her. He helped her, holding her arm and taking her leather valise.

"From up there I thought you were Tomás Carreño," she said, sliding to one side and slipping out of Lituma's hands. "That's why I waved like I knew you."

"No, I'm not Tomás," he said, feeling stupid because of what he had said and at the same time filled with sudden joy. "You can't know how happy I am to hear a Piuran talk again!"

"How do you know I'm Piuran?" she asked in surprise.

"Because I'm one, too," said Lituma, extending his hand. "From deep in the heart of Piura, you bet. Corporal Lituma, at your service. I'm head of the post here. Isn't it incredible for two Piurans to run into each other in these barrens, so far from home?"

"Tomás Carreño is here with you, isn't he?"

"He went down to the village for a minute, he won't be long."

The woman sighed with relief, and her face looked happy. They had reached the shack, and she dropped onto one of the sacks filled with dirt that the corporal and his adjutant, with the help of Pedrito Tinoco, had wedged between the boulders.

"That's good," she said with some agitation, her chest rising and falling as if her heart would burst from her mouth. "Because if I made this trek for nothing . . . The Huancayo bus left me so far away. They told me it was an hour to Naccos. But it took me more than three to get here. Is that the village down there? Is that where the highway's going to be?"

"That's where it was supposed to be," said Lituma. "They stopped construction, there won't be any highway. A huayco came down a few days ago and did a lot of damage."

But the subject did not interest her. She stared uneasily at the path up the hill.

"Can we see him coming from here?" There was something familiar about her appearance and gestures as well as her voice. "Piuran girls even smell better," Lituma thought.

"As long as it doesn't get dark first," he warned. "The sun sets early this time of year, you can see it's almost gone down. You must be dead after that little trip. Would you like a soda?"

"Anything's fine. I'm dying of thirst," she replied, nodding. She was observing the tin roofs of the barracks, the stones, the slope dotted with patches of grass. "It looks nice from here."

"It's better from a distance than up close," the corporal said without enthusiasm. "I'll bring your soda right away."

He went to the shack, and as he took a bottle from the pail they kept outside to cool their drinks, he was able to look the visitor over at his leisure. Even splattered by mud and with her hair uncombed, she was terrific. How long had it been since he'd seen a good-looking broad like her? The color of her cheeks, her neck, her hands, brought a flood of images from his youth back home in Piura. And oh baby, what eyes. Half green, half gray, half I don't know what. And that mouth with those full lips. Why did he have the feeling he knew her, or at least had seen her? How great she must look dressed up in a skirt, high heels, earrings, her lips painted a fiery red. The things you lost shut away in Naccos. It wasn't impossible, he might have run into her sometime, somewhere, when he was living in a warm, civilized place. His heart beat faster. Was she Mechita? Was she?

He came back with the soda, and an apology. "I'm sorry, we don't have any glasses. You'll have to drink straight from the bottle."

"Is he all right?" the woman asked between sips. A trickle of liquid ran down her neck. "He hasn't been sick?"

"Tomasito is a rock, he doesn't get sick," Lituma reassured her. "He didn't know you were coming, did he?"

"I didn't tell him, I wanted to surprise him," she said with a mischievous smile. "Besides, letters probably don't even get up here."

"Then you must be Mercedes."

"Carreñito told you about me?" she asked, turning to look at him with some uneasiness.

"Well, a little." Lituma nodded, feeling uncomfortable. "I mean, a lot. He talks about you every night. In this wasteland, with nothing to do, telling secrets is the only thing left."

"Is he very angry with me?"

"I don't think so," said Lituma. "Because, speaking of secrets, I know that some nights he talks to you in his sleep."

He was immediately ashamed of having said that and quickly looked for cigarettes in his tunic. He lit one, awkwardly, and began puffing on it, exhaling the smoke through his mouth and nose. Yes, she was the girl Josefino rented to La Chunga for a night, the one who disappeared afterward. Mechita. When he had the courage to look at her again, she was very serious, watching the slope. There was concern in her eyes. "No wonder you cried for her so much, Tomasito," Lituma thought. Damn, what a small world.

"Is it just the two of you here?" Mercedes asked, gesturing toward the post.

Lituma nodded, exhaling.

"And we're leaving soon, thank God and the huayco. We couldn't have stood it much longer." He took another deep drag on the cigarette. "The post is closing. The camp, too. They've already started moving out whatever's left. There won't be a Naccos anymore. Wasn't there something in the Lima newspapers about the huayco? It destroyed machinery, buried a steamroller, ruined six months' work. Luckily, nobody was killed. Tomás will tell you all about it, he watched the rockslide from here. These are our last few days in Naccos. I got caught in the huayco farther up the mountain and it almost pulled me down in its sled."

But Mercedes had only one thought in mind. "If he's dreaming about me, he can't hate me so much for what I did."

"No, Tomasito really loves you. I've never known anybody who was in love the way he is with you. I swear."

"Did he tell you that?"

"He implied it," the corporal answered prudently. He looked at her out of the corner of his eye. She was still very serious, her gray-green eyes examining the hillside from one end to the other. "The wonderful things Tomasito must have seen in those eyes, looking at them up close," he thought.

"I really love him, too," Mercedes whispered, not looking at Lituma. "But he doesn't know it yet. I came to tell him."

"You'll make him happier than he's ever been in his life. What Tomasito feels for you is more than love. I swear, it's like an obsession."

"He's the only decent man I ever met," Mercedes murmured. "You're sure he's coming back, aren't you?"

They were both silent, watching the bottom of the hill, waiting for Tomás. It was growing dark down below, and they would not see him until he had climbed halfway up the slope. It was beginning to turn cold, too. Lituma saw Mercedes button her coat, raising the collar and huddling into it. What luck his adjutant had, an ordinary Civil Guard and some phenomenal woman went to the trouble of coming all the way to this damn hole to tell him she loved him. So, you're sorry you left him. Did she have the four thousand dollars with her? You're going to faint with joy, Tomasito.

"You were very brave to come on your own from the road, right through the middle of the barrens," the corporal said. "The trail isn't marked, you could've gotten lost."

"I did get lost." She laughed. "Some Indians helped me. They didn't speak Spanish and we had to use sign language. Naccos! Naccos! They looked at me like I came from another planet, until they caught on."

"You could've run into real trouble." Lituma tossed the cigarette down the hill. "Didn't anybody tell you the terrucos are in this zone?"

"I was lucky," she acknowledged. And added, with no transition: "It's funny you recognized my Piuran accent. I thought I'd lost it. I left Piura a long time ago, when I was still a kid."

"You can never lose that Piuran lilt," said Lituma. "It's the prettiest accent I know. Especially in women."

"Could I wash up a little and fix my hair? I don't want Carreño to see me looking like this."

Lituma was about to say, "You look terrific," but he restrained himself, feeling intimidated.

"Sure, how stupid, I didn't even think of it," he said, getting to his feet. "We have a basin, water, soap, and a little mirror. Don't expect a bathroom, everything's very primitive here."

He led her inside the shack, and his pride was slightly wounded when he saw the disillusionment, sorrow, or disgust with which Mercedes examined the two rumpled cots, the suitcases that served as seats, the washing-up corner: a chipped basin on a barrel full of water, with a small mirror hanging from the wardrobe that held the rifles. He filled the basin with clean water, handed her a new bar of soap, and went to find a dry towel on the line outside. When he left, he closed the door behind him so she would feel more comfortable. He returned to the spot where he had been talking to Mercedes. A few minutes later, the figure of his adjutant emerged from the darkness that was moving up the hillside. He held his rifle in his hand, leaning forward as he climbed the hill in long strides. What a surprise you have waiting for you, boy. This will be the happiest day of your life. When he was just a few steps away, he saw that the guard was smiling at him, holding up a piece of paper. "The message from Huancayo," he thought as he stood up. Instructions from headquarters. And good news, judging from Tomasito's face.

"I bet you can't guess where they're sending you, Corporal. I mean, Sergeant."

"What? I've been promoted?"

The boy handed him the sheet with the construction company letterhead at the top.

"Unless somebody's pulling a dirty trick. They're sending you to Santa María de Nieva as head of the post. Congratulations, Sergeant!"

There was not enough light to read the radiogram, and Lituma barely cast a glance at the black scratching on a white background.

"Santa María de Nieva? Where's that?"

"In the jungle, near the Upper Marañón." The boy laughed. "But the funniest thing is where they're sending me. Go on, take a guess, you'll die of envy."

He seemed very happy, and Lituma felt a combination of jealousy and fondness for him.

"Don't tell me it's Piura, don't tell me they're sending you to my hometown."

"That's right, to the Castilla district commissary. My godfather kept his word, he got me out of here even sooner than he said."

"It's your lucky day, Tomasito." Lituma patted him on the back. "Today you won the lottery, your luck changed today. I'll put you in touch with my friends, the Invincibles. Just don't let those bandits corrupt you."

"What's that noise?" said the guard in surprise, pointing at the post. "Who's in there?"

"Believe it or not, we have a visitor," Lituma said. "Someone you know, I think. Go take a look, Tomasito. Don't worry about me. I'm going down to the camp to have a few farewell anisettes with Dionisio and the witch. And you know what? I'm really going to tie one on. So I don't think I'll be back tonight. I'll sleep wherever I get tired, in the cantina or in the barracks. With all the booze I plan to drink, any place will feel like a bed of roses. See you tomorrow. Go on, say hello to your visitor, Tomasito."

.

"What a surprise, Corporal, sir," said Dionisio when he saw him come in. "Haven't you left Naccos yet?"

"I stayed so I could say goodbye to you and Doña Adriana," Lituma joked. "Is there anything to eat?"

"Soda crackers and mortadella," replied the cantinero. "But there's plenty to drink, at wholesale prices. I'm liquidating my stock."

"Great," said Lituma. "I'm going to be here the whole night and drink myself blind."

"Well, well." Dionisio smiled from behind the bar with surprise and satisfaction, piercing him with his glazed eyes. "The other night I saw you a little tight, but that was after the scare the huayco gave you. Now you've come to get drunk on purpose. It's never too late to start living."

He filled a glass with pisco and put it on the bar, along with a small tin plate of stale crackers and slices of mortadella.

Señora Adriana had come to the bar and, leaning her elbows on the counter, stared openly at the corporal with her usual brazen coldness. There were only three other patrons in the small, half-empty room, drinking beer out of the same bottle; they stood and talked, leaning against the back wall. Lituma murmured "Cheers," raised the glass to his lips, and drank it down in one swallow. The tongue of fire licking at his belly made him shudder.

"Good pisco, isn't it?" Dionisio boasted, quickly filling the glass again. "Smell it, smell its bouquet. Pure grape, Corporal, sir!"

Lituma inhaled. And, in fact, in its burning aroma he could detect a kind of base of fresh clusters of grapes that had just been cut and brought to the press, ready to be trampled by the expert feet of the Ican winemakers.

"I'll always remember this hole," murmured Lituma, talking to himself. "Even in the jungle I'll be picturing what happened here in the dead of night, when everybody was falling-down drunk."

"Are you starting in again on the missing men?" Doña Adriana interrupted with a gesture of annoyance. "Don't be a pain, Corporal. Most of the laborers have gone. And with the huayco, and the company shutting down, whoever's left in Naccos has other things to think about. Nobody remembers them. You forget, too, and enjoy yourself for once in your life."

"It's no fun to drink alone, Doña Adriana," said the corporal. "Won't you two join me?"

"What do you think?" answered Dionisio.

He poured another glass of pisco and toasted the corporal.

"You always showed up with a face as dark as night," declared Señora Adriana. "And took off as soon as you got here, like a soul with the devil after him."

"A person would think you were afraid of us," continued Dionisio, patting him on the shoulder.

"I was," Lituma acknowledged. "I still am. Because you're mysterious and I don't understand you. I like people to be transparent. By the way, Doña Adriana, why didn't you ever tell me those stories about pishtacos you tell everybody else?"

"If you came to the cantina more, you would've heard them. You don't know what you missed, being so standoffish!" And the woman burst into laughter.

"I don't get angry because I know you say things about us but don't mean to offend." Dionisio shrugged. "A little music, let's get some life in this graveyard."

"Graveyard's the right word." Lituma nodded. "Naccos! Son of a bitch, every time I hear the name my hair's going to stand on end. Excuse my language, señora."

"You can say whatever you want if that livens you up a little," the cantinero's wife said, accepting his apology. "As long as people are happy, I can stand anything."

She gave another bold laugh, but it was drowned out by a burst of music on Radio Junín. Lituma sat looking at Doña Adriana. In spite of her witch's hair and rumpled clothes, at times he could see something like a trace of past beauty. Maybe it was true, maybe she had been a looker when she was young. But never anything like Mercedes, never like the Piuran who was taking his adjutant to paradise right this minute. Was she Meche or not? Those mischievous eyes flashing gray-green, they had to be Meche's. You could understand Tomasito's falling head over heels in love with a woman like her.

"Where's Guard Carreño?" asked Señora Adriana.

"Having the time of his life," he replied. "His girlfriend came to see him, all the way from Lima, and I gave them the post for their honeymoon."

"She came to Naccos by herself? She must be a pretty tough woman," remarked Doña Adriana.

"And you're dying of envy, Corporal, sir," said Dionisio.

"Sure," Lituma acknowledged. "Because on top of everything else, she's a beauty queen."

The cantinero filled their glasses and poured a drink for his wife. One of the three men drinking beer began to sing in a husky voice, following the words of the huayno that was playing on the radio: "*Oh, my dove, my pretty little dove . . .*"

"A Piuran." Lituma felt a pleasant inner warmth, and now everything seemed less serious and important than before. "A worthy representative of Piuran womanhood. You're damn lucky they're sending you to the Castilla district, Tomasito! Cheers, everybody!"

He took a drink and saw Dionisio and Señora Adriana wetting their lips, too. They seemed pleased and intrigued at his getting drunk, something he had never done in all his months in Naccos. Because, as the cantinero said, the night of the huayco didn't count.

"How many people are left in camp?"

"Just the watchmen for the machinery. And a few who are too stubborn to leave," said Dionisio.

"And you?"

"What's there for us to do here if everybody's leaving?" said the cantinero. "I'm an old man but I was born with itchy feet, and I can work anywhere."

"People drink everywhere, so you can always make a living."

"And if they don't know how to drink, we'll teach them," said Doña Adriana.

"Maybe I'll get a bear and train him and go back to the fairs and do my act." Dionisio began to hop and growl. "When I was young I had one that read cards and swept and picked up pretty girls' skirts."

"I hope you don't run into the terrucos on your travels, that's all."

"The same to you, Corporal, sir."

"Can we dance, lady?"

One of the three men had come over and, swaying slightly, took hold of Doña Adriana's hand, which was resting on the bar. Without a word, she began to dance with him. The other two men had come to the bar as well and were clapping in time to the huayno.

"So, you two will leave and take your secrets with you." Lituma tried to look into Dionisio's eyes. "In a little while, when we're good and tight, will you tell me what happened to them?"

"It wouldn't mean anything." Dionisio was still imitating a heavy dancing bear. "The drink would make you forget everything afterward. Take a lesson from our friends here and cheer up. Your health, Corporal, sir!"

He raised his glass encouragingly, and Lituma drank with him. It was hard to cheer up with everything that was going on. But although the serruchos' drinking had always seemed melancholy and taciturn to him, the corporal envied the cantinero, his wife, the three laborers drinking beer. As soon as they had a few, they forgot their troubles. He turned to watch the couple dancing. They were barely moving, and the man was so drunk he didn't even bother to follow the music. Glass in hand, Lituma moved closer to the other two.

"You stayed behind to close down the camp," he began. "Are you watchmen?"

"I'm a mechanic, they're blasters," said the older one, a small man whose disproportionately large face had wrinkles like scars. "We leave tomorrow to look for work in Huancayo. This is our goodbye to Naccos."

"Even when it was full of people, the camp was like limbo," Lituma said. "Now that it's empty, and with all the boulders from the huayco and the barracks smashed in, it's really depressing, isn't it?"

He heard a stony little laugh and a half-whispered comment from the younger man, who wore an iridescent electric-blue shirt under his gray sweater, but then Lituma became distracted because the man dancing with Doña Adriana was angry about something.

"Why are you pulling away from me like that, lady?" he protested in a nasal voice, trying to press his body against hers. "Are you going to tell me now you don't like to feel it? What's the matter with you, lady?"

He was of average height, with a prominent nose and restless, sunken eyes that burned like coals from alcohol or emotion. Over his faded overalls he wore one of those alpaca sweaters women from the Indian communities knit and take down to sell at the fairs, and over that, a jacket that was too tight. He seemed imprisoned in his clothing.

"You take it easy and keep your hands to yourself or I won't dance," Señora Adriana finally said with no anger, pushing him back a little and watching Lituma out of the corner of her eye. "Dancing is one thing, but what you want is something else again, you old goat."

She laughed, and the men drinking beer laughed, too. Lituma heard Dionisio's hoarse guffaw at the bar. But the man who was dancing had no desire to laugh. He stood, swaying, and turned toward the cantinero, his face blazing with rage.

"Go on, Dionisio," he shouted, and Lituma saw greenish foam in his contorted mouth, as if he were chewing coca. "Tell her to dance! Ask her why she doesn't want to dance with me!"

"She does want to dance, but what you want is to feel her up." Dionisio laughed again, still moving his hands and feet as if he were a bear. "They're two different things, or don't you know that?"

Doña Adriana had gone back to the bar and was standing behind it, next to her husband. From there, with her elbows on the counter and her head resting on her hands, she observed the discussion with a frozen half smile, as if it had nothing to do with her.

Abruptly, the man seemed to lose interest in his own anger. He staggered to his companions, who held him up to keep him from falling. They handed him the beer. He took a long drink from the bottle. Lituma could see his eyes flashing, and when he swallowed, his Adam's apple moved up and down in his throat like a small caged animal. The corporal went to lean on the bar, too, facing the cantinero and his wife. "I'm drunk," he thought. But this was a joyless, heartless intoxication, very different from drinking in Piura with his brothers, the Invincibles, in La Chunga's little bar. And at that moment he was certain she was Meche. "It's her, it's her." The same girl Josefino had seduced, the one he had pawned so he could go on with the game, the one they had never seen again. Son of a bitch, a lot of water under the bridge since then. He was so involved in his memories he did not know just when the man who had gone too far with Doña Adriana came to stand next to him. He looked furious. He faced Dionisio in a boxer's stance.

"And why can't I feel her up when I dance with her?" he said, slamming his hand on the counter. "Why is that? Go on, explain that to me, Dionisio."

"Because the law is here," replied the cantinero, pointing at Lituma. "And when the law's around, you have to behave."

He was trying to joke, but Lituma could detect, as always when Dionisio spoke, something mocking and malicious behind his words. The cantinero looked back and forth, at him and the drunk, in amusement.

"Law or no law, cut the bullshit," the drunk exclaimed, not even bothering to glance at Lituma. "We're all equal here, and if anybody thinks he's a big shot, to hell with him. Don't you always say that drink makes us equal? So that's that."

Dionisio looked at Lituma, as if to say: "Now what are you going to do? This concerns you more than me." Doña Adriana was also waiting for his reaction. Lituma could feel the eyes of the other two men fixed on him.

"I'm not here as a Civil Guard but as an ordinary customer," he said. "This camp's closed down, so let's not have any trouble. Let's have a drink instead."

He raised his glass and the drunk docilely imitated him, solemnly raising his empty hand: "To your health, Corporal."

"That woman with Tomasito now, I knew her when she was a kid," said Lituma, his mouth slack. "She's even better now than she was in Piura. If Josefino or La Chunga could see her, they wouldn't believe how good-looking she is."

"You're a pair of liars," said the drunk, in a rage again, pounding the bar and bringing his face close to the cantinero in an antagonistic way. "I tell you right to your face. You can scare everybody else but you don't scare me."

Dionisio took absolutely no offense. His expression, somewhere between excited and peaceable, did not change, but he stopped imitating a bear. In his hand he held the bottle of pisco with which he had periodically been filling Lituma's glass. He very calmly filled another glass and handed it to the drunk with a friendly gesture.

"What you need is something good to drink, compadre. Beer is for people who don't know what's good, who like to bloat and belch. Go on, try it, smell the grape."

"This Mercedes can't be Meche," Lituma thought. He had made a mistake, the alcohol had confused him. Through a kind of fog he saw the drunk obey, taking the glass that Dionisio handed him, inhaling the fragrance and sipping it slowly, his eyes half closed. He seemed to calm down, but as soon as he emptied the glass he became angry again.

"A pair of liars, but I could call you something worse," he bellowed, and again he brought his menacing face close to the impassive cantinero. "So, nothing was going to happen? Everything happened! The huayco came, the highway shut down, we all got fired. All the horrible things, and we're worse off than before. You can't mess with people and then just sit back and watch the game from a box seat."

He was breathing heavily, and his expression changed. He

opened and closed his eyes and looked around suspiciously; was he worried at having said what he said? Lituma observed the cantinero. Dionisio impassively filled the glasses again.

Señora Adriana came out from behind the bar and took the drunk by the hand. "Come on, let's dance, so you won't be so mad anymore. Don't you know getting mad is bad for your health?"

The song on the radio could barely be heard through the static and continual interference. The man began to dance a bolero, hanging on to Doña Adriana like a monkey. Through the persistent fog Lituma saw that as the drunk pressed against her he ran his hands over her buttocks and rubbed his mouth and nose along her neck.

"Where are the others?" he asked. "Those guys who were just drinking beer over there."

"They left about ten minutes ago," Dionisio said. "Didn't you hear the door slam?"

"Don't you care if they manhandle your wife like that right under your nose?"

Dionisio shrugged. "Drunks don't know what they're doing." He laughed excitedly, inhaling from the glass he held in his hand. "Besides, what difference does it make? We'll give him ten minutes of happiness. Look how he's enjoying himself. Aren't you jealous?"

The man had stopped dancing and was almost on top of Señora Adriana. His feet did not move, his hands ran over her arms, shoulders, back, breasts, his lips searched for her mouth. With a bored, slightly disgusted expression, she let him do as he pleased.

"He's like an animal." Lituma spat on the floor. "How could I be jealous of something like that?"

"Animals are happier than you and me, Corporal, sir." Dionisio laughed and became a bear again. "They live to eat, sleep, and fuck. They don't think, they don't have worries like us, and that's our misfortune. He's paying a visit to his animal now, just see if he isn't happy."

The corporal moved a little closer to the cantinero and took him by the arm. "What were those horrible things?" he said, stressing each syllable. "The things they did so nothing would happen, so everything that happened wouldn't happen. What were they?"

"Ask him, Corporal, sir," answered Dionisio, making slow, clumsy movements, as if obeying the commands of a trainer. "If you believe what a drunk says, then you can let him tell you all about it. Satisfy your curiosity once and for all. Make him talk, beat it out of him."

Lituma closed his eyes. Everything was spinning inside, and the whirlwind was going to swallow up Tomasito and Mechita too, embracing at the very moment they loved each other most.

"I don't care anymore," he stammered. "It's over, case closed. I have a new post. I'll go to the Upper Marañón and forget about the sierra. I'm glad the apus sent the huayco down on Naccos. I'm glad they stopped work on the highway. Thanks to the apus, I can get out of here. I've never been so miserable in my life as I was here."

"Well, well, the pisco's bringing up the truth," said the cantinero approvingly. "Like it does to everybody, Corporal, sir. At this rate, you'll pay a visit to your animal, too. What'll it be, I wonder. A lizard? A hog?"

The drunk had begun to shout, and Lituma turned around to look. What he saw sickened him. The man, bundled into his jacket-prison, had opened his fly and held his sex in both hands. He showed it, dark and erect, to Doña Adriana, and shouted with a thickened tongue: "Worship it, lady. Get down on your knees, put your hands together, and say: 'You're my god.' Don't play shy with me."

Lituma was shaken by a fit of laughter. But then he felt like vomiting, and doubts about Mercedes still whirled in his head. Was she or wasn't she that girl in Piura? Son of a bitch, it was too much of a coincidence. Did that fool say something about horrible things?

Señora Adriana turned and went back to the bar. Here she was again, leaning her elbows on the counter, looking with absolute indifference at the drunk with the open fly, who stood in the middle of the empty room, contemplating his sex with a defeated expression.

"You were talking about horrible things, Corporal, sir," said Dionisio. "There's one. Have you ever seen anything more horrible than that little black prick?"

He guffawed, and Señora Adriana laughed, too. Lituma did the same, to be polite, because he had no desire to laugh. Any second now, he would begin retching and puking.

"I'm taking this asshole out of here," he said. "He isn't funny anymore, and he won't leave you alone for the rest of the night."

"Don't worry about me, I'm used to it," said Dionisio. "It's all part of the job."

"How much do I owe you?" asked the corporal, reaching for his wallet.

"Tonight it's on the house." Dionisio stopped his hand. "Didn't I tell you I was liquidating the stock?"

"Thanks very much, then."

Lituma walked over to the drunk. He took his arm, and with no violence began to move him toward the door. "You and I are going outside for a little fresh air, compadre."

The man put up no resistance. He quickly closed up his fly.

"Sure, Corporal," he said in a choked voice. "People understand each other when they talk."

•

An icy darkness waited for them outside. There was no rain, and the wind was not blowing as on other nights, but the temperature had plummeted since the afternoon, and Lituma could hear the blaster's teeth chattering, could feel him shivering as he huddled into his straitjacket clothing.

"I guess you're sleeping in the barracks the huayco left standing," he said, supporting him by the elbow. "I'll walk with you, compadre. Let's hold on to each other. In this fog and with all the potholes, we could crack open our skulls."

They moved slowly, staggering, stumbling, in darkness that the myriad stars and the pale half-moon failed to lighten. After a few steps, Lituma felt the man double over, clutching his stomach.

"Do you want to puke? Go on, you'll feel better. Go on, try, get rid of that shit. I'll help you."

The man leaned over, shuddering as he heaved, and Lituma stood behind him, pressing on his stomach with both hands, as he had done so often with the Invincibles back in Piura, when they left La Chunga's bar good and drunk.

"You're poking me in the ass," the blaster protested suddenly in a faint voice.

"You'd like that." Lituma laughed. "You dumb bastard, I don't like men."

"Neither do I," bellowed the other, between heaves. "But in Naccos you become a faggot, and even worse."

Lituma felt his heart pounding. Something was eating at this guy and he wanted to spit that out, too. He wanted to get it off his chest, tell somebody about it.

The blaster finally straightened up with a sigh of relief. "I feel better now." He spat and stretched his arms. "It's fucking cold out here."

"It's enough to freeze your brains," Lituma agreed. "Let's get moving."

They linked arms again and began to walk, cursing whenever they tripped over a rock or sank into mud. At last the barracks loomed in front of them, denser than the darkness that surrounded it. The wind could be heard whistling around the hilltops, but down here everything was quiet and peaceful. The effects of the alcohol had worn off, and Lituma felt clearheaded and lucid. He had even forgotten about Mercedes and Tomasito making love up there in the post, and about Meche from so many years ago in the little bar on the sandy ground near the Piura Stadium. A decision sputtered inside his head, ready to explode: "I've got to get it out of him."

"Okay, let's smoke a cigarette, compadre," he said. "Before we go to sleep."

"Are you going to stay here?" The blaster seemed to have sobered up too.

"I don't feel like climbing all the way up there now. Besides, three's a crowd, and I don't want to interrupt the happy couple. There must be a spare bed in here."

"A cot, you mean. They already took away the mattresses."

Lituma heard snoring from the far end of the barracks. The man dropped into the first bunk on the right, next to the door. With the help of a match, the corporal found his bearings: there were two bare wooden cots next to the one occupied by the blaster. He sat down on the closer one, took out his pack, and lit two cigarettes. He handed one to the laborer and said in a friendly voice: "Nothing like the last smoke when you're in bed, waiting to fall asleep."

"I may be drunk, but I'm not an idiot," said the man. The corporal saw the end of his cigarette glow more brightly in the dark, and a mouthful of smoke blew right into his face. "Why are you staying here? What do you want from me?"

"I want to know what happened to those three men," said

Lituma, very softly, surprised at his own boldness. Wasn't he risking everything? "I'm not going to arrest anybody. I'm not sending any reports to headquarters in Huancayo. Nothing to do with the service. I just want to know, compadre. I swear. What happened to Casimiro Huarcaya, Pedrito Tinoco, Medardo Llantac, alias Demetrio Chanca? Tell me while we smoke this last cigarette."

"Not on your life," the man rasped, breathing heavily. He moved in the cot, and it occurred to Lituma that now he would jump up and run out of the barracks and hide with Dionisio and Doña Adriana. "Not even if you kill me. Not even if you pour gasoline on me and set me on fire. You can torture me the way you do the terrucos, if you want. But I won't talk."

"I won't touch a hair on your head, compadre," said Lituma, very slowly, exaggerating his amiability. "You tell me, and I'll go away. You leave Naccos tomorrow and so do I. We each go our own separate ways. We'll never see each other again. After you tell me we'll both feel better. You'll get rid of what's eating you, and so will I, it's been gnawing at me all this time. I don't know your name, and I don't want to know. I only want you to tell me what happened. So we can both sleep at night, compadre."

There was a long silence, broken by sporadic snores from the rear of the barracks. Occasionally, Lituma saw the tip of the blaster's cigarette flare, and a cloud of smoke would rise and sometimes tickle the inside of his nose. He felt calm. He was absolutely certain the guy was going to talk.

"You sacrificed them to the apus, didn't you?"

"The apus?" asked the man, moving in the cot. His restlessness affected the corporal, who felt an urgent itch traveling over various parts of his body.

"The spirits of the mountains," explained Lituma. "The amarus, the mukis, the gods, the devils, whatever they're called. The ones that live inside the hills and make bad things happen. Did you sacrifice them so there wouldn't be a huayco? So the terrucos wouldn't come to kill anybody or take people away? So the pishtacos wouldn't dry out any laborers? Was that the reason?"

"I don't know Quechua," the man said hoarsely. "I never heard that word before. Apu?"

"Wasn't that the reason, compadre?" Lituma insisted.

"Medardo was my paisano, I'm from Andamarca, too," said the man. "He used to be the mayor. That's what fucked up Medardo."

"The foreman is the one you feel bad about?" asked Lituma. "I guess the others matter less than your paisano. The one that gets me is the little mute, Pedrito Tinoco. Were you good friends, you and Demetrio, I mean, Medardo Llantac?"

"We knew each other. He lived with his wife up there on the slope. Scared to death the terrucos would find out he was here. That time in Andamarca he got away by the skin of his teeth. Do you know how? He hid in a grave. We talked sometimes. These Ayacuchans and Abanquinos and Huancavelicans were always on him, telling him: 'Sooner or later, they'll get you.' Telling him: 'You living in Naccos makes it dangerous for all of us. Go on, get out of here.' "

"Is that why you sacrificed the foreman? To get in good with the terrucos?"

"Not just for that," the blaster protested in great agitation. He smoked and exhaled steadily, and it was as if his drunkenness had returned. "Not just for that, damn it."

"Why else?"

"Those motherfuckers said he'd already been convicted, that sooner or later they'd come and execute him. And since we needed somebody, better somebody who was on their list and would die soon anyway."

"You needed human blood, isn't that what you mean?"

"But it was a big lie, they cheated us," the man said angrily. "Didn't we lose our jobs? And do you know what they're still saying?"

"What are they saying?"

"That we didn't give them all our recognition and that's why they were offended. According to those motherfuckers, we would've had to do even more things. Understand?"

"Sure I do," whispered Lituma. "What could be more horrible than killing the albino, the foreman, the little mute, for some apus nobody ever saw, when nobody even knows if they exist?"

"Killing was the least of it," shouted the man in his bed, and Lituma thought whoever was sleeping at the back of the barracks would wake up and tell them to shut up. Or sneak over and close the blaster's mouth for him. And because he'd heard what he'd heard, they'd take him to the abandoned mine and throw him down the shaft. "Aren't there killings everywhere? Killing is the least of it. Isn't killing just routine, like pissing or taking a shit? That isn't what fucked people up. Not just me, a lot of the ones who left already, too. It was the other thing."

"The other thing?" Lituma felt cold.

"The taste in your mouth," whispered the blaster, and his voice broke. "It won't go away, no matter how you rinse it out. I can taste it now. On my tongue, on my teeth. In my throat. I can even feel it in my belly. As if I'd just finished chewing."

Lituma felt the cigarette burning his fingers, and he dropped it. He stamped out the sparks. He understood what the man was saying, and he did not want to know any more.

"So, that too, on top of everything else," he murmured, and he sat with his mouth open, panting.

"It doesn't go away even when I sleep," declared the blaster. "Only when I drink. That's why I drink so much. But it's no good for me, it's bad for my ulcers. I'm shitting blood again."

Lituma tried to take another cigarette, but his hands shook so much he dropped the pack. He looked for it, groping around the damp floor covered with gravel and matchsticks.

"Everybody took communion. I didn't want to, but I took communion, too," the laborer said in a rush. "That's what's fucking me up. The stuff I swallowed."

Lituma finally found the pack. He took out two cigarettes, put them in his mouth, and then had to wait until his hand could hold a match and light them. He handed one to the man, not saying anything. He saw him take a drag, another foul-smelling mouthful of smoke blew in his face, he felt the itch in his nose.

"And now I'm even scared to go to sleep," said the blaster. "I turned into a coward. I never was one before. But can anybody fight his dreams? If I don't drink, I have nightmares."

"Do you see yourself eating your paisano? Is that what you dream?"

"I'm hardly ever in the dreams," explained the blaster, with absolute docility. "Just them. Cutting off their balls, slicing them, eating them like some kind of delicacy." He retched, and Lituma heard him hunch over. "But when I'm in the dream too, it's worse. Those two come and tear mine off with their hands and eat them right in front of me. I'd rather drink than dream that. But what about my ulcer? You tell me if this is any kind of life, damn it."

Lituma stood up abruptly. "I hope you get over it, compadre," he said, feeling dizzy. He had to lean against the bunk for a minute. "I hope you find work where you're going. I guess it won't be easy. I don't think it'll be easy for you to forget this, either. You know something?"

"What?"

"I'm sorry I tried so hard to find out what happened to them. I'd be better off just suspecting. I'll go now and let you sleep. Even if I have to spend the night outside so I won't bother Tomasito. I don't want to sleep next to you or near those guys snoring back there. I don't want to wake up tomorrow and see your face and have a normal conversation with you. Son of a bitch, I'm going to breathe a little air."

He stumbled to the door of the barracks and walked out. He felt a blast of icy air, and despite his confusion, he could see the splendid half-moon and the stars shining in a cloudless sky, still shedding their clear light on the craggy peaks of the Andes.